"HERE I AM."

"Here you are."

He stared at her for three more heartbeats, as if he wanted nothing more than to look. His dark eyes held hers and a strange heat pooled low in her belly.

"We didn't come here to talk," he told her.

No, they'd come for an entirely different purpose that had her blood rushing and her heart pounding and her legs trembling.

"Come on, Josie." Long, strong fingers laced through hers and she forgot everything except the way his skin warmed hers and sent little tingles through her body. "Show me what you can do."

Other *Love Spell* books by Kimberly Raye:
ONLY IN MY DREAMS
SOMETHING WILD
FAITHLESS ANGEL

Midnight Kisses

KIMBERLY RAYE

LOVE SPELL BOOKS ◆ NEW YORK CITY

LOVE SPELL®

February 2000

Published by

Dorchester Publishing Co., Inc.
276 Fifth Avenue
New York, NY 10001

If you purchased this book without a cover you should be aware that this book is stolen property. It was reported as "unsold and destroyed" to the publisher and neither the author nor the publisher has received any payment for this "stripped book."

Copyright © 2000 by Kimberly Rangel

Cover Art by John Ennis, Ennisart.com

All rights reserved. No part of this book may be reproduced or transmitted in any form or by any electronic or mechanical means, including photocopying, recording or by any information storage and retrieval system, without the written permission of the Publisher, except where permitted by law.

ISBN 0-505-52361-2

The name "Love Spell" and its logo are trademarks of Dorchester Publishing Co., Inc.

Printed in the United States of America.

For Debbie Villanueva.
For all of your support and understanding.
I'm so lucky to have you as my friend.

Midnight Kisses

Chapter One

Were there *any* good men left in the world?

The question echoed through Dr. Josephine Farrington's mind as she sat on the patio at *Le Naturale*, one of Chicago's hottest health food spots, and stared across an overflowing platter of bean sprouts and watercress at the man who sat opposite her.

Archie Witherspoon.

He was the chief accountant for Three Kisses, Inc.—the toy company where Josie headed the Research & Development department—and the latest prospect in her search for the perfect life mate.

Josie, in her most secret, private fantasies had always envisioned a tall, dark and handsome man with killer eyes and a sexy smile and a bad-boy streak. And hands . . . Large, strong, skilled hands. Like the *ER* version of George Clooney on a Harley.

Arthur, all five-feet-five-inches of him, with his short dishwater-brown hair, pale complexion and perfectly knotted bow tie, reminded her more of Don Knotts. She wasn't even going to mention the motor scooter parked outside near the curb or the clear nail polish glistening on the ends of his short, stubby fingers.

But after six months of serious searching, complete with enough first dates to qualify her for some kind of desperate single woman's record, Josie wasn't going to write him off simply because he didn't measure up to her fantasy man.

In fact, she was boosting him up her list of potential mates because he *wasn't* her fantasy man.

Josie knew the difference between fantasy and reality.

Fantasies were fueled by lust—and she knew firsthand that lust didn't make for lifelong commitment. Compatibility did that, and while Archie didn't make her want to rip off her sensible cotton panties and go orgasmic at one glance, he'd already aced five of Josie's Ten Compatibility Commandments.

He was a health-conscious, classical-music-loving, nonsmoking, white-collar professional ready to settle down and start a family.

Archie ate a piece of watercress dipped in

bean curd and dabbed at his mouth with the corner of his napkin before smoothing it over his lap.

Josie's gaze dropped to her own lap, to the neatly spread napkin. *Compulsively neat.* Hello number six.

Six out of the ten. That put him one over her only other serious prospect, Mitchell Remington, a brilliant nonsmoking cardiac surgeon desperate to marry and make babies before he turned forty.

Josie could sympathize. Her thirty-fifth birthday—a major traumatic event that would make her the oldest single woman working at Three Kisses if she didn't do something *now*—was just around the corner.

One month.

She fought down a wave of rising panic. She would make her deadline to meet and marry before then. She'd already licked the meeting part. As for the marrying . . .

First she had to decide between Archie and Mitchell.

Archie was definitely leading the race, despite the nail polish. He was probably just a closet nail biter. Besides, as well as being compatible, he was nice, financially solvent, and he'd asked her out for date number two. *And* he hadn't brought his mother this time.

Hey, a girl had to give credit where credit was due.

He ate several more pieces of watercress in the same ritual fashion—eat, dab, smooth—

11

before eyeing her side of the platter. "You're not going to eat yours, are you? Mother couldn't make it tonight, so I told her I'd bring a doggie bag."

On second thought . . .

"You're here at nine o'clock on a Friday night," said the thirty-ish redhead sitting behind the security desk at Three Kisses, Inc., when Josie walked through the door later that evening. "Which means only one thing."

"I'm a dedicated scientist in the middle of a major breakthrough on the Tinkling Tina doll?"

"He brought his mother." Phyllis wasn't just a tall and pretty redhead. She was a perceptive one.

Josie shrugged. "She had previous plans." She handed a take-out container filled with bite-size wheat-germ cakes to Phyllis, the night security guard and Josie's confidante when it came to her love life. Or lack thereof. "But he assured me she'd be ready, willing and able for date number three before he rushed home to watch the *Tonight Show* with her."

Phyllis sniffed at the bag, then wrinkled her nose. "How can you eat this stuff?"

"It's good for you."

"The only thing good for me is a megadose of sugar and caffeine." She put the bag aside and reached for a half-eaten bowl of Cocoa Puffs. Taking a big bite, she chewed and swallowed, following it up with a swig of Diet Coke.

"You should try it some time. It might light a fire under you and make you give up all these boring losers you've been hooking up with."

"They're not losers."

"They're boring," Phyllis pointed out.

"Boring can be good."

"So sayeth the woman who specializes in the subject. You need to get a life, Josie. Get yourself a hot dress. You've got the figure for it."

"My butt is too big."

"Men like a little cush for the push."

"And my boobs are too small."

"Nothing a Wonderbra can't fix."

"And my thighs are too wide."

"That's what girdles are for. And no man is going to be looking at your thighs if you let that long blond hair of yours down and doll yourself up in spandex or leopard-print or something ultra sexy. Men don't focus in on flaws. They go for the all-over picture. You should shed that stiff-looking image, go to a nightclub and live it up. The night is young. *You're* young."

If only.

"I hope you at least told Archie where to get off," Phyllis went on. "He's bad enough on his own without bringing his equally boring mother." When Josie just shrugged, Phyllis gave her a pointed stare. "You did tell him to take a flying leap, right?"

"Not exactly."

"As in you let him down easy?"

"As in we're going to a poetry reading at the

13

libary next weekend. His mom composes her own." She shook her head. "I'm pathetic, huh? Not for going out with Archie, though—he's turning out to be just what I'm looking for in a man. Although he is a little too attached to his mother."

"Cord syndrome. She hasn't cut him loose and he doesn't have the balls to do it himself." Phyllis ate another spoonful of Cocoa Puffs. "And you're not pathetic. A little desperate maybe, but still a notch up from pathetic. Pathetic is not having a date—boring loser or otherwise—for seven months, six days and four hours."

"Roger hasn't called?"

"Not for seven months, six days and four hours." She sighed, a low, pitiful sound that roused the four Doberma pinschers from their lounging spot in front of the lobby TV and a *Ricki Lake* rerun. They whimpered and wagged and licked at Phyllis who gave them each a wheat-germ cake and a pat.

"It's good to see that you're not obsessing." It was supposed to be a joke, but Phyllis didn't crack a smile.

She simply sighed again, louder this time. "I'm spending so much time at my local video store, I'm one rental away from a free box of Milk Duds."

"You really miss him, don't you?"

"Are you kidding? I'd had it with all his snoring and burping and I won't even mention what he did at my mother's house after he ate three bowls of her five-alarm chili." She shook her head. "I've had better sex all by myself. What I miss the most is having a warm body waiting at home."

Amen to that.

"Someone to talk to," Phyllis went on. "Laugh with, smile at. Someone to just *be there*." Phyllis ate another bite of cereal. "You'd think," she said around a spoonful, "that with all the modern-day technology, someone could invent the perfect man. A guy with a great body and a great face, minus the disgusting bodily noises."

"I already have." Josie pointed to the full color poster depicting Hunky Hank, the company's newest action figure.

Hank was the latest edition to the REAL series of dolls Three Kisses had launched on New Year's Eve. What made the REAL dolls so special was that they looked and felt *real* thanks to Josie's latest brainchild, aptly named S.K.I.N.

S.K.I.N.—Synthetic Kollection of Integrated Neurosystems—was a breakthrough plastic that looked and felt like real skin. Not only did it have a natural elasticity, but it warmed to the touch. Miss Kiss, the launch doll created with the new synthetic had only been on the market a few weeks and already her demand had far exceeded the Tickle Me Elmo craze. The synthetic contained actual sensors that sent a message to a microprocessor implanted in the doll's head, which triggered the appropriate programmed response. In other words, the doll could actually "feel"—and act on that feeling.

"Granted, I like the strong, silent type and he's got muscles to die for, but twelve inches tall isn't my idea of perfection." Phyllis grinned. "Now twelve inches *long* . . . Hello, Mr. Perfect."

"I like 'em twelve inches myself," said the sixty-something man who rounded the corner, briefcase in hand. "There's nothing like a foot-long with extra onions and chili to really rev up the old system."

Phyllis winked at Josie before turning a smile on Arthur Kiss, the chief executive officer of Three Kisses and resident weiner connoisseur. "Can't say that I've tried any with onions and chili, but it sounds interesting. So what's up, Mr. Kiss? You pulling a late nighter, too?"

"Can't let the grass grow under my feet." His gaze shifted to Josie and his smile widened. "Both of my chief scientists hard at work on a Friday night? Am I a lucky son of a gun, or what?"

Both, as in Marvin Tannenbaum, a top-notch scientist and the resident artificial-intelligience expert.

S.K.I.N. had been Josie's brainchild, but Marvin was the one who did the actual physical construction. He was brilliant, quiet and reclusive, and Josie had exchanged little more than pleasantries with him during the six months he'd been at Three Kisses.

Marvin wasn't much of a talker.

"So where is he?" Josie asked.

"Locked up in his laboratory, as usual, bless his productive soul. Speaking of which, please tell me you're here to work on the Rappin' Rhonda doll? I need a finished product first thing Monday morning."

"Geez, Mr. K., Josie's got a life, you know. Her existence doesn't revolve around this place. She's on a manhunt."

"A manhunt?" His gaze shifted to Josie. "You're hunting for a man? Is this true, Josephine?"

"I thought it high time I explored my options."

"Meaning," Phyllis cut in, "her biological clock is ticking and she's starting to get desperate."

"I'm not desperate. I'm simply looking for more than just twelve inches." Josie wanted someone who would like and respect her for who she was. Someone who wouldn't be disappointed once the lust faded, because of who she wasn't. "Speaking of ticking," Josie glanced at her watch, "I've got a doll up in my lab that isn't getting any younger. I should go work on her."

He nodded enthusiastically. There were only two things that never failed to nab Arthur's attention. Work and food.

"Get to it, Josie!" He waved his briefcase before saying goodnight and leaving.

"Do you believe that guy?" Phyllis said once he was out of earshot. "He leaves us here slaving away while he waltzes home."

"Well, you *do* work the night shift."

"That's beside the point."

"Which is?"

"*You* don't." Phyllis looked at her pointedly.

"Tonight I do." She left Phyllis and headed up the elevator to her office attached to the Research & Development lab and play area where the toys were tested by average kids who attended a play session for two hours on Mondays, Wednesdays and Fridays. Inside, she flipped on the lights and turned to Rhonda.

She waited for the rush of excitement that always came with each project. Work had always been her number one priority. Her passion. Her end all and be all. Her life.

Or it had been up until six months ago when she'd added the final ingredient and created the revolutionary S.K.I.N.

She'd been working late, as usual, and had made the discovery long after everyone else had already closed up shop and headed home—with the exception of Marvin Tannenbaum who'd been barricaded inside his neat-as-a-pin laboratory with his Do Not Disturb sign posted on the door. Josie had shouted in triumph to Phyllis, the Dobermans and a startled cleaning lady, before rushing home to her apartment.

She'd never really noticed how dark, how quiet, how utterly *empty* her place was until she'd walked in, almost ready to pop with her good news, and found no one to share it with except her upstairs neighbor, the elderly Mr.

Babcock. And he'd already been sound asleep, so she'd had no one to listen to her, to smile at her, to pat her on the back and tell her she'd finally done something worthwhile.

No one, because Josie had always been too busy with her work, too driven, too focused, to have time for a goldfish much less a man.

Until now.

She booted up her computer and pulled up the design specifications for Rhonda. Her fingers flew across the keyboard, making physical adjustments based on the most recent research data. But Josie's attention refused to completely focus, an all-too-frequent occurrence since she'd made the breakthrough on S.K.I.N.

She'd spent the past fifteen years designing toys for a living and doing the occasional research project for Maloy Laboratories, a leading plastics manufacturer. It was just such a project that had led to the discovery of the new molecular base that had inspired S.K.I.N. and confirmed that, despite her chosen profession as a toy maker, she was every bit the famous Joseph Farrington's daughter.

Her father was an MIT professor and one of the leading researchers on biochemical reactants. It had looked to all that Josie would follow in his footsteps. After all, she'd attended Walter Smythe School for the Gifted, then gone on to MIT to major in both chemistry and physics.

But after graduating from college at the tender age of eighteen, Josie had chosen a different path. While she'd shared her father's passion for work, she'd wanted to leave Cambridge, to start fresh someplace where she wasn't known as Knowsey Josie. The egghead. The brainiac. The freak.

She'd wanted a normal life, and she'd found it with Three Kisses.

Her gaze went to the pictures lining her wall. Dozens of smiling faces stared back at her. All of the children she'd worked with throughout her time in various research play groups. Over the years, she'd watched them fall in love with her projects, shared in their excitement and wonder. The children had more than made up for her emotionally lacking childhood. She'd played with them, laughed and smiled with them.

But now she wanted more.

She wanted to laugh and smile with her very own children, while she was still young enough to enjoy them. She didn't want her only legacy to be a revolutionary plastic skin-substitute, though it *was* a legacy—a big one she'd never anticipated, despite all the late nights she'd put in developing the formula.

Not only had the synthetic impacted the toy industry, but it had intrigued the medical community, as well. As soon as the first doll had launched, Three Kisses had been contacted by several pharmaceutical companies interested in obtaining the patent to offer the synthetic for use in everything from routine cosmetic procedures to reconstructive surgery for burn victims.

Josie had gladly made a deal with Johns Hopkins and given the medical center exclusive rights to S.K.I.N. in return for its agreement to make the synthetic available to all those in need, regardless of economic status. Her synthetic was relatively cheap to produce, and Josie didn't want any profiteering bureaucrats to inflate the price.

This discovery marked the achievement of a lifetime, the peak of her career.

Professionally, things couldn't get much better for Josie Farrington.

Personally, however, they couldn't get much worse, and she had a freezer full of Single Sensation health food dinners to prove it.

No more.

She was trading those Single Sensations in for Delectable Duets and finding herself a significant other *before* she hit the big three-five, and Josie was notorious for not missing a deadline.

She'd initially approached the task the way she did any endeavor—by doing research. She'd taken Dr. Sophia Erickson's seminar on finding the perfect life mate. After weeks of lectures and lab time spent customizing her very own Ten Compatibility Commandments, Josie had set out to find her man and settle down.

Her thoughts shifted to Archie and Mitchell. She was well on her way with two hot prospects. All right, so they were more luke-warm than hot, but a high rating on Josie's lus-tometer wasn't one of the Ten Compatibility Commandments.

Josie's heart went out to women the world over. Dating with a clear, concise plan of action was difficult enough. She couldn't begin to imagine what things would be like without benefit of Dr. Sophia and her seminar.

Standing in the employee lounge she'd heard her share of war stories regarding cat-astrophic dates. There was the boring date with the guy who talked nonstop about his hobby—collecting napkins from truck stops all over the country. The blind date with the guy who sucked his teeth. The infuriating date with the guy who argued politics all night. The depressing date with the guy who plotted revenge against his cheating ex. The date that qualified more as a lesson in tacti-cal manuevers with the guy who had fast hands. And lips. And she still hadn't gotten over the news of what he'd tried to do with his big toe.

Someone out there *should* make the perfect man and give women the world over a much-needed break.

A man who was kind, sensitive, sexy and everything every woman hoped for in a—

Her thoughts braked to a shattering halt as a thought struck her. A crazy, outrageous, ridiculous thought she would have pushed away immediately if she hadn't just spent the past few hours talking about tax dividends and Archie's mother. Mutual funds and Archie's mother. Rolling over IRA's and Archie's mother.

Her gaze went to the Hunky Hank doll sitting on her desk and she reached out. Fingertips trailed over his miniature chest, his sculpted biceps. He was so small, yet so perfect. So solid and warm and *real*.

And he talked, too.

Okay, so he snarled. And growled. And made annoying grunting noises whenever she touched his stomach, but he was an action figure, after all. Not a six-foot-tall Romeo eager to sweet-talk a woman. The voice came courtesy of a microcomputer chip that could be programmed to say anything.

Anything.

Like how great she looked wearing her ratty old MIT sweatshirt. And how great she smelled when she'd been hunched over a chemical burner all day. And how the glasses she wore made her look sexy instead of smart. And how she really, really didn't need to worry about her weight because her hips were just the right size.

"I'm losing it," she blurted to Hank, but she didn't quite believe it.

After a few more strokes of Hunky Hank's muscles and some serious contemplation of the coming Saturday spent listening to Archie's mom read haiku on the joys of potty training her son, she reached a decision.

The idea was crazy and outrageous and totally ridiculous. At the same time, it was the best she'd had in a long, long time.

If Josie couldn't find the man of her dreams, she would make him.

Chapter Two

Matthew Taylor was not in the habit of walking around his laboratory stark-naked.

But this was in the interest of science, after all. Particularly, the Chicago Science Expo being held at McCormick Place. The expo was one of the biggest, most reputable science fairs in the country, and it was scheduled for next month. It would be Matt's prime chance to reveal his breakthrough.

He adjusted one of the more than two hundred heat sensors attached all over his body—he'd had to peel off every stitch of clothing to find enough space for all the connections—and watched the numerical display race across his computer screen.

Body heat.

That's what this was all about. A renewable, timeless source of energy that would exist for as long as man did, despite environmental conditions or the depletion of available resources. The concept of using human heat as a new energy source seemed far-fetched, yet at the same time, so obvious. Man walked and talked and generated heat. It seemed only logical to channel that heat, to convert it into a viable source of fuel, and Matt had done just that.

He glanced at Harry, the robotic dog sitting in the far corner. Minutes ago, Harry had been wagging his tail courtesy of Matt's body heat converter and the energy he'd stored up last night.

The printer whirred, cranking out the individual temperature readouts for all two hundred sensors while they absorbed his heat and sent it to the small generator sitting next to his computer. This was just the beginning, of course. He knew it wasn't realistic to have to wear the cumbersome sensors every time he wanted to store energy; he'd started to develop a smaller version of the converter. A mini-converter that could be implanted in the dog. Then all that would be required was a human touch directly on a specially designed pad Matt had built into the fur covering Harry's stomach. He would be able to stroke the dog's belly and fuel him up at the same time. Until then . . .

He spent the next fifteen minutes going about his normal activities. Adjusting his glasses. Drinking water. Working on his latest project for Three Kisses, Inc., an action figure in progress. Leaning over his worktable and making a few adjustments on the Rappin' Rhonda chip. He did a couple of jumping jacks and even ran in place for a few painful seconds that made him rethink this naked business.

Next time, he'd forfeit a few sensors and wear underwear. Or at least a jockstrap. It might take longer to store up the required amount of energy, but at least he wouldn't be doing damage to one very vital part—even if it was *this close* to shriveling up and falling off from lack of female contact.

Playing the quiet, dedicated, geeky scientist didn't do much to attract the opposite sex.

Which was exactly the point. Matt Taylor had morphed into Marvin Tannenbaum and taken the job at Three Kisses because nerdy Marvin was least likely to attract anyone's attention. Keeping a low profile and his true identity a secret was Matt's key to success. To his future.

Not to mention, sweet Josie Farrington didn't so much as spare him a passing glance.

All the better, he told his ego. Josie Farrington seemed like a forever kind of woman, and Matt couldn't, wouldn't give any woman forever.

Even the talented and driven Dr. Brainiac Farrington.

He'd expected her to be talented. Before Matthew Taylor had dropped out of his old life

27

and re-emerged as Marvin Tannenbaum, he'd done his research. Over the past fifteen years, Three Kisses had gained a reputation as an industry leader, all thanks to the talent of Josie Farrington.

It was her drive that had most surprised Matt. After all, she made *toys* for a living rather than doing something monumental like designing plastics for the space shuttle.

But she'd turned out to be every bit as serious and dedicated as any other scientist he'd ever met, and Matt knew plenty of them. She treated every project as if world peace rested on the outcome and he couldn't help but admire her. And want her.

From afar, of course.

Contact with anyone didn't figure into his plan, and so Josie was completely off-limits.

She was also sexy as hell in her starched white lab coat and her black-rimmed glasses, and she was standing in his doorway—

His thoughts screeched to a furious halt. Holy hell, she'd barged in on him while he was naked. While he . . . His thoughts scattered for a split second before scrambling back into place.

Christ, he was *naked*!

His heart pounded against his chest as he jerked open the nearest cabinet door, which barely reached to mid-thigh. He grabbed a sheet of paper and started to strategically back toward his clothes.

Meanwhile Josie didn't so much as blink one

pretty green eye, much less look up at him. She simply waltzed by, her attention fixed on the clipboard in her hand as she murmured, "I need you."

He stopped mid-step. The words sparked all sorts of erotic thoughts that he had no business entertaining with a woman who didn't even realize he was naked. He grabbed a second sheet of paper. If she didn't quit sucking on the end of that pen, he'd need a whole ream before he made it to his pants.

Okay, so technically he wasn't *naked* naked. He had on a green bouffant cap to disguise his dark hair and more than two hundred strategically placed sensor pads that covered nearly every major part of his body. All except for *the* major part, growing more major by the second, particularly when he caught a whiff of her perfume—a deep, musky scent much too sexy for a scientist. A burst of heat shot straight to his groin.

The paper trembled in his hands, and his computer beeped at the sudden rise in body temperature, drawing Josie's attention and giving Matt a chance to snatch up his pants and duck behind a nearby file cabinet that reached clear to his chest.

He ripped sensors from his legs and stifled a cry of pain as the sticky pads took hair and all with them. He managed to shove one leg inside his god-awful polyester pants before she turned back to him. She couldn't actually see anything incriminating, not with the file cabinet in the way. That, coupled with the fact that she wasn't even looking should have sent relief pumping through him. After all, being caught naked was sure to spark suspicion; quiet, reclusive Marvin wasn't the walk-around-naked type, even if it were in the interest of science.

Instead, he felt a surge of irritation that she could overlook him so easily.

Count your blessings, buddy.

He should have. When Matt had come up with the idea of using the Marvin Tannenbaum persona to repair his damaged reputation, he'd vowed to keep a low profile, to stay distant and aloof from any and everyone because his time at Three Kisses was limited. Not to mention he was notorious in the scientific community. Josie, being the brilliant, informed woman she was, was sure to have heard of him and seen his picture at one time or another. The last thing he wanted was to be recognized.

But he hadn't spend his early-morning hours doing all those push-ups and stomach crunches so she could walk right past him and not bat even one of her pretty green eyes.

He was daring the devil, but he couldn't help himself. He cleared his throat.

Her head snapped up and she looked at him for all of two heartbeats before pink flooded her cheeks and she whirled, putting her back to him.

"I, um, I didn't realize—" She gulped. "Do

you know you're naked?" She shook her head. "Uh, of course you do. I mean, who wouldn't?"

"An experiment," he explained, shoving his other leg into his pants. He pulled the trousers up slowly and deliberately, seeing her shoulders tremble as the glide of fabric and the rasp of his zipper filled the air. "I'm channeling body heat as an energy source." And he was doing a damned fine job because from the frenzy of his computer, his body temperature had shot up remarkably thanks to Josie and that quick two-second look.

Slipping on his shirt, he left it unbuttoned as he walked across the room and punched the Pause key on his computer. The printer skidded to a halt.

"So what's up?" *Besides me, that is,* a silent voice whispered as he turned on her, watching the flush creep up her neck as he buttoned his shirt. "Rappin' Rhonda needs more flexible arms? Hunky Hank needs biceps that ripple? Ice-Cream Ivan needs a mouth that doesn't drool?"

"Actually, it's me." She peeked over her shoulder and, seeing that he was fully dressed, finally turned. A deep blush still pinked her cheeks, and he had the sudden thought that Josie hadn't walked in on too many naked men before.

A thought that pleased him a hell of a lot more than it should have.

"I need something."

"Which is?"

She licked her lips nervously, confirming the No Naked Men theory regarding her past. "A man."

Then again . . .

"The perfect man," she went on. "And you're the only one for the job."

Ha, those stomach crunches *had* paid off.

"You can build anything," she rushed on, cutting off the path of his dangerous thoughts. "While I've got the know-how and I can certainly design him, you would be the one to actually build—"

"Hold on a second. Let me get this straight. You want to *build* a man?"

"The perfect man. We've been looking to branch out, to find something that will appeal to the adult set, something other than the standard board games."

"I think there are other companies making toys for the adult market."

She cut him a glance. "I'm talking technology, not blow-up dolls. He'll have an intellect, as well as a nice smile, a great face and a good body—not that I think he should look like he's pumped up on steroids or anything. Muscular's nice, but too bulky makes me think of sumo wrestling, which stirs thoughts of those diaper-looking underpants, and how sexy are those?"

He arched an eyebrow at her. "Sexy, huh?"

Her cheeks turned a dark shade of pink. "Not that this guy is for sex. He's strictly a companion. Like a puppy, but much nicer to look at, and with a little interactive software, he'll be able to carry on a conversation—"

"A *man*?" he cut in, trying to register what she was telling him. "You want to actually build a man?"

"Not me, *we*. You're the structure expert. I'll be doing the design and some of the programming."

"For a man?"

"The perfect man." She must have read the disbelief on his face. "You don't have to look so shocked. It's not like I'm suggesting we commit one of the seven deadly sins. It'll be like Hunky Hank, only larger. Six feet. Maybe six-two. And much smarter. And no snarling." When he shook his head, she added, "We can do it, you know."

"I'm sure we can."

With her S.K.I.N. to perfect the outside, and Matt's new body heat generator to fuel the inside, forget this being "just another toy, only larger." Their *man* could be the first of a new breed of artificial intelligence.

"We make everything from baby dolls that eat, drink, wet and poop, to toy soldiers that walk and talk and respond to voice commands. Why not a life-size man?"

"The question isn't *why not*, but *why*? There are already life-size robots out there."

"Are you talking about Lester?" She shook her head. "You have to be kidding."

Lester was the most recent model designed by SpaceTek, one of the country's leading robotics manufacturers and Matt's previous employer.

"He's nearly six feet tall," Matt pointed out, "And he walks and talks and carries out programmed orders."

"And he looks like a giant tin can."

"Alloy, not tin."

"Not to mention he's got a great big electrical outlet for a butt."

Only because SpaceTek, while holding the patent on Matt's sensor pad, didn't realize what they had. They were too focused on the precious pads and their use in medical applications such as fever reduction to see the bigger picture. Matt hadn't developed the pad in and of itself. The heat sensor had been a stepping stone to something much bigger.

To Matt's breakthrough body heat converter.

"Electricity was the most obvious power source," he pressed. Obvious, but not practical. The first blackout, and bam, Lester would be useless. While he would probably be able to keep going with a battery pack, it wouldn't be for long. Harry, on the other hand, only needed the touch of a human being to juice him up.

"I'm not talking about a tin can—" At his pointed look, she amended, "an *alloy* can that walks and talks and acts like a man. Our robot will look like one of our dolls, only life-size. *That* will be a first, and a major contribution to women everywhere. Think of the potential."

But Matt was already thinking. A life-size man to actually demonstrate his converter would be much more convincing than Harry, and the perfect way to show the world that Matt Taylor wasn't a thief. He'd been framed and where he hadn't been able to prove his innocence, he could prove his brilliance.

The more impressive the evidence, the better. "I'm in."

Chapter Three

She'd seen Marvin Tannenbaum *naked*.

Sort of.

He hadn't been wearing clothes, but he had been wearing two by two sensor pads over most of his body.

Most.

Josie tried to stifle the wave of heat that worked its way up her neck as she sat in her office and folded wedding invitations for the bride-to-be, Samantha Skye, one of her closest friends and the vice president of marketing for Three Kisses.

Embarrasment. That explained the strange heat that had swept through Josie this past weekend each and every time she'd thought about Marvin. About his bare chest and his rippled abdomen and his . . .

Funny, how she'd barely glimpsed him, yet the image seemed branded into her head. He was more muscular than she'd ever imagined, with dark silk that covered his chest and swirled into an enticing line that bisected his abdomen, surrounded his navel and funneled to his—

"They ought to give out directions with these things," Sam snapped, effectively killing Josie's thoughts.

Thankfully.

Sam, with long blond hair and a body that would have made Pamela Anderson envious, perched on the corner of Josie's desk and attempted to fold the trifold wedding invitation, complete with insert, for the fifth time, and ended up with the top flap on the bottom and the bottom flap on top.

"Hand it over." Josie folded the invitation, slid the insert into its appropriate space, then plopped it into the growing stack on her desk.

"Thanks." Sam shook her head. "I don't know what's wrong with me. I'm not usually all thumbs."

"I know." Usually Samantha Skye was all fingers. Capable, able fingers that did everything in record time. Until Jake Morelli had walked into her life. "You're getting married in two weeks and you've had only a few days to do what takes most people an entire year. You're entitled."

"I should have gone with a single card, no fold and no inserts. I hate angsting over all this stuff. There are so many decisions. The food, the flowers, the dresses. I've been a bridesmaid eight times and I've got eight ugly outfits to show for it."

Josie knew the feeling. She had her own closetful of bridesmaids' dresses, and the war stories to go along with them. The last wedding, she'd given a helpful suggestion and the bride—Tina up in sales—had declared to the other eight bridesmaids that Josie didn't like the dress. She'd spent the entire evening getting hate looks from a row of women decked out in purple tulle complete with matching parasols.

No, thank you. Josie could be a team player just like anyone else. This was Sam's game, her call.

"I want this to be a mutual decision," Sam went on. "I want you to actually *like* the dress. To want to wear it again. I want a win/win situation for all parties involved."

"Your MBA roots are showing."

"I'm serious. I want to pick something we both like."

"As in color?"

"Color and style."

"Why don't you just pick what *you* like. I promise I'll be all right with it."

"No, no. I really want you to pick something you like."

"But it's your wedding."

"And you're wearing the dress."

"It's traditional for the bride to choose the wedding color."

"The wedding's in less than two weeks. I still haven't picked out my dress, my Granny's wearing chartreuse, my flower girl is my dog. I'm just now sending out my invitations. Does this sound like a traditional wedding to you?"

Josie smiled. "Chartreuse would be fine."

Sam did the nose-wrinkling thing again. "You actually like chartreuse? Because Jake's sister hates chartreuse, but if you really like it—"

"Only if you do," Josie cut in. "Do you?"

"Only if you do."

The comments hovered in the air for a long moment as each woman tried to read the other. Personally, Josie hated chartreuse, but if Sam and the other girls really liked it, she would wear it. *If* . . .

"Not that it's any of my business, but chartreuse is a real pukey color."

The comment came from Felicity, a twenty-something brunette with big brown eyes and a smile that looked as if it had come straight out of a Crest commercial. Felicity, Josie's research assistant, spent her days running after the group of five-year-olds currently exploring the wonders of the new Rappin' Rhonda doll on the other side of the bay window that overlooked the play room.

"Now coral," Felicity went on. "There's a hot color."

"Coral?" The minute the word came out of Sam's mouth, Josie mentally scratched coral off her list. "This is a wedding. Why coral?"

"Weddings are prime, grade-A places to meet hot men, so it's really a good idea to look as hot as possible, especially for Josie."

"She doesn't have to look hot. She's bringing a date." Sam's gaze swiveled to Josie's. "You did ask someone, didn't you? This is my moment of true glory. I can't rest easy knowing one of my best friends is mateless *and* dateless."

"I was going to mention it to Archie, but I wanted to talk to you first. I know you wanted an even number of dinner guests, but if he comes, his mother comes, too, which might throw the table seating off."

"Girl, you need to dump that mama's boy," Felicity said. "Find yourself a man who knows how to treat a woman under sixty-five."

"That's right. Take my cousin, J. T." Sam had been talking up her hottie cousin for the past six months, ever since Josie had announced her new quest in life—finding a compatible man.

Unfortunately, Sam's idea of compatible meant a nice horizontal fit rather than an emotional one. "He's handsome, financially solvent and never been married."

"And why is that?" Josie asked. "He's thirty-something and never been married. What's wrong with this picture?"

"You're thirty-something and have never been married," Sam pointed out to Josie.

"Smacks of ugliness to me," Felicity said. At Josie's sharp look, Felicity added, "No offense. It's different for women. We're not losers. We're just choosey."

"Well, J. T. isn't a loser, either," Sam told them. "And he's not ugly. He's gorgeous and single and dances at one of the hottest women's clubs in Chicago."

"Aha," Felicity said. "He's a player."

"One of the best. J. T. loves women and he likes to have fun, and if there's one thing you need in your life," Sam pinned Josie with a stare, "it's a little fun. You're taking this single thing way too seriously."

"Easy for you to say. You're about to tie the knot with the man of your dreams."

"Before I met Jake, the last thing I wanted was to settle down. I was enjoying life, relishing my freedom. You spend so much time cooped up in that lab, it's no wonder Archie's the best you can come up with when it comes to prospective husband material."

"Archie is the end result of months of research, and he isn't the only one I've come up with. There's Mitchell. He's also the perfect prospective life partner."

"And just as boring as Archie. Why are you so hung up on getting married? You're young and vivacious."

"I'm *this close* to thirty-five." To being the

only thirty-five-year-old unmarried woman at Three Kisses.

No.

She wasn't hitting her birthday without at least an engagement ring. A down payment on more to come. Her house in the suburbs with kids, lots of kids.

"All the more reason to live it up," Sam went on. "You're in the sexual prime of your life. When's the last time you grabbed a guy and kissed the hell out of him?" At Josie's silence, Sam went on. "Kissing's fun, Josie. Dating's fun." She wiggled her eyebrows. "Dating hot guys you have no serious interest in is even more fun."

"But J. T. doesn't sound like my type."

"He isn't. That's the point." Sam pinned her with another stare. "I'm giving him your phone number and don't even think about arguing. You don't have to marry the guy. Just let your hair down, smile a little, and enjoy yourself."

"And don't start burping up all those big words like you've just swallowed a copy of *Science Digest*," Felicity added. "Guys don't like girls who are smarter than they are."

"That's probably a good idea," Sam said. "J. T. is very macho. You wouldn't want to threaten his manhood. Just keep it simple and have a good time."

"And think lewd, lascivious sex," Felicity added. At Josie's arched eyebrow, the woman added, "Hey, I believe in positive reinforcement. I think, therefore I have."

"I don't even know this guy. He hasn't even asked me out. He hasn't even *called*, for heaven's sake."

"He will," Sam reassured her. "He will."

Tonight's the night.

The Rod Stewart song pushed into Matt's head, and he immediately shoved it back out.

Tonight was no different from any other, he told himself as he headed down the hallway toward his laboratory. Even if his heart was pounding and his muscles were tense and he could practically smell her soft, musky scent though he was a good hundred feet from his destination.

From her.

Tonight he and Josie were meeting for the first time to go over plans for the new project, and since Arthur Kiss had detained him a good half hour talking about next year's lineup of toy bull-dozers, Matt was late. Josie was already there.

Ready and waiting.

In a strictly professional sense, of course.

Business.

That's all Josie Farrington meant to him, all he would allow. Especially since she made him forget his Marvin persona and slip back into the old Matt, as he'd discovered last night. She was dangerous to his sanity and his privacy, and both were crucial for Matt to pull off this charade.

Even more, she wasn't his type. Josie Farrington was a sugar-cookie woman if he'd ever seen one and, therefore, a definite no-no.

He'd developed his sugar-cookie rule while growing up next door to Mr. and Mrs. Garrett. Every Saturday, Mrs. Garrett would bake cookies while Mr. Garrett stood out back and diced up firewood. Afterward, he would haul the wood to the back porch and she would meet him with a plate of home-baked goodies. They would stare lovingly into each other's eyes, sit side by side in their rocking chairs and eat cookies.

To this day, Matt could still smell the sweet scent of warm sugar and hear the creak of wood as Mr. Garrett moved back and forth.

The last Matt had heard, Mr. and Mrs. Garrett were still married, still holding hands, still meeting on the back porch to eat cookies and rock. They oozed commitment, something Matt wanted no part of.

While he thought women were the greatest thing since chocolate-covered peanuts, he wasn't interested in splitting wood for one or eating her cookies. A quick tumble in bed was all he had time for, and he made sure the women he bedded wanted the same thing.

He gravitated toward the professional, I'm-too-busy-with-my-career types who had no expectations other than a good time. That much Matt could certainly deliver. But there was no way he was giving more before he was good and ready.

If he ever found himself good and ready.

He wasn't making the same mistake his father had made. John Taylor had been the best high school quarterback to ever play football in the state of Texas. He'd had talent. Potential. A bright future ahead of him complete with a ticket out of dead-end Little Creek, straight to the University of Texas and a full scholarship. Then a few heated moments in the backseat of his daddy's Chevy had changed his life forever.

John Taylor had gotten Norma Louise Fisher pregnant, and that had been the beginning of the end. His father, family-oriented and old-fashioned, had forced him to take responsibility, to give up his scholarship and its questionable future to stay home and own up to his mistakes. To be a man and forget his foolish dream of playing professional ball. John, always desperate for his father's approval, had buckled. And at his parents' insistence, he'd married Norma—and he'd spent the rest of his life blaming her for ruining his future.

Matt stifled a surge of bitterness. Not him. He wasn't settling down until he was ready, until he'd done everything he wanted to do and could give himself totally, completely to his family. He wouldn't alienate his wife, and he certainly wouldn't take out his bitterness on an innocent child.

No regrets.

And no attachments, he reminded himself as

a picture of Josie pushed into his mind. The last thing he needed was to get close to anyone. His time at Three Kisses would be over in a few months and he'd be out of here, back at SpaceTek, back on top.

Business.

That's all Josie meant, and Matt wasn't going to think otherwise.

He wasn't going to think about peeling away her heavy lab coat and unbuttoning her conservative sweater and sliding those beige slacks down her long legs and—

A small sob interrupted his dangerous fantasy and he came to a dead stop. His gaze shifted to the open doorway that led to the Research & Development playroom.

Another small, high-pitched sob and he walked inside. A few quick visual scans and he found the source of the noise. A small boy sat in the corner, tears gliding down his face.

"Say, buddy, what's the matter?"

The little boy's head jerked up and tear-filled eyes met Matt's. "My daddy didn't pick me up."

"Did you tell someone?"

He nodded. "Miss Felicity's trying to call. I'm s'posed to wait here until she comes back, but I've never been in here by myself." His voice lowered and an ominous tone crept in. "It's kinda scary."

Matt thought about Josie waiting in his lab and his heart pounded harder. If he didn't show, she was liable to think he'd forgotten, to leave before he had a chance to see her and smell her sweet scent—

He settled himself on the floor and reached for an electric-powered airplane he'd put together last week.

"Actually," he said, starting the propeller. "I think being here alone is pretty cool."

"Really?" The boy wiped at his face.

Matt nodded. "Nobody to fight with over toys."

A small smile crept over the boy's face. "No girls."

"Exactly."

Unfortunately.

Matt shoved aside the ridiculous thought. He needed to see Josie Farrington in a professional sense; the last thing he needed was to see her as a "woman," even if it was the first thing he wanted.

Because it was the first thing he wanted.

"My name is Ethan," the boy said, lifting huge eyes to Matt. "And I like dogs. Not that I have one. But I want one."

"My name is Marvin, and I think dogs are pretty neat, too." He winked and smiled, and before he could stop himself, he reached out and his thumb flicked away the stray tear. "I don't have one either, though. It's good to meet you, Ethan."

So much for no attachments.

Then again, it was just for a little while. Just a few minutes until Felicity returned. Besides, Matt owed the kid. He was an excellent diversion. At this moment, he could be sitting next to Josie Farrington, and while she smelled a lot sweeter, she was a hell of a lot more dangerous.

"You're late." Josie glanced up from a pile of analysis sheets and pinned Matt with a stare when he finally walked into the laboratory a good half hour later.

"Something came up." Just that very second, as a matter of fact. When he'd taken one look into her greener-than-green eyes and felt a jolt of heat straight to his *something*.

Distance, he warned himself, making a bee-line for his computer station, eager to put his hands to good use before they acted on their own agenda and started undoing all those big buttons on her lab coat.

He could feel her gaze on him, watching and stirring. He stiffened and turned on her with the ultimate Marvin look—a sour expression that indicated deep, deep thought and said plainly. *I don't have time for you.*

The look was Matt's primary weapon when acting as Marvin. It was, he hoped, a seemingly natural gesture residual from years of focus, dedication, and lack of interest in the opposite sex. Matt, this time, had to put every ounce of energy into making the look believable.

Instead of turning away, Josie's gaze narrowed and concern flashed in her eyes. "Are you okay?"

"Of course I'm okay." He must be doing something wrong. It had worked like a charm before, sending everyone around him scurrying out of his way. Matt scrunched up his nose as if he'd just bitten into a lemon and tried harder.

"You don't look okay."

"I'm fine."

"You don't look so fine."

"I've never been better."

"You don't look—"

"It's focus." He shoved his glasses up onto his nose for good measure. "Dammit, woman. I look focused."

Christ, he was losing it.

Marvin would never say *dammit, woman*. He'd modeled this character on an old college friend, a roommate who had never said much of anything. He'd been quiet, calm, reserved and severely introverted. He drew in a deep breath and fought the urge to shout.

"I'm *focused*," he said through clenched teeth.

"You look nervous to me. Have you had any coffee? Because I noticed your coffee cup and while I usually try not to preach, all that caffeine can really do crazy things to the nervous system."

If only it was just coffee. He thought about Marvin and his obsessive-compulsive tendencies, including a stringent diet. "It wasn't my cup. I never touch the stuff."

At the admission, a smile crept across Josie's face, sending another burst of heat to a place that had no damned business heating, period. Not where Josie Farrington was concerned.

"Can we just get to work?" he muttered, wiping the expression from her lips.

"Fine." She flashed him a puzzled look before her face grew serious. "Here's the proposal for the project, including the time-frame prospectus."

"ADAM," he read the name on the first page. "Pretty clever."

"He was the first man, and our ADAM will be the first artificial man of his kind. By my calculations, we should be able to have a prototype ready for the National Toy Symposium in six months."

He shook his head. "ADAM is going to be finished in time for the Science Expo. If we introduce him at the toy symposium, that's how people will see him. As a toy. An animated blow-up doll. Introducing him at the Science Expo will lend more credibility." And give Matt a chance to prove his innocence to the very people who'd blacklisted him six months ago and driven him underground to finish his body heat converter in secrecy.

The Expo was his chance at redemption. At revenge.

"You've got a point," she said, seeming to contemplate the situation. "Though I don't want him seen as something so high-tech he's beyond the average person. We could coordinate with marketing to make sure the media— both newspaper and television—covers the unveiling. That would give him more exposure and emphasize his enormous possibilities."

"Sounds good." The more media that witnessed Matt's moment of glory, the better. "Let's get to work."

They spent the next few hours combing over the proposal and making adjustments. Matt tried to keep his mind on business, but every once in a while his gaze slid toward Josie.

She sat in front of her laptop, her glasses riding low on her nose, her hair pulled back into its usual loose braid. Her expression was one of serious intent, a small wrinkle marring the patch of skin between her eyebrows. He had the sudden urge to reach out, to smooth the frown with his thumb and see if her skin felt as soft as it looked. As it smelled.

His nostrils flared and the soft musky scent filtered through his head, stirring his senses, his—

"Are you okay?" Her gentle voice shattered the thought and drew his attention. His gaze collided with hers.

"Fine." He gave the puckered look another try. After all, Matt was persistent.

Josie wasn't the least bit put off. "You don't look fine."

"I'm fine."

"But—"

"*Fine.*" At least that's what Matt told himself. With any luck, he might eventually start to believe it. Otherwise, these were going to be the longest two months of his life.

Chapter Four

". . . go for bachelor number one, I tell ya. Number one!"

Josie heard the familiar voice drifting from her apartment the minute she reached the third-floor landing. Anyone else who lived alone might have turned and gone straight to a pay phone to call the cops and report an intruder. But Josie wasn't just the youngest resident among the over-sixty set that inhabited the Michigan Avenue brownstone. She was also the only one with cable TV.

While Josie subscribed primarily for the science channel, she also received everything from the golf channel to the twenty-four hour

Gameshow Network—a favorite of the spend-thrift seniors in her building, particularly her next-door neighbor and resident handyman, Elijah Babcock.

"Hi, Mr. Babcock," she said as she pushed open the door to find the seventy-something-year-old man parked on one end of her beige sofa. A re-run of *The Dating Game* blazed on her TV. A half-empty bowl of granola sat on her coffee table next to a large wrench and her remote control.

"Hey there, little lady." He grabbed a handful of granola, popped it into his mouth, and pushed to his feet. His face puckered as he chewed. "How can you eat this stuff?"

"Granola is healthy."

"And tasteless. I got two words for you—pork rinds. Now there's a snack."

"I'll remember that the next time I'm at the Healthy Mart. So what are you doing here so late?"

He retrieved his wrench and motioned to the kitchen. "Just changing that S pipe under your sink."

Since Josie had had the cable hooked up, her apartment had skyrocketed to the top of Mr. Babcock's maintenance list. If it wasn't her S pipe, it was her leaky toilet or the knock in her dryer or a strange humming in her refrigerator, or the invisible mouse he still hadn't been able to catch, despite his best efforts. Just last Saturday, he'd shown up with a *TV Guide*, a six-pack of root beer, and three cans of Cheeze

Whiz, the last of which he'd sworn would nab the little bugger. But after three hours and six episodes of *Wheel of Fortune*, he still hadn't caught the rodent.

Not that there was one. The mouse, along with her S pipe and her O-ring and all the other repairs, were Mr. Babcock's excuses to watch her TV.

"I hate to keep you up so late. The sink could have waited until tomorrow."

"No trouble." He shrugged. "I just got my second wind."

She smiled. "Just in time for *The Dating Game*, I see." His favorite, though he enjoyed everything from *Wheel of Fortune* to *The Price is Right*.

"They got celebrity guests on tonight." His gaze shifted to the TV where a platinum blonde was capering about, dressed in go-go boots and brilliant blue eyeshadow. "Why, Goldie Hawn looks just like my Priscilla did back then. Man, but she was a looker." Priscilla was the late Mrs. Babcock. She'd died of heart failure more than ten years ago, and she was one of the main reasons Josie put up with Mr. Babcock and his game shows. Not that she'd been personally acquainted with Priscilla. The woman had long since passed on by the time Josie had moved into the brownstone. But whenever the old man mentioned his dearly departed wife, a soft, lovesick expression flashed in his eyes.

That, and a look of overpowering loneliness. While Josie wasn't the least bit familiar with the first emotion, loneliness she knew all too well.

"She certainly is pretty." Josie left her briefcase by the door and unbuttoned her coat.

"And stubborn." He frowned as he watched Goldie make her decision. "If I said it once, I said it a dozen times. *Number one.*" He punched the Off button on the remote and went to retrieve his toolbox from the kitchen. "So why are you out so late?"

"New project." She followed him out to the kitchen and braced herself for the coming lecture.

"It ain't right for a young girl to be roaming the streets at this ungodly hour."

"I didn't roam the streets. I came straight home."

"It's still an ungodly hour. Anything can happen. You got that Mace I picked up for you?"

"In my purse."

"What about the whistle?"

She indicated the nylon rope around her neck and the small piece of metal that hung suspended.

"Good girl," he said and a small spiral of warmth went through her. Mr. Babcock might be nuttier than a pan of pecan muffins, but he was also sweet and caring. He constantly nagged her about being cautious, but he also left the newspaper on her doorstep every morning, took out her trash and had even programmed her VCR to record *Chemistry Tonight*. The least she could do was let him

56

appropriate her TV to watch his nightly game shows.

"So the sink is in working order now?" she asked, even though she'd made tea and done dishes just that morning.

"That's how it looks, but don't be fooled by appearances." He tossed the wrench inside the toolbox sitting on her small, round kitchen table and slammed the lid shut. "It might look and run okay, but I've still got to put in a new O plug." He held up a piece of black rubber. "This'll do away with that squeaky sound it's been making."

She turned on the faucet. "I don't hear anything."

"Sure you do." He leaned in close to the stream of water for several seconds. "There. That's a squeak if I ever heard one."

"I still don't hear anything."

"Don't fret," he went on as if she hadn't said a word. He cut the water off and patted the knob. "I'll get over here tomorrow night and get this puppy runnin' real nice and quiet."

She arched an eyebrow at him. "*Price is Right* marathon?"

A grin crinkled his old face. "*Family Feud* is hosting famous TV families." He hefted his toolbox and started for the front door. "The Carringtons from *Dynasty* are going up against the *Eight is Enough* bunch."

"Sounds like fun."

"All in a day's work, little lady. All in a day's work."

Kimberly Raye

"Speaking of work," Josie murmured as she closed the door behind Mr. Babcock. Her bones ached with exhaustion, but she wasn't nearly ready to call it a night and climb into bed. Instead, she retrieved her briefcase.

While she'd written the initial proposal for ADAM, Marvin had made several brilliant and invaluable suggestions, which she intended to implement tonight when she started on the actual design.

Josie pressed the message button on her answering machine and turned to unpack her briefcase, organizing everything into nice, neat piles on her coffee table while the first message played.

"This is Samantha. What do you think about teal? Jake likes teal but he doesn't have to wear it. You do. Call me."

While Josie loved her friend, she couldn't help but envy her. Sam had found Jake living in the apartment below her. No seminar. No research. No fruitless searching for a man who met each of the Ten Compatibility Commandments. Just a knock on the door downstairs and, bam, instant life partner.

Beep.

"It's Sam again. What about lavender? Royal purple? It's an evening wedding, but we could go either way because I want you to be comfortable. To wear the dress again. I want to break the ugly bridesmaid's dress cycle. Call me . . ."

The only person living above Josie was Mr.

58

Thompkins, the eighty-something square dance caller for the local senior's home. While he was single—he'd outlived five wives—he didn't come close to meeting even one of the Commandments.

Josie needed a man with a comparable IQ who was dedicated, neat, health-conscious, ready to settle down, a white-collar professional, not too flashy a dresser, a lover of classical music, and a nonsmoker. While those qualifications only added up to nine, she wasn't fool enough to think she could actually find a man who met number ten.

That would be pushing things a bit too far.

Nine out of ten would more than make her happy.

Beep.

"Hello, Josephine. This is Dad. I've finally wrapped up that exothermal gravitational hand for NASA, so I'm heading off for a weekend of relaxation. I'll be at the Summers Institute, sitting in on a seminar on polymer nuclides. I hope work is going well. The department is still buzzing over your invention. That's my girl!"

She was, indeed, every bit her father's daughter. That was the only explanation for the fact that Josie had spent her entire adult life with her head buried in her work.

Joseph Farrington was one of the most brilliant research scientists at MIT and a total workaholic. After his divorce from Josie's mother when Josie was five, he'd turned to work to distract him from his lost marriage. Since then, he'd been so consumed, so driven that he'd never remarried. He lived in a cramped house cluttered with equipment and computer readouts and old science journals, and smelled of mothballs and antiseptic. Work was and always would be the center of his universe. Up until six months ago, Josie had been following in his footsteps.

But she wanted more. A husband and kids. A real family. For the first time in her life.

As if some cosmic force were listening in on her desperate thoughts, the answering machine beeped again and Archie's message came over the line.

"Hi, Josie. Bad news. Can't make our poetry date. Mom has laryngitis from doing too much karaoke and she doesn't think she'll have her voice back in time. But how about dinner? Saturday night. Our place. Seven sharp."

Our place.

As in more than one. As in he lived with his mother.

Josie leaned her head back against the sofa, closed her eyes and fought back a wave of despair.

So, he lived with his mother. So what? Living alone was not one of the Ten Compatibility Commandments. If it had been, she would have bypassed Archie for Mitchell, the thirty-nine-year-old cardiac surgeon desperate to have kids before his sperm dried up, or so he'd told her during the starting five minutes of their first date.

Being ready to settle down *was* one of the Commandments, so the dates with Mitchell had progressed to two, then three. They were holding steady at four with no commitment as of yet since she'd yet to rule out Archie. But Josie knew that Mitchell wouldn't wait forever. He'd taken to playing the New York Symphony's version of the mating of the whales whenever they were in his car.

While she liked his enthusiasm, she couldn't quite picture herself waking up to him every morning. Or going to bed with him. Or *being* in bed with him.

Not that sex had anything to do with anything. Sex could be misleading. People married all the time on the basis of great sex—marriages that usually ended in divorce because mating simply couldn't take up twenty-four hours of the day. People had to talk to each other, to interact, and in order to do so, they had to like and respect each other.

She liked and respected both Mitchell and Archie, even if they didn't make her toes curl with one glance.

Beep.

"What about hot pink? Do you like hot pink? It's Sam. Call me . . ."

Beep.

"I've got one word—lemon. Sam, here. Call—" The message cut off as the phone rang.

Josie snatched up the receiver. "Please stop obsessing about this. It's not good for your nerves. I'll waltz down the aisle naked if that's what you want."

"Is that a promise?" The deep, compelling voice rumbled over the line and a tingle swept the length of Josie's spine.

She sat up straighter. Heat rushed to her cheeks. "I—I'm sorry. I, um, thought you were someone else."

Laughter rumbled, so deep and soothing and *stirring*. "A lucky someone from the sound of things."

Her cheeks burned hotter. "No, no, she's just a friend. She's getting married and she's been stressing, trying to pick the right dress color even though I could care less. I just want her to be happy."

"Suggest red. Samantha loves red."

"How do you . . . ?" The question faded as realization clicked and she remembered Sam's vow to give Josie's phone number to her cousin. This was the cousin. The cute cousin. The cute cousin with the terribly sexy voice.

Her hands trembled as she clutched the receiver. "Red, you say?"

"She likes red. She's always wearing something red."

Josie searched her mind. Sure enough, she came up with an image of Sam from that afternoon. She'd had on a taupe suit with a red scarf. And the day before, she'd worn a red heart-shaped pin, and the day before that, some red earrings.

"Red," she said. "Thanks."

"Anytime."

Silence settled for a few frantic heartbeats and Josie had the strange feeling he was debating whether or not to hang up.

"So," she blurted before he had the chance. "Is that the only reason you called? To make suggestions for Sam?"

"Actually, I just called to hear your voice." The words slid into her ears and sent a rush of warmth through her body.

She searched for a deep, sexy murmur. If he looked half as good as he sounded—and Josie knew from Sam that he did—she wasn't about to scare him away with her plain old boring voice. "And?"

"And what?"

"What do you think? Do I pass the voice test?"

"That depends. Do I?"

"Definitely," she blurted before she could think better of it. She didn't want to seem too eager. She *wasn't* eager she reminded herself. "I mean, you sound really nice."

"Nice?" His soft chuckle whispered over her senses and her heart pounded faster.

Pounded? Oh, God, her heart was pounding. And she was tingling. And there was this heat . . .

"Josie?"

"Hmmm?" She realized he was still waiting for an answer to his question. *Nice*? "Great," she clarified, marveling at the sensations rushing through her. "You sound really great."

"And you sound nervous. Am I making you nervous, Josie?"

"Not at all." Despite her pounding heart, he wasn't making her nervous. Anxious and excited and a multitude of other feelings she couldn't begin to name, anything, everything, but nervous.

"I was working late tonight. I've got this new project in the works, a multifunctional form of artificial intelligience that . . ." Her words faded as she remembered Felicity's comment about burping up big words. "I—I just get really worked up at the start of a new project."

More silence ticked by while she prayed that she hadn't gone too far and insulted his manhood. It was crazy because she didn't have time for this . . . this *lust.* Still, she couldn't make her heart calm and she certainly couldn't put down the phone.

"What else gets you worked up?"

The question, so low and sexy, sent a thrill to her when the only thing on her mind should have been hanging up. The men she'd actually slept with—the very few and far between—had never asked her such intimate questions, and this was a stranger.

Not a total stranger, mind you. He was Sam's cousin. But she'd still never met him face to face. Never even talked to him until now.

Hang up, she told herself.

Instead, her hand tightened on the receiver.

While she'd never met him, she couldn't help but feel this strange connection to him. A familiarity. "This is going to sound crazy, but it's almost like I know you."

"You do."

"I don't mean just as Sam's cousin. I mean *know* know you."

There was a slight pause, as if he were searching for something to say. "Sam's probably told you so much about me," he finally murmured. "That's probably why you feel like you already know me."

"Maybe." That could account for the strange sense of familiarity. That and the fact that she liked the sound of his voice. There was just something so compelling about the deep, husky tone. Something intimate.

"The sound of your voice," she heard herself say.

"What?"

"That's what gets me worked up. The sound of your voice." She couldn't believe the admission had passed her lips. Josephine Farrington never, ever said such bold things. She'd never had the urge to say them. But they were, after all, just talking. It wasn't as if she'd ripped off her clothes right in front of him.

Oddly enough, she felt as if she had.

Silence stretched for a long moment; she had the distinct impression he was smiling.

"I'm glad," he finally murmured. "Sweet dreams." The phone clicked and Josie was left with a pounding heart, a tingling body and enough heat to rival a major nuclear reaction. Josie, who never pounded or tingled or warmed for any man.

And this wasn't even a man. It was a voice. A *voice* for heaven's sake.

What was wrong with her?

What was wrong with him?

Matt slid the receiver back into place and damned himself a thousand times. He'd meant to call just to make sure she'd gotten home all right. After all, they'd worked very late and while he'd wanted nothing more than to walk her home, he'd held back. Getting close to her was a bad idea. But letting her wander the streets of Chicago after dark was unconscionable.

So he'd called.

Then he'd heard her voice and something had come over him.

Stupidity, a voice whispered. Pure stupidity. In an instant, he'd forgotten the no-nonsense nasal sound of Marvin's boring monotone and had simply talked to her as Matt—and she'd mistaken him for someone else.

Thankfully.

The last thing he needed was to get into an intimate conversation with Josie Farrington. An intimate *anything*, for that matter. His success depended on keeping his identity a secret. The farther he stayed from everyone at Three Kisses, the less chance of discovery. Not to mention that he would return to the real world, to the old Matt Taylor, in a little more than two months. The fewer relationships he formed, the easier leaving would be and the less his chance of discovery in the meantime.

Matt slid off his T-shirt and tossed it to the floor of his cluttered apartment.

Not that leaving would be difficult in any way, shape or form. He couldn't wait to leave. He was tired of the disguise, of treating every book lined neatly on the massive bookshelf in his lab—from *Brain Food* to *The History of Polyester*—as the gospel according to Marvin Tannenbaum.

It had been the gospel to the real Marvin, Matt's ex-college roommate and every bit the geek Matt was doing his best to emulate. Marvin was off in Switzerland on a research project that had him living isolated up in the Alps with nothing but a mess of books and a computer. His old pal was in isolationist heaven. Marvin had always been content to make discoveries for himself in obscurity; Matt had wanted the world to see.

To notice.

And they would. All he had to do was keep his head and remember that those books on his shelf represented the man he was supposed to be in public. A man who never ate pizza and drank beer and longed to do something real with his hands.

He *was* doing something, he reminded himself.

In between the dolls and the miniature cars, he'd spent the past six months perfecting the body heat converter. Now all he had to do was complete ADAM and reveal his invention to the world, along with his true identity. SpaceTek and the entire scientific community would see that he wasn't a thief. Matt was every bit a top-notch scientist.

The converter would prove that.

If Jack Donovan, the real thief and Matt's nemesis, didn't catch up to him first.

"Tell Madame Maureen what it is that you need to find."

"Actually," Eve Malone walked into the third-floor apartment that belonged to her landlady—hairdresser by day and fortune-teller/witch by night—and debated the answer to that question.

On one hand, she needed a plunger. That's what had sent her running up to Madame Maureen's red-velvet house of cosmic energy—aka Apartment 302—in the middle of the night to find the older woman decked out in a psychadelic mumu and two dozen Mardi Gras beads.

On the other, Eve hadn't spent the past six months searching for the infamous Dr. Matthew Taylor to let such a prime opportunity pass her by. Even if she did think Maureen Grabowski was a few bottles of sangria past sober. Six months would make any woman desperate.

Besides, Eve had nothing to lose by asking.

"A man," she told Madame Maureen, sliding into the chair opposite the woman seated at a round table covered in red and fringed with matching tassles. "I need to find a man."

"Ah, but of course." Madame Maureen, a fiftyish woman with steel-blue hair anchored with a brightly colored purple scarf, reached behind her to a shelf overflowing with bottles and jars. She unscrewed the lid of one, retrieved a silver goodie and set it in front of Eve. "The kiss of luck. Eat this and you'll find the man of your dreams."

"I don't want the man of my dreams." She pushed what looked like an ordinary Hershey's kiss back toward Madame Maureen.

The *last* thing Eve needed in her life was a dream man. She'd been there, done that. Thanks to her husband, the late Burt Malone, a wanna-be private investigator, part-time tournament bowler and cheating scumbag, Eve had learned her lesson where men were concerned.

Never again.

But this was different. This was strictly business.

"I'm looking for a particular man."

She gave Madame Maureen all the specifics on Matthew Taylor, brilliant scientist and the only silver lining in Eve's cloudy future.

"So, can you help?"

"I don't know."

"Please, Maureen. You're my last chance." And that was the only reason Eve—whose idea of a religious experience consisted of standing in the shoe department at Saks and simply taking a deep, rejuvenating whiff—

would even consider consulting a self-proclaimed fortune-teller/witch, even if said fortune-teller/witch was her upstairs neighbor and the only link between a stopped-up toilet and happiness.

She didn't believe in magic or little green men or things that went bump in the night. Just as she didn't place an ounce of faith in love and fairy tales and happily-ever-afters. Eve even had her doubts when it came to a higher power. If there'd been someone Upstairs watching over her, she wouldn't be in this mess. Widowed at the ripe old age of twenty-eight, with five dollars in the bank and five thousand dollars' worth of credit card bills—thanks to Burt—she wasn't exactly sitting pretty. Not to mention she'd hocked everything worth anything and borrowed the rest to come up with enough money to pay for his funeral.

Her mind rushed back to the night of his death. She could still see him in the front seat of his car with Sherril Shapiro. One minute Eve had been watching them getting it on via a pair of binoculars. The next, she'd seen the car explode into a giant ball of flame, courtesy of Sherril's jealous boyfriend, and just like that, the eight most miserable years of Eve's life had come to a blazing end.

Okay, so maybe there was a higher power.

After all, after eight years of cooking and cleaning; of listening to Burt badmouth her and her cat, Twinkles; of finding panties in his pocket and lipstick on his collar; she figured she'd more than earned her freedom and a second chance.

Matt Taylor was that chance. Her future. Her ticket to financial freedom.

But first she had to find him.

"Come on, Maureen. Try to pick up some vibes or something. *Anything*. Is he still in the city? The suburbs? Has he fled the country?"

"Geography really isn't my specialty." Maureen pushed the chocolate kiss back at Eve. "I specialize in love potions." She wiggled her eyebrows. "Just gobble it up and you'll have the first man you meet begging at your feet. Guaranteed."

Eve's stomach grumbled at the prospect. Not at the begging man part. She was more interested in the gobbling. Dire financial straits meant tightening her belt when it came to groceries and she hadn't had the luxury of a candy bar in days.

She summoned her courage and pushed the foil-wrapped candy back at Madame Maureen. "I'll give you a ten percent discount on a pedicure if you give me some answers."

"I didn't know you gave pedicures." The woman stared her down. "Sixty percent," she finally said.

"Forty-five."

"Fifty."

"Deal." It was a huge discount, but Eve had been surviving on discounted beautician work, so this was hardly any worse than she'd *been* doing. And maybe this would help.

After rummaging beneath the table, the woman pulled out an apple-size crystal ball and sat it on a piece of satin in the center of the table. Closing her eyes, she chanted for several long moments before her eyes snapped open and she stared into its glassy depths.

Eve held her breath, waiting. She didn't believe in such things, but maybe . . . Just maybe . . . "What do you see?"

"A man." She peered closer, her eyes widening. "Yes, yes, it's a man all right."

"Is it him?"

"Maybe."

"Is he in Chicago?"

"Possibly."

"Will I find him?"

"Very likely."

"Will Madonna settle down and marry Jerry Falwell?"

"Who knows." Madame Maureen sighed, retrieved a bottle of sangria from the sideboard behind her and took a long swig, ending on a burp. "Boy, am I tired. Dealing with the Other Side is hard work.

"That's it?"

"You still get the blessed kiss," the woman said, motioning to the candy. "And since this is your first visit, I'm upping your name on the tenants' list. The plumber will get to your toilet first thing Monday."

Rather than try to shove the kiss back at Maureen yet again, Eve stuffed it into her coat pocket and frowned. "But you didn't tell me anything solid."

"There are no solids on the Other Side. Sometimes the link is fuzzy. Sometimes it's clear. I did my part. You wanted answers, I gave you some."

Before Eve could form a reply, Madame Maureen slid off her outlandish velvet purple sandals and plopped her legs onto the table.

"There's something growing on that little toe," she told Eve, pointing to her foot. "But don't worry. It's not contagious . . . I don't think."

Eve took one look at the woman's feet and came *this close* to running the other way. But a deal was a deal, and Eve Malone always kept her word.

After eight years with Burt and total financial ruin, her word was all she had left. That and a broken toilet, and a girl had to do what a girl had to do.

Chapter Five

What else gets you worked up?

The words slid into her ears, as smooth and hypnotizing as the large, strong hands that slid over her body, fingertips stroking and searching and setting her on fire.

"That," Josie murmured as he touched the tender side of her neck, just below her ear. "Mmm, and that." He licked the frantic beat of her pulse. "That, too." His fingertips stroked the underside of one breast. "Oh, and *that*," she gasped as his tongue flicked at the hard tip of one nipple and sensation bolted through her.

And then she opened her eyes.

Her heartbeat hammered and her blood rushed as she glanced around and realized she'd been having a dream. A very intense, erotic dream.

Darn it.

Josie spent the next half hour prowling her kitchen. She ate an entire honeydew melon and a few granola bars, but nothing could satisfy the craving deep inside.

A *craving*, of all things.

Josie didn't believe in cravings. She was a firm believer in mind over body, and while the body might want certain things, it was up to the mind to control that want, and her mind had always had a firm dictatorship.

Until now.

Her hormones were launching an all-out rebellion, and for the first time, Josie could understand Phyllis' need for Cocoa Puffs. Not that Josie was spiraling down the processed-food drain just yet. She had her own form of comfort. Her work.

Settling on the sofa, she pulled out her laptop. The screen flickered and ADAM's image appeared. Josie set about making the numerous calculations needed to compute the required amount of material. With any luck, she and Marvin could start on the actual physical structure at the beginning of next week.

But as she worked, her mind kept going back to the dream. To the hands touching her neck and breasts and . . . Her pulse quickened and a hunger gnawed at her, and for the first time in her life, her work wasn't enough.

She wanted more.

She wanted *him*.

She tried to push the memory of his voice away, but it stayed with her, replaying, making her nerves buzz, her body feel tight and itchy and *desperate* until she gave up the computer and went in search of something cold to drink.

She needed relief.

She felt her forehead. She was actually feverish.

Josie shrugged off her robe without even bothering to fold it and put it away. Instead she jerked open the refrigerator and simply stood there, letting the cold air wash over her.

She'd been attracted to men before. She'd even had a steady boyfriend in college. Her lab partner in biochemistry. They'd studied together and even had sex a few times, but nothing—not his kisses, or even his quick, efficient lovemaking—had ever made her feel as anxious, as needy as she did right now. *Nothing* had ever made her peel off her robe and stand naked in front of an open refrigerator.

Lust.

Heavens, she was in *lust*, of all things, despite the fact that at this point in her life, she didn't want to fall into lust. She wanted to fall into compatibility. To find the perfect lifemate, even if he didn't stir a fourth of what J. T. made her feel.

Lust was misleading. It clouded the facts and made people think they were right for each other when they couldn't have been more wrong. Her own parents' divorce had taught her that. They'd met and married in a few weeks, and spent the following five years trying to recapture what they'd had.

But they hadn't been able to—because it hadn't been something precious they'd shared, simply lust. Once that lust had been spent, there'd been nothing left but two people who didn't have anything in common.

Her mother and father had met one night at a club where her mother had been auditioning and her father had been celebrating his most recent discovery—how to bond nuclide proteins. Her mother had been a wanna-be country and western singer, while her father had been a teaching assistant at his alma mater. Her mother had loved George Jones; her father only listened to Mozart. Her mother liked the Movie of the Week and her father watched nothing but documentaries. Her mother had been a smoker, her father a non-smoker, her mother an innie, her father an outie.

In every aspect, they'd been opposites and while they'd shared a child, it hadn't been enough to keep them together. Her mother had left and headed for Nashville while her father had taken a professorship.

Josie had grown up spending the school years with her father and the summer with her mother who'd given up her dreams of being the next Tammy Wynette, to sing background for a recording studio, a job she still held today. She'd married a handsome guitarist and settled two blocks from the Grand Ole Opry. While Josie flew down once a year and her mother made the occasional trip up, they weren't as close as other mothers and daughters. Josie was too much like her father, which meant, despite being the same sex, she and her mother had little in common.

Which was why Josie wasn't basing a major life commitment on anything other than compatibility. Lust felt good for a little while, but the feeling faded.

That's what she told herself as she took a deep breath, gathered up her robe and slammed the refrigerator door.

But two hours later, after tossing and turning, her body burning up despite the ice-cold comfort blowing from the air-conditioning vents, she started to wonder if maybe, just maybe there was something to this lust business.

She was sweating, for heaven's sake. Tingling. *Wanting.*

You don't have to marry the guy. Just have a little fun.

Sam's words echoed in her ears, refusing her any peace until she finally admitted the truth. Her friend was right. She *didn't* have to marry the guy. She wouldn't. But fun . . .

Josie had spent her entire life with her nose buried in a book. She'd missed out on so much—parties and picnics and football games and school carnivals and all the other events that most kids enjoyed during a lifetime.

79

Why should she miss out on a little old-fashioned bone-melting, knee-trembling lust?

After a lifetime spent dedicating herself to her work, she deserved a little fun.

"Okay, everybody. It's fun time." Josie made the announcement to the group of five-year-olds scattered throughout the R&D play area. "Since everybody's been so good and there have been no fights—"

"Tommy pulled my hair."

"And Missy stepped on my feet."

"And Julie spit at me."

The comments echoed through the group and Josie amended: "Since everybody's still alive, we'll put away the toys and do something really fun." She smiled. "A new project." The news met with a round of applause and youthful excitement.

Josie had started organizing one small chemistry project a week to share with the kids after one of them had asked her why she sat around with a clipboard and never did any real work. She'd explained that the clipboard was part of her work. The kids hadn't understood and so she'd decided to give them a demonstration of what a chemist actually did.

She'd first demonstrated basic chemical analysis with paper chromatography using blotting paper and black ink. That was six months ago. She'd been performing simple experiments to a rapt audience ever since.

"Does anyone remember what we did last week?"

"We made bread," one of the children called out.

"That's right. We used yeast, which has starches and sugars that decompose rapidly into carbon-dioxide gas and ethanol, which result in gas bubbles that cause the yeast to distend—"

"What's de-com-pose?"

"Yeah, what's dis-tend?

"Decompose means to separate into constituent elements, while distend refers to the state of gathering in volume and size and . . ." Her words trailed off as she noted the glazed looks of the children. Felicity's comment about burping up *Science Digest* terms echoed through her head. "Yeast gets bigger, which makes the dough bigger, which enables us to make a really big loaf of bread."

Realization dawned on the small faces that surrounded her and she breathed a sigh of relief. She didn't have to burp if she didn't want to.

"Can we make a chocolate cake next time?" one of the kids asked.

Josie shrugged. "Chocolate might taste good, kids, but it's really bad for you. How about if we make a carrot cake?"

Ethan made a face. "I like chocolate cake."

"I like chocolate fudge cake."

"Well, I like double chocolate fudge with chocolate chips."

"Well, I—"

"How about paste?" Josie cut in. "Does anyone like paste?" A dozen hands shot into the air. "Good because today we're going to make paste. Paste is a product that forms from a chemical reaction between starch and water."

"Can we make red paste? Red is my favorite color."

"Blue is my favorite color."

"Dark blue is my favorite color."

"Super dark blue is my favorite—"

"We can make any shade of paste we want by adding pigmenta—I mean, color." No burping, she reminded herself. "But first we have to mix our basic compound. Now, we start with water and starch and just to make our paste more adhesive, a dropper filled with natural tree sap . . ."

Thirty minutes later, Josie handed each child a small container of paste to take home to show his parents.

"What about yours?" The question came from Ethan, a small blond-haired boy with wide blue eyes and freckles. He lingered behind after all the children had filed out and motioned to the paste left over in a beaker. "Don't you want to take some home to show your mommy?"

"My mom doesn't live with me anymore."

"My mom doesn't live with me either." His head dropped. "She yells at my dad a lot. And he yells back. I don't think they like each other anymore."

"Why, I'm sure they do." She knelt down beside him and adjusted the collar of his shirt. "Sometimes grown-ups get so mad that they just forget they like each other."

"I think they forgot they like me. My mommy doesn't come around. My dad says she's too busy trying to glue her head together."

"I think that's *get* her head together."

Tear-filled blue eyes lifted to hers. "The last time I saw her, it didn't even looked cracked. I think she just doesn't want me."

"Sweetie, I'm sure she wants you. She just needs some time. Meanwhile, you've got your daddy to take care of you."

"He doesn't come home until late and he's so tired, he forgets to read to me. He forgets everything." His head dropped and he eyed his sneakers. "He forgot to pick me up the other day. I don't think he likes me anymore either."

"I'm sure that's not true. When I was a little girl, my mommy had to leave, too, and my daddy was really sad. He didn't have much time for me then because he was so busy with his work, but that didn't mean he didn't love me."

Josie had blamed herself when her mother had walked away, and then she'd blamed herself when her father had buried himself in his job. It wasn't until years later that she'd finally understood he'd been working so hard as a way of escaping his own pain.

She wouldn't, couldn't do that to her own child, which was the very reason she'd taken Dr. Sophia's Perfect Life Mate seminar.

Marriage equaled forever in Josie's book, especially since she wanted kids of her own. Of course, before she could start the kids, she had to pick the father.

Archie or Mitchell or—

There was no *or*.

Archie or Mitchell, end of discussion.

"I'm sure your daddy didn't mean to forget. It was just an accident. Remember when you spilled your apple juice on Jenny's new dress?" Ethan nodded. "It was a bad thing, but you didn't mean to do it . . ." Her words faded as she noted his small smile. "Okay, bad example. How about the time you smashed bananas in Winnifred's braids . . ." Another smile. "Ethan Callahan. Did you smash those bananas into poor Winnie's braids on purpose?"

"I wouldn't answer that, buddy. You'll just incriminate yourself."

The deep resonant voice sent her heart into overdrive and her head snapped up. It couldn't be—

It wasn't.

She found Marvin standing in the doorway and realized the strange familiarity had just been her own wishful thinking. She'd been hearing the voice all day, anticipating it, and so she'd projected it onto Marvin who was hardly the deep, rumbling, melt-your-bones type.

With his tie and dress shirt and black slacks covered with a white buttoned-up lab coat, he was more the stuffy scientist type.

Rightly so.

He *was* a stuffy scientist, even if he did have a strong jaw, nice lips, a decent nose and she had seen him naked—sort of. His black wire-framed glasses sort of lent him a Clark Kent air. The green bouffant cap, however, killed the entire Superman analogy and yanked him back down to Jimmy Olsen status, and then only *if* he shed the cap.

Her gaze met his and she had the sudden incredible urge to pull his hat off just to see what lay beneath. Did he even have hair? Was it as dark as his eyebrows? Short or long? Thick or thin?

She forced the questions aside. Marvin's hair was the least of her problems and the fact that she'd seen him naked was a memory best forgotten.

Her attention shifted back to Ethan. "I'll make you a deal. I'll take my paste home if you take yours home. You make me something and I'll make you something. Then we can exchange gifts next time after everybody leaves. Sort of like secret pals."

Ethan's gaze shifted to Marvin. "It won't be a secret if Mr. Marvin knows."

"I promise I won't tell." Marvin winked and grinned in very un-Marvin-like fashion, and Josie marveled at the transformation it made of his face. He looked softer, more approach-able. Maybe even handsome . . .

"I'll need the preliminaries on ADAM before

you leave." The frown returned as his gaze shifted to her and he did that awful pucker thing with his eyebrows.

Maybe handsome was stretching things a bit. More like tolerable. Borderline ugly.

"You have finished the preliminary designs, haven't you? I've got other projects and I think we should get started right away, and I hope you gave some serious consideration to the size issues we discussed."

Definitely ugly. And pushy. And irritating. *On purpose.*

She ignored the strange thought. Marvin had no reason to provoke, except maybe out of professional jealousy. Lord knew Josie had dealt with her fair share of that, and always in a calm, cool and dignified fashion.

"Listen, buster." *Adios calm, cool and dignified.*

Even as she felt her temperature rise and heard the annoyed note in her voice, she couldn't stop it. There was just something about him that made her heart work faster and her blood pound.

"I'm finished and the designs are already in your lab, and there are no size issues. My design. My choice."

If she didn't know better, she would have sworn she saw a glimmer of laughter in his eyes, but then his frown deepened. "I'll have a look and we can go over them tomorrow."

"Fine."

"Fine," she ground out, grabbing her beaker

of paste and her briefcase. "Come on, Ethan. I'll walk you down to the lobby to wait for your dad."

As Josie walked by Marvin, her heart gave a frenzied *bam, bam, bam*.

Anger, she told herself. And dread. It was going to be the longest month or two of her life.

Starting with an endless night.

She puttered around her apartment later that evening and tried to forget all about the phone and the fact that it hadn't so much as beeped once.

Not that she was waiting. It was better if J. T. didn't call at all, since she really didn't have time to waste on a no-end relationship. No matter how titillating. He shouldn't call. She didn't want him to call. In fact, she hoped with all her heart that he didn't—

Rrring!

She snatched it up before it could make it to a second ring. "Hello?" she said breathlessly.

"What about blue?" Sam asked.

"What?"

"Blue? For the bridesmaid's dress. You like blue, don't you?"

"Do you like blue?" Josie asked.

"Only if you like blue . . ."

This had to stop. "I like red," she said, sending up a silent prayer that Sam's cousin had been right, even if he had forgotten how to dial the phone. The jerk.

"Red? What shade of red?"

87

"Vivid red."

Silence floated over the line and Josie could actually see Sam chewing her bottom lip. "Really?" she finally asked. "You're sure about this?"

Actually . . . *Stop it.* She was going with red, for better or for worse. She gathered her courage. "I'm positive. I love red. I live for red."

A big sigh floated over the line and Josie's fingers relaxed on the telephone.

"Red is my absolute favorite color," Sam finally said. "This couldn't be more perfect. I knew letting you pick the color would be for the best. Now we'll both be happy. It's win-win all the way. So what style were you thinking of?"

Style? "What styles do you like?"

"Whatever you like."

Here we go again . . .

Josie spent the next ten minutes going back and forth on the phone before she finally managed to hang up. And then only after promising to decide by tomorrow.

She'd barely slid the receiver into place when the phone rang again.

"Whatever you want," she blurted.

"Is that a promise?" The deep, familiar voice rumbled over the line and for a moment Josie's heart stopped beating altogether.

It was him.

Chapter Six

"It's you," Josie blurted.

"Expecting someone else?"

Josie managed to quiet her pounding heart long enough to draw air into her lungs. "Actually, I wasn't expecting anyone. I mean, it's late."

"And Archie would never call this late."

"How do you know . . . Sam," she finally finished. "She told you about Archie, didn't she?"

He hesitated, as if he didn't want to answer. A strange niggle of doubt went through her.

"It's okay. She told me all about you, too. Archie's a little unconventional, but he's a nice guy."

"Whose mother probably tucked him into

bed hours ago." There was no mistaking the laughter in his voice.

"For your information—"

"—Archie is the perfect man for you. I know, pussycat. You've already told everybody at Three Kisses as much."

"But you called me anyway."

"Yes." The one word sizzled across every nerve ending and sent a rush through her. A *rush* of all things, and at nothing more than one word. Life was definitely not fair.

Why couldn't Archie make her rush or tingle or *something*.

"I know all this life-mate stuff probably sounds kind of crazy."

"You know what you want. Nothing wrong with that."

I'm not so sure anymore. No sooner had the thought crossed her mind than she realized she'd actually said it out loud.

"And why aren't you sure?"

Because she was glad he'd called. He made her feel things, and at nothing more than the sound of his voice, that no man had ever made her feel. Least of all perfect Archie. This man made her rush and tingle and *want*, and even though she had no business feeling such things for a man so totally wrong for her, she couldn't help herself.

She felt them.

She felt *him*.

Her nipples tingled, her blood rushed and Sam's words echoed through her head.

You're not going to marry the guy. Just have some fun.

"You haven't answered my question." His deep voice pushed into her thoughts. "Why aren't you sure about what you want?"

"I am. I mean, I know what I want in a life mate."

"Upper-middle-class background. High IQ. Conservative job. Yearly subscription to *Biology Today*. A love of classical music. And an Oedipus Complex."

She couldn't help the grin that tugged at her lips. "Very funny, and it's *Science Digest*, not *Biology Today*."

"That's what you want, who you want, for the future." His voice deepened and took on a serious note. "But what about now? Who is it you want right now, Josie?"

You. The word was there on the tip of her tongue but she held back. This guy was all wrong for her. A playboy type who went through women the way she went through a bag of trail mix.

A *right now* kind of guy.

Just have some fun. Sam's words echoed through her head, joining the deep, even breaths of Mr. Right Now who waited on the other end of the phone for her answer.

"Why not?" she blurted. "It's not as if Archie and I are engaged or even going steady," she rushed on. "I mean, we've hardly even kissed and when we did, it wasn't more than a quick peck because his mother cleared her throat.

91

Not to mention, I'm a good person." She was babbling now, desperate to justify her actions to herself as well as him. "I volunteer every Thanksgiving and Christmas at the Lake Street Mission. I donate all the prototypes for my toys to the local children's shelter. I even let Mr. Babcock auction me off at his Single Seniors' Bachelorette auction last year."

"How much did you bring in?"

"Fifty dollars."

A low whistle followed. "For seniors, that's pretty serious money."

"That, and a dozen half-price coupons for denture cream."

"We're talking serious investment."

"I spent two hours every evening for an entire week helping old Mr. Peters—he's the man who bought me—figure out crossword puzzles. Not to mention that last year alone, I visited ten local schools to promote national science week. And I always donate my old clothes to the Red Cross. Don't you think all that entitles me to a little fun?"

"Meaning?"

"Well, Sam's always talking about how..." Great. Just when she made up her mind, she lost her nerve. She took a deep breath and searched for the words. "I mean, I know how you are."

"And how am I?"

"Wild."

Silence carried over the line, followed by a low, deep chuckle that did even more terrible things to her. She actually burned so fierce, she trembled, and at just the sound of his *voice*.

She couldn't begin to imagine what it would be like to be touched by him. Kissed by him.

"And a little crazy," she added.

Exactly how she felt at the moment. She hadn't even seen the guy in person, but it didn't seem to matter. She wanted him, and for the first time in her life, she was acting on that want. Just for a little while. Just for tonight.

"What else have you heard?"

"That you're . . . friendly with the ladies."

"And you want to be my friend?"

"Yes." There, she'd said it. For the first time in her life, at the ripe old age of soon-to-be thirty-five, she'd propositioned her first man. "I mean, as long as we understand each other. This is just . . . I know you don't want to get serious, and neither do I, so this will be just—"

"—a little *fun*."

"Exactly. So," she licked her lips and fought back a wave of doubt. "What do you say—" The question faded into the beep of her other line. "Darn it."

"Your other line is beeping."

"I know." *Beep*. "So what about us getting together?"

"Tomorrow night." The line clicked, and he was gone.

Josie sat there for a few frantic heartbeats and tried to contemplate what had just happened. She'd just propositioned a man. Even more, he'd accepted.

Tomorrow night.

Anticipation, so hot and sweet, bubbled

inside her, making her entire body burn and ache and—

Beep.

She clicked over. "What?"

"Josie?" Sam's voice floated over the line. "Are you okay?"

"Let's see . . . My heart is pounding. I'm having a major hot flash. And about the only thing in my kitchen cabinets is a box of Wheaties. What do *you* think?"

"Sounds good," Sam said distractedly. "Now what about a fitted dress? Like a shift?"

Josie sank back against the sofa, closed her eyes and prayed for strength. "Do you like shifts?"

"I do if you do."

Here we go again . . .

He was crazy. That was the only explanation for what he'd just done. Calling her again. Agreeing to meet her.

Forget crazy. He was friggin' certifiable.

Because of her. A few seconds of her sweet voice, and his damned intentions had flown south, straight into one helluva hard-on. It had been so long, too long since he'd had a woman, much less one as sexy, as smart, as irresistible as Josie Farrington.

A little *fun*.

She wanted him, a fact he couldn't ignore because he wanted her just as much.

Temporarily, of course. Long enough to slake the lust eating at his common sense and

distracting him from what was really important—his work, the physical proof that Matt
Taylor wasn't a liar or a thief.

He was a dedicated scientist and, most of all,
a man of his word, a reputation he'd fought too
long and hard for to give up without a fight. He
couldn't afford to get sidetracked right now,
not with his future riding on the next month.
Josie's proposition, however crazy, offered the
only solution.

*Right. And how do you intend to meet her,
talk to her, be with her and still keep your identity a secret? Make that two identities? She can't
know it's Marvin, and she sure as hell can't
know it's you.*

True, but then Matt hadn't gained notoriety
as a creative genius for nothing. He had an IQ
off the charts. He would think of something,
and quick. Then he would give them both a
night to remember.

Just one, hot, sweet, breath-stealing night,
and all his troubles would be over.

What's a girl like you doing in a place like this?
The cliché echoed through Josie's head as
she stood inside the doorway of The Mask, one
of Chicago's most notorious night spots and
not the sort of place that conservative, boring
Dr. Josephine Farrington usually frequented.

Black strobe lights blasted a swirl of purplish
color across a crowded dance floor overflowing
with people wearing trendy clothes and masks.
She had seen everything from handheld feather-

decorated opera glasses to full monkey faces, all of which were handed out at the door in keeping with the club's name. Otherwise, it was like every other club she'd glimpsed on late-night MTV dance shows. Lots of smoke. Lots of noise. Mega-loud music surrounded her, pulsed through her and made her heart beat faster.

Or maybe it was the excitement doing that.

For all her misgivings, she couldn't suppress a tiny thrill because she was really here, and she was really doing this—even if a small part of her longed for flannel pajamas and a pint of strawberry yogurt.

She stared down at the pink handheld mask she'd been offered at the doorway. She really should hold it over her face, but she hadn't worn her glasses. Her vision, under the best lighting circumstances, fell far short of twenty-twenty. Put a cluster of feathers and rhinestones in her way, on top of the club's dark interior, and she was sure to miss him. There was no way she was doing that.

She hadn't spent an entire day with a stomach full of butterflies for nothing. She'd felt the first flutter that morning when she'd opened the card delivered to her lab along with a dozen red roses, and a note that read:

> *Tonight*
> *Ten sharp*
> *The Mask.*

No signature. No initials. Nothing.

Yet she'd known.

Just looking at the bold handwriting had sent a wave of heat through her. She'd made up her mind then and there to go through with the meeting, in spite of the nagging voice that insisted she wasn't the sort to go around meeting strange men.

She wasn't, but then that was the very reason she found herself in her present situation. If she'd been the adventurous, go-for-the-gusto-and-the-man type, if she'd spent her time listening to all the giggling in the girls' bathroom rather than working on her science homework, she wouldn't have reached the ripe old age of thirty-four and counting without ever experiencing a knee-melting kiss or sweaty palms or butterflies in her stomach. Or *lust*.

Pure, simple, uncomplicated lust.

Not to mention that J. T. wasn't really a complete stranger. She'd talked to him twice and what's more, she knew Sam. While her friend had warned her of his womanizing ways, she'd never mentioned anything about him being a serial killer.

Just in case, Josie had given in to a moment of temporary paranoia by telling Mr. Babcock where she was going and with whom. That way, on the slim chance that J. T. did turn out to be a nut, at least they'd know where to start looking for her body.

She forced the thought away and tried to stifle the urge to bolt into the nearest bathroom and take cover. Her nervous fingers plucked at her clingy leopard-print dress—the end result of an afternoon spent combing dozens of stores for the hottest outfit she could find. She didn't want him disappointed, and the real Josie with her tailored slacks and conservative blouses was sure to leave a man like J. T. wanting.

Not in this getup, a voice reassurred her. With long sleeves and a hem that ended just below the knee, it wasn't so much the cut that made the dress so risqué and a guaranteed man-pleaser. It was more the utlra-clingy fabric and the slit that ran clear to her . . .

She *was not* naked, she told herself for the hundredth time, and she *was* doing this. End of debate.

Shifting her attention, she concentrated on scanning the trickle of people coming through the doorway. Blurry people. Where were a good pair of contacts when you needed them?

Floating at the bottom of her septic tank, that's where. Josie was all thumbs when it came to contacts and she'd ripped at least sixty pairs over the past few years. So many that she'd finally given up and realized she was doomed to wear glasses forever.

Except for nights like tonight. Bad vision aside, she hadn't traded a nice, quiet evening at home so she could show up for a rendezvous with Mr. GQ looking like a major geek. Tonight was about chemistry. Sparks. Attraction.

Okay, there was a man . . . Her heart started pumping until he moved closer and she realized he had red hair and a major beer belly.

Her gaze jumped back to the doorway. Too blond. Too female. Too . . . With three-inch stilletos, an ice-cream-cone-shaped bustier and enough leather to outfit an entire Harley Davidson reunion, Josie wasn't sure what it was, except that it couldn't be the tall, dark and ultramasculine man from the phone.

Unless the nut theory pans out and he turns out to be half-stud, and half-female dominatrix.

A closer look and relief swept through her. It wasn't him. She could breathe again.

Her nostrils flared and the tempting aroma of warm male with just a hint of cologne pushed past the stale stench of cigarette smoke. Her heart fluttered and she knew it was him even before she heard his low, familiar voice.

"I hope you haven't been waiting too long."

"All my life," she murmured to herself, drinking in another deep breath and relishing a surge of giddy excitement.

"What did you say?

"Nothing. I was just . . ." Her words faded into the sudden thunder of her heart as she turned and came face-to-face with her destiny.

Chapter Seven

Based on Sam's description, Josie had pictured tall, dark and handsome. But never, except in her wildest, most private dreams, had she pictured tall, dark and *Zorro*.

She blinked, but he didn't disappear. Dark, mesmerizing eyes stared back at her through the twin eyeholes of the black trademark mask. A day's growth of stubble shadowed his firm jaw and outlined a sensual mouth. Black, silky hair flowed loose to his shoulders, blending into his black silk shirt. Black jeans and boots completed the outfit.

This Zorro wasn't carrying a sword, however.

Instead, he held up a long-stemmed red rose. "To go with the twelve I sent you this morning," he said, handing her the flower. "You look really great, Pussycat."

She couldn't help herself. "You called me that the other night. Why?"

"Josie and the Pussycats." At her blank look, he added. "Haven't you ever seen the cartoon?"

"I never watched much TV while I was growing up."

"Where did the name come from?"

"My father used to read European history to unwind." He didn't look the least bit surprised and something warm unfurled inside her that had nothing to do with lust and everything to do with *like*. While she'd always been proud of her father, he was a far cry from the typical dad. "He's a professor at MIT. He teaches biochemistry and has been studying reactants for the past ten years. Anyhow, he had a thing for Napolean's Josephine, and here I am."

"Here you are."

He stared at her for three more heartbeats, as if he wanted nothing more than to look. His dark eyes held hers and a strange heat pooled low in her belly, a reaction Josie had never experienced before when exchanging glances with a man.

"I picked red," she blurted, suddenly afraid of the fierce attraction between them. Afraid and excited and ... Geez, it was hot in here. "For the dress color," she rushed on. "I picked red, but now Sam wants me to choose the style. If I've learned one thing from standing up in fourteen weddings, it's to keep my mouth shut. I don't suppose you have any suggestions?"

"Only one."

"An A-line?"

"That we save the style discussion for another time." His dark gaze collided with hers. "We didn't come here to talk about Sam."

No, they'd come for an entirely different purpose that had her blood rushing and her heart pounding and her legs trembling.

"Come on, Josie." Long, strong fingers laced through hers and she forgot everything except the way his skin warmed hers and sent little tingles through her body. "Show me what you can do."

The comment brought to mind a dozen very erotic images, none of which Josie had even a fourth of experience with in real life. "I really can't do very much." So much for a clingy dress to wow him. But the last thing she wanted was to start *showing* and have him be disappointed. "I mean I've been with men before, but we never... They never... I never..."

He tugged her close, a grin curving his sensuous lips. "*Never?*" She shook her head and his smile widened. "And here I had you figured for another Ginger Rogers."

"Ginger Rogers..." The name echoed through her head and heat flooded to her cheeks. "Dancing. You're talking about dancing."

He winked again and gave her a knowing look. "Was there ever a doubt?" His gaze darkened and his smile eased. "Come on, Pussycat. Let's dance."

Pussycat. The name slid into her ears and prickled her feminist sensibilities, but at the same time, a warmth spread through her. She'd spent her entire life enduring all sorts of nicknames, everything from The Brain to Einstein. Pussycat was a welcome change, especially the deep, romantic way it rumbled from his lips.

He led her onto the crowded dance floor. They worked their way through a sea of gyrating bodies, off to the side where the music wasn't quite so loud.

A seductive rock ballad drifted from the massive speakers. He tugged her close and plastered them together from chest to thigh, holding her securely with one arm tight around her waist.

The other hand crept up her spine, as if memorizing every bump and groove through her clingy dress as he worked his way up. With a few deft movements of his fingers, her hair unraveled from its loose braid and spilled down her back. His hand cradled the base of her scalp, massaging for a few blissful moments that had her melting against him.

Matt felt the press of her soft breasts against his chest and nearly groaned out loud. Holding her, feeling her was so much more than his fantasies. Those had been intense, but this . . . This was heaven. And, at the same time, it was hell because he couldn't tamp down the rising need that had him drawing her even closer, wanting to hold her, to inhale her.

He put one foot between hers and pressed his thigh even closer to her body. Despite their clothes, he could feel her. Her heat scorched and teased him with a delicious friction as they moved to the slow, heard-pounding rhythm.

"I've never been much of a dancer," she breathed into his ear when she accidentally stepped on his foot. Her hands tightened on his chest, knotting his shirt as she held on to him to catch her balance. And damned if that one action didn't turn him on even more than the closeness of her soft body, the wondrous scent of her golden hair.

He wanted to believe she didn't do this very often, that he was the first, the only. Crazy. A woman like Josie, career-minded and driven, didn't go in for the relationship scene any more than he did. This was exactly the sort of thing she would do. Maybe not often, but enough that he shouldn't feel such a rush of pure masculine possessiveness.

After all, she'd met him here. Tonight. A man she hardly knew. Sure, she thought he was Sam's cousin, but one she'd never actually seen.

She'd obviously done this before, despite her sugar-cookie first impression.

He wanted to believe that, but when he

looked into her eyes, it was difficult. Innocence glittered there so hot and bright, mixed with wonder and an awe that turned him inside out. The smile she offered up made his gut tighten and his arms close around her protectively.

"J. T.?"

The name slid into his ears and he stiffened, pushing aside the ridiculous feelings. Christ, he was acting like a lovesick kid. He wasn't. This was desire, pure and simple lust and he was a grown man.

And she was all woman. His woman.

For tonight anyhow.

"Are you okay?" Worry laced her question and he forgot all about his conflicting feelings and concentrated on her, on the tickle of her hair against the backs of his knuckles, the heat of her skin creeping through the thin fabric of her dress, the way she brushed his erection with every slight sway and sent a throbbing pulse from his head to his toe. "I didn't mean to step on you, but I've never really done much dancing."

"Me either."

"But I thought you danced for a living?"

Too late, he realized his mistake. She thought he was someone else. Sam's cousin. J. T. the *dancer*.

What kind of dancer? A dozen possibilities came to mind and Matt chose his next words carefully. While he didn't particularly like deceiving her, he'd come this far and he wasn't going to back out now. He wanted her and she wanted him. She'd talked to him, flirted with him, and she was dancing with him, even if she didn't realize his name. It was still *him* that she wanted.

"This isn't your average dancing," was all he said.

"I guess not. I mean, you probably do a lot more moving when you dance. More bumping and grinding. And gyrating. I bet you gyrate a lot."

Gyrating was the best idea he'd heard in a hell of a long time. With a little move to the left and one to the right, he could really get in close and feel her, the teasing friction of Miss Josie practically straddling his leg, sending shudders through his body.

"Is this one of your dancing outfits?" She reached up and fingered the edge of his mask.

"Yes." He caught her wrist, his fingers circling. He urged her hand away, his thumb rubbing a lazy circle against her pulse beat. She trembled. "This is my dancing outfit."

Hey, it was his and he *was* actually dancing. Hence, his *dancing* outfit.

"So where do you dance?"

"Around." While he was playing this charade through to the end, he wasn't keen on lying to her. As for evading her, that qualified more as sin by omission.

"Around where? I've never been to very many clubs, but I know the area. I would love to check out one of your shows."

Shows? "Downtown," he blurted.

Kimberly Raye

"Downtown where? Grant Park? Navy Pier?"
"Yeah."
"Which one?"
"Damn, but you ask a lot of questions," he muttered, and then he did the only thing he could with her staring up at him so expectantly, her eyes bright with curiosity and innocence and a sizzling desire that called to his own.

Chapter Eight

Matt didn't mean to take things slow.

He wanted her, she wanted him. There was no sense in playing games and hiding his intent behind soft, teasing kisses. Get down to business with a little warm-up dancing, then it was out of here, on to someplace dark and quiet and private. Very private, to sate the lust that had been eating away at him for the past few months.

But the minute his hungry mouth touched hers and he felt her trembling lips, her surprised gasp, he forgot all about a quick, fierce warm up. He wanted only one thing at that moment.

For Josie Farrington to soften in his arms, to

part her luscious lips and let him savor the sweetness inside. For her not to be afraid.

Afraid?

He forced the thought aside. Sure she was stiff and trembling, no doubt because she was as hard-up as he was. Women like Josie were dedicated workaholics. She'd probably been on the chastity wagon as long as he had and the stress had her wound tight.

She just needed to relax and while he was so near to bursting by just drinking in her scent, he could slow down a little.

He splayed one hand at the base of her spine, his thumb rubbing lazy circles as he held her close and sucked her bottom lip into his mouth. He licked and nibbled until she made a soft mewling sound and her hands slid around his neck.

Her body pressed into his and her lips parted. He deepened the kiss, his tongue sliding into her mouth, teasing hers until she joined in and gave as good as she got.

Better.

He'd always liked kissing, but this went way beyond *like*. The taste, the touch, the feel of her, her heat pressed against his thigh, scorching him through denim and silk, overwhelmed him and made him want—no, *ache* for more.

For her.

Here. Now.

He pulled away and struggled to get himself under control. Otherwise, he'd never make it the fifteen minutes to the nearest hotel, up the stairs, out of his clothes—

"My knees trembled."

"What?" It took a second for him to realize she was staring at him in dazed awe.

"My knees . . ." She shook her head. "Forget trembled. They *shook*."

He knew the feeling. "Come on." He enfolded her hand in one of his and cupped her elbow, steering her around. "Let's get out of here."

"What about the preliminaries?"

"It's time for the main event." He steered her around and guided her toward the front exit. The last thing Matt wanted was an audience, and as tight as he was strung, he was afraid that's exactly what was going to happen. He needed to kiss her again. And touch her. And—

"But I was sort of enjoying the preliminaries."

"Then you'll really enjoy the main event."

"I—I'm sure I will, but a few more dances couldn't hurt."

"Sweetheart, it could hurt a lot more than you think." And Matt had the throbbing body part to prove it. He was too hot already, too hard, too wired. He guided her off the dance floor, toward the front entrance.

"But I really like this song."

"I'll hum it for you."

"And I really need a drink."

"We'll pick up something along the way."

"And I could really use a good bowl of peanuts."

The last comment brought him up short. He turned and stared down at her, the last few comments piercing his passion-fogged brain. "Peanuts?"

She nodded furiously. "Honey-roasted. You'll love them." Before he could blink, she pulled away from him and started toward the bar.

He watched her bypass three bowls of peanuts, round the bar, and disappear into the ladies' room, before he finally admitted the truth, which had been niggling at him since the first moment he'd touched Josie Farrington.

Despite the dress, the breathy "I want you," she was just as innocent as his damned conscience had been telling him all along. Just as innocent as she'd claimed, despite the fact that she'd come here to meet him.

So what? She still wants you.

She did. He saw it in her green eyes, felt it in the way she responded to his kiss. She wanted him, and he wanted her. Whatever reservations she had didn't matter.

Yes, they did.

He didn't want her to feel even a moment's hesitation with him, for whatever reason.

The realization hit him and he knew then and there that he felt more for her than lust. He actually *cared*. He didn't know why or how it had come about. Maybe because she'd haunted his dreams for so many nights, or because she looked after Ethan until his father managed to pick him up, or because she didn't spare Marvin the geek a second glance, and Matt had never been able to resist a challenge. Maybe all three.

. He didn't know. The only thing certain was that he wouldn't be able to walk away the morning after and get on with life as if he'd never touched, tasted or *felt* sweet Josie Farrington. One night with her wouldn't be nearly enough.

Unfortunately, that was all Matt had to give.

"Peanuts?" Josie stared at her reflection in the bathroom mirror. "Your IQ is 180. You graduated from MIT at eighteen. You're a member of Mensa, for Pete's sake. A man wants to take you home to bed and you offer him *peanuts*?"

"I like peanuts myself," said a girl who exited one of the stalls and walked up to the sink next to Josie. At least six feet tall, she wore nothing but black. Black turtleneck, black pants, black motorcycle boots, black lipstick and coordinating nail polish. " 'Specially when Ralph sucks them out of my belly button, but if you're really looking for a turn-on in the sack, try strawberries. They're firm enough to stay put, but not uncomfortable if you use them in certain areas, if you know what I mean."

A very vivid image popped into Josie's mind. She turned an even darker shade of red and nodded. "Um, yeah. Thanks for the tip."

"Sure thing." Miss Tall, Dark and Beatnik dried her hands and left Josie to splash water onto her over heated face.

She'd offered him nuts. Geez, he probably thought *she* was a nut.

The two bowls she'd consumed while waiting for him churned in her stomach and her father's voice echoed through her head.

You are what you eat, dear.

Geez, she *was* nuts. She had a gorgeous guy waiting for her who didn't bring his mother along on dates, and here she was hiding out in the bathroom thinking about her father.

Yes *that* was definitely nuts.

She splashed more water onto her face and reached for a paper towel. So she'd run away and he probably thought she was a lunatic, but all was not lost. She would simply get herself together, march back out there and finish what she'd started by having agreed to this interlude in the first place.

One night.

One incredible, heart-pounding night to satisfy her curiosity for the rest of her structured, predictable, boring life.

Boring? Hey, she wasn't exactly Miss Excitement, but *boring* seemed a bit harsh. She'd always thought of herself as conservative. Sedate. Placid.

Boring.

Okay, she was boring. Usually, but not tonight. Tonight she was following her instincts, letting the chemistry spark, making memories.

Drawing a deep, shaky breath, she dried her

face, gathered her courage and traded the bright fluorescent bathroom lights for the dim interior of the club.

She blinked, scanning the surrounding men before she spotted his back a few feet away. Before she could give in to another panic attack, she walked up to him and tapped him on the shoulder.

"I know you probably think I'm crazy, but I really do want to do this. I've been wanting to do this my entire life. I've always heard about the toe-curling phenomenon, but I've never witnessed it up close. It threw me for a curve, but I'm ready to pick up where we left off and get on with tonight. Just tonight. As much as my toes curled, you're not my type and I'm really not yours, which is why hot tawdry sex between us would be absolutely perfect and why I wouldn't mind seeing your act up-close and personal, in the privacy of—" Her words stumbled to a halt as he turned to face her.

"You're the Lone Ranger," she blurted, staring up at the strange man she'd just propositioned.

He grinned. "Technically I'm not really *lone* tonight. I'm with someone. But if you're game, I think I could talk her into a threesome."

"Three's definitely a crowd." The deep voice rumbled behind her, and Josie turned to find Zorro standing there. His warmth seeped into her, upping her already blazing body temperature.

The Lone Ranger shrugged and said, "Can't

win 'em all," before turning back to his conversation.

"Do you always go around propositioning men you don't know?" Zorro asked when she finally stopped wishing for the floor to open up and swallow her and managed to turn and face him.

"Usually I stick to the ones I know." Good comeback. Definitely a nine on the flirty scale. She gave herself a mental thumbs-up.

Zorro didn't look nearly as pleased. "And do you know a lot of men?"

"That depends." She licked her suddenly dry lips and his gaze followed the motion.

"On what?"

"On whether or not we're qualifying the term."

"We're qualifying. *Know*, as in—"

"—the 'Hi, how are you' sense?" She forced a laugh. "Dozens."

"I was thinking more along the lines of the *Hi, let's get naked* sense."

"Oh." She licked her lips again. "I'd have to say—" *dozens, hundreds, thousands—* "not many." *Great, Josie. Why don't you just confess to being the next candidate in line for a miracle birth?* "Boy, it's awful hot in here." Before her traitorous lips blurted out any more ugly truths, she threw herself into his arms and kissed him.

It was a hot, openmouthed kiss that left them both stunned for three fast, furious heartbeats before he grabbed her hand and ushered her from the club.

Josie didn't put up a moment's resistance, no matter how her heart thundered at just the contact of his palm against hers, their fingers entwined. She followed him, grateful for the cool night air that rushed at them the moment they stepped outside. He was so hot, so male, she needed all the help she could get.

"Your place or mine?" she asked as he hailed a cab.

He stared at her, his dark eyes flashing a dozen different emotions as indecision played across his features, as if he couldn't decide. "Yours."

While she'd succesfully remade herself into a superhot bombshell, her apartment was still ultraconservative. Sedate. Placid. *Boring.*

"I don't—" The protest faded as a cab screeched to a stop in front of them. She could always hope they'd be too busy for him to notice the volumes on nuclides and proton reactors lining her bookshelves.

He held open the door for her. She climbed in while he gave the driver her address. Before Josie could so much as blink, he shut the door and she found herself alone in the backseat of the cab.

"Aren't you coming?" she asked through the partially open window.

His only answer was one last hot, open-mouthed kiss. Just as he broke the contact, his mouth slid toward her ear and he whispered, "Sweet dreams, Pussycat." Then he leaned back from the window and signaled the driver.

"Wait—" But the cab was already pulling away and Josie was left to wonder what had just happened.

She'd been dumped by Zorro.

So, she'd been dumped by Zorro.

There were worse things that could happen. Mass hysteria. Nuclear winter. Mr. Babcock, minus his glasses, in possession of a firearm—

Josie did a double-take, but there was no mistaking the old man who yanked open her door and shoved the barrel of a very dangerous-looking BB gun into her face.

"Get your hands off that girl or you'll be singing soprano, buddy!"

Josie's purse fell as her hands jumped into the air, her heart nearly hammering out of her chest. "Easy, Mr. Babcock. I'm alone."

"Alone?" Mr. Babcock lowered his gun a few inches and peered past her. "Are you sure?" He scanned the corridor before a knowing look crept over his face. "Oh, I get it. You're *alone*." He winked and stepped past her as she bent to retrieve her purse. "Ain't a soul nearby." He crept down the hallway toward the stairwell. "Nobody lurking nearby, hiding in the alcove . . . Gotcha!" Mr. Babcock jumped toward the spot beneath the stairs and aimed. "Goshdarnit."

"I'm really alone."

He propped the barrel of the BB gun on his shoulder and marched back toward her. "I thought he might be making you say that to throw the old watchdog here off."

"There is no he."

"He stand you up?" He hefted the gun and stroked the barrel. " 'Cause I'll be happy to hunt him down and give him a piece of Bambi right here."

If only she had Zorro's address.

She retrieved her purse and walked into her apartment, Mr. Babcock following. "What were you doing in my apartment?"

"I was worried about you, so I let myself in to keep an eye on things 'til you came home." He gave her a condemning stare. And make sure that VCR of yours recorded *'Chemistry Tonight'*. Besides, *Jeopardy* reruns are on tonight, so I thought I'd keep an eye out for that mouse."

"You ain't got any Ritz crackers," he went on. "I had to bring down a box of my own." He snatched up the half-eaten box of crackers. "And you ain't got no Cheez Whiz. Lucky for you the brown stuff in that jar was mighty tasty, otherwise, I wouldna had no strength to go defending your honor and trying to catch that mouse."

"Brown stuff . . ." The words faded as her gaze snagged on the familiar jar. "You ate my polyglucose reaction."

"Damned good, too." He burped. "Sleep tight."

After Josie had shut the door behind Mr. Babcock and cleaned up what was left of this week's experiment for the children, she shed the purportedly irresistible ultra-sexy dress and stuffed it back into the box. Before she headed in to work tomorrow, she was taking the leopard print back to the store and demanding a full refund.

But first, she had to get through the night.

Sweet dreams, Pussycat.

She'd have sweet dreams, all right. Plotting the many detailed ways she'd like to give Mr. Zorro a piece of her mind.

All ended with her riding off into the sunset with George Clooney or Brad Pitt or some other hunky guy, none of whom made her toes curl or her palms sweat or her body tremble even once.

Ugh.

Where was a bowl of Cocoa Puffs when you really needed one?

"Here." Josie thrust the box of Cocoa Puffs at Phyllis early the next morning as she walked into Three Kisses just as her friend was finishing up her night shift.

"What is this?" Phyllis peered into the box. "Some organic look-alike?"

"It's the real thing. Two hundred calories and I'm walking proof. I only had a small handful of the stuff, dry, but I can already feel the sugar rushing to my hips."

Phyllis gave her a knowing look. "He didn't call?"

"We met last night."

"And?" Her curiosity turned to disappointment as she eyed the box. "Not good."

Actually, it had been too good. Which was the very reason Josie was having such a hard time forgetting about Zorro and his kisses and his touches and . . . and *nothing*, because she'd gone home alone.

Not for long, she vowed to herself. While she was at an impasse when it came to Archie and Mitchell, she'd gone through her seminar notes and based on Dr. Sophia's advice, devised a tie-breaker. The Ultimate Goal test.

She would ask each man for their ultimate goal, the culmination of their life's work, the meaning of life itself, and whichever man came the closest to matching her own Ultimate Goal, would be the one. Her perfect life partner. *The* one.

Just as soon as she got around to it.

Meanwhile, she had work to do. She spent the rest of her day at her computer and finished the simulation for ADAM. Who needed Zorro when she had the ideal male specimen right at her fingertips?

Chapter Nine

"*That's* your idea of the perfect man?" Marvin adjusted his glasses, leaned over Josie's shoulder and stared at the image on the computer screen. His warm breath brushed the back of her neck and a tingle skittered up her spine. *Excitement.*

Excitement?

Of course. She was unveiling ADAM for the first time. There was bound to be the usual rush of pride, followed by the usual jolt of adrenaline that accompanied the beginning of every project.

"You have to be kidding," Marvin said, quickly pumping up the adrenaline a notch until she upped the emotion meter from excited to irritated.

"What's wrong with him?"

"For one thing, his hair's too long." Marvin leaned forward and elbowed her out of the way as his hands went to work on the computer. "There, that's better."

Josie watched as the figure's hair shrunk to a crew cut. "Are you kidding? He looks like G.I. Joe . . . Not that a G.I. model is completely out. Once we do the initial ADAM we can change the design and make other models. But this one needs more hair." She pushed Marvin out of the way and stabbed a few keys. The hair started to grow again.

"He's too muscular."

"He's just right."

"He looks like a pit bull." He punched a few buttons. "And why are his lips so big?"

"They're not big. They're sensuous. I got those lips off the cover of GQ."

"No real guy has lips like that." He keyed in a few commands and the lips thinned. "Or eyes that green. And why is he so big?"

"He's not big. If you'd look at the scale chart, you would realize he's just a little more than six feet."

"I'm not talking about his height." His gaze riveted on a certain part of anatomy and heat flamed in Josie's cheeks. "Five inches is average. He's at least twice that."

"For your information, six is average."

"Says who?"

"*Cosmo*. And for the record, my guy isn't a fraction over nine."

"*Our* guy." Marvin stabbed a key and the body part in question started to shrink. "And six is better. In fact, I think five would do. Come to think of it, why does he need one at all—"

"Look, Marvin." She elbowed him out of the way and leaned protectively over the keyboard. "I appreciate your input, but I think I should have autonomy as far as the design goes."

"Because it's your idea?"

"Because I know what women want." She punched a few keys and the hair started to grow again. "Long hair, for starters." Not that she, herself, was a stickler for long hair. Shoulder-length would do just fine, or even a few inches shorter. Maybe a little tousled, framing a shadow-stubbled jaw and brushing the edges of a black mask—

Attention, Josie! This is your common sense calling!

She forced aside the Zorro image and reached for the keyboard to repair the damage Marvin had done. "He needs his hair. Women want the romantic fairy-tale type and long hair says romantic. They don't put Fabio on all those romance novel covers for his intellectual appeal. And we definitely need the full lips. And a few more muscles here and here. . . . As for size, and just to show you that I do value your opinion, I'll make a concession . . . since size isn't all that important anyway—"

"What makes you think I don't know what women want?" The deep voice whispered in her ear, so deep and familiar and stirring.

The hair on the back of her neck stood on end for a paused heartbeat until she glanced over her shoulder at Marvin. Geeky Marvin with his Coke-bottle glasses and his severe frown. "No offense, Marvin, but you don't exactly look like an expert when it comes to the opposite sex."

"And how do I look?"

"Well," she eyed him. "Stuffy, for one thing."

He frowned. "Stuffy?"

"And introverted."

The frown deepened. "Introverted?"

"And anal, and much, much too serious all the time. You need to loosen up."

"Like you?" He fingered the starched white collar of her lab coat. "If this were any stiffer, you'd cut yourself up."

"This is just a uniform. For your information, I wear jeans when I'm at home. Soft, wrinkled jeans . . ." Her words faded as she noticed the direction of his gaze. Her attention shifted to her hands poised above the keyboard, fingers stiff and white and so tense she looked ready to crack a knuckle. She snatched her hands into her lap and glared at him. "I'm talking about attitude. About life beyond this laboratory. When was the last time you went on a date?"

"A while."

"One week? One month? One decade?"

"Two years."

"That's exactly what I'm talking about. How do you propose to know what women want if you haven't been with one in more than two years?"

"I didn't say I haven't been with a woman."

"Yes, you did. You just said—"

"—that I haven't had a *date* with a woman in two years. Not that I haven't *been* with one. There's a difference."

"Oh." His meaning sank in and her gaze snapped up to collide with his. "*Oh.*"

His grin was slow and . . . *wicked.* That was the only word that came to mind. Ridiculous, of course. Guys named Marvin didn't do anything wicked. They were stuffy, introverted, anal. They slicked their hair back and wore geeky glasses and mismatched neckties that cut off their circulation and made their Adam's apples bulge.

And they looked pretty darned good naked.

She forced the unbidden thought to the back of her mind and tried to calm her heartbeat down to a respectable level. "I still think I'm a better judge. Who better to design every hardworking *woman's* fantasy, but a hardworking woman?"

"You've got a point." He perched on the edge of the desk and trained his thick glasses on her. "So tell me your fantasy. Besides the long flowing hair, the green eyes, bulging muscles and nine inches."

"I do not fantasize about nine inches." She shook her head.

Kimberly Raye

"Or any of those other things. It's not really about looks." At Marvin's doubtful expression, she added, "Just because I want ADAM to have a nice package doesn't mean I sit around fantasizing about it. Women's fantasies aren't so much visually oriented, as they are emotional. It's not about what a man looks like, but the way he makes a woman feel."

"And you know this because . . . ?"

"Research."

"*American Medical Journal, Science National, Discovery?*"

"*Cosmo.*"

"Didn't that magazine win the Lost in Space award last year at the American Association of BioPhysics convention?"

"Not *Kosmo. Cosmopolitan.*"

"The fashion magazine?"

"I'll have you know they do some very informative polls—"

"One of which revealed this interesting phenomenon about men and women," he finished for her. "That men think in terms of looks and women think in terms of character."

"Exactly."

"A nine-inch character."

"Okay, so maybe I got a little carried away. I could scale him back to eight."

"Seven."

"Seven and a half."

"It's a deal."

"So what about you, Marvin? Do you fantasize?"

"Fantasies are a waste of brain power." Despite his words, there was no mistaking the twinkle in his blue eyes . . . Blue?

She peered closer. Yes, beyond the thick glasses were a pair of very vivid blue eyes. Almost as vivid as . . .

Ridiculous. She was still mooning over Zorro and her imagination was getting the best of her. Marvin as Zorro?

Her gaze hooked on him, from his bouffant cap and his geeky glasses to the clunky shoes peeking past the edge of brown polyester slacks.

As if he noticed her interest, his brows drew together and he turned away from her. "It's late. I've got work to do." He sat down on the stool in front of his body heat converter and started to work. "You finish the actual design while I complete the base skeleton. Then we'll get started on the external structure."

So much for him revealing his deepest fantasies.

Not that Josie really cared. After all, Marvin's fantasies, *if* he even had any, were irrelevant. It was the female fantasy Josie was more concerned with. She wanted ADAM to represent the female ideal. Prince Charming. Don Juan. Sir Lancelot.

Zorro.

Disappointment welled inside her and her hands went to the keyboard. Maybe Zorro was the ideal for some women, but not her. ADAM was definitely getting long hair. Long, *blond* hair. And *green* eyes. Dark, brilliant green. As far from blue as she could get.

Fifteen minutes later, when she had ADAM looking more like Fabio than her masked man, she stopped and studied the results.

What the hell? Maybe she'd try a Zorro mask on him. Just to see.

"Now *that's* a dress."

Actually, it looked more like a car cover to Josie. "Don't you think it's a little . . . full?" It was the closest Josie had come to an objection in the three hours she'd been trying on dresses at Special Occasions, the biggest bridal shop in Chicago.

Sam eyed her. "You think it's too full?"

"I didn't say *too* full, just that it's full."

"And perfect." Regina Morelli, Sam's future mother-in-law and the only woman brave enough to accompany Sam to the bridal shop and actually give an opinion, shook her head. "Full is good. You young things run around with so much hanging out. You need to leave something to the imagination."

Josie eyed her reflection. This dress left everything to the imagination except the color of her hair.

"Why, in my day and age, we covered up," Regina went on. "The boys back then knew they wouldn't get the milk for free. Not until they plopped down cold, hard cash for the cow." She rounded Josie, eyeing the red creation from all angles.

"Speaking of milk . . ." Sam wiggled her eyebrows and grinned. "How did your date go with J. T.?"

"It didn't go."

"What do you mean?"

"We didn't really hit it off."

"You're kidding?"

"Actually, I hit it off. He just took one look"—okay, so a few long looks and even a kiss, but Josie wasn't about to add hurt to humiliation—"and ran the other way. I guess I wasn't his type."

"You're breathing; you're his type," Sam said.

"You're making me feel so much better."

"I didn't mean it that way."

Josie arched an eyebrow.

"Okay, I meant it that way. But only because J. T. isn't the type to turn women down. Any woman."

"You said he grew up. Maybe he's turning over a new leaf."

"And maybe white doves will fly out of my butt and save me the trouble of renting them for the wedding. I said he grew up. He didn't die. There isn't a woman alive who isn't his type."

Except Josie.

She fought back a wave of hurt at the depressing thought. So she was different? Different was good. Not many women had an IQ that exceeded their body weight. No, most women had boyfriends and husbands and families and could care less about their IQ. Most women . . .

Except Josie.

"Do I have *reject* stamped on my forehead?"

"Forget J. T. He's a total loser. Why, he hasn't even RSVP'ed for the wedding and I have to give a head count tomorrow!" She waved a hand. "You're better off without him."

"He's really not going to the wedding?" At Sam's nod, Josie sent up a silent prayer of thanks. There was a God, and Josie now had proof positive that He was a She.

"He probably has to work or something. Saturday nights are the busiest at Buns-A-Rama. Forget him. Let's talk about something more important."

"World peace?"

"Who you're bringing to the wedding."

"I thought I'd just go alone."

"You *have* to bring a date. Just get out there and ask someone. Anyone. Come on, Josie. The tables are set up for two. It's the latest romantic thing. You have to have a date, otherwise, you'll be eating with Jake's Great-Grandma Angela."

"That doesn't sound so bad."

"Forget bad. It borders on the *Twilight Zone.*" At Josie's questioning stare, Sam added, "She's got an invisible friend named Guido."

"Not to mention, she likes to take her teeth out and show them around the table," Jake's mother added.

"But I'll be the only one at the table."

"Exactly. Nuts," Regina Morelli scoffed. "My husband's side of the family is completely nuts." She crossed the room to retrieve an old, frail woman wearing orthopedic shoes and a flower-print dress. "Come here, Mama, and tell us what you think of this bridesmaid's dress. It's sweet, don't you think?"

The woman circled Josie several times. "I think it sucks," she finally said, blowing the entire sweet grandma image completely out of the water. "She looks like a fire truck with arms."

Regina threw her arms up. "Let's see *you* pick out something."

"Why, I don't mind if I do."

A half hour later, Josie stood wearing tight red spandex. "I look like a stuffed sausage."

Great-Grandma Grace took one look and her face crinkled into a smile. "That's the whole point, doll. You want to meet a nice Italian fellow, you have to play on his weaknesses. My Vito, God rest his soul, was a sucker for an Italian sausage sub."

"My Frank loves Italian sausage and pasta," Regina offered.

"Jake does like Italian sausage pizza," Sam chimed in.

Great-Grandma Grace gave her an I-told-you-so look. "We'll go with the red spandex," she told the salesclerk, effectively closing the subject and sentencing Josie to an evening dressed as a stuffed sausage, which at least wouldn't have been so bad if she'd had a sexy Italian pining away for her.

As it was, her options were few.

Archie—with his eat-for-life regime—didn't even like sausage. Nor did vegetarian Mitchell. Not to mention, she'd yet to decide which man she liked more and asking one out rather than the other was liable to give the wrong idea. Namely that she'd decided which to target as her potential life mate.

She needed someone she had no interest in. Someone who had no interest in her. Someone safe.

Someone who looked really great naked.

Chapter Ten

"I don't think this is such a good idea," Marvin told Josie the next night when she laid out her plan.

"It's perfect. You're going and I'm going. We'll just go together."

"First off, I'm not going, and second, if you need a date, why don't you just ask someone? Women ask men out all the time."

"That's just it. This is not a date. A date implies interest, and I've got two men who already think I'm interested. I don't need to muddy the waters by adding a third."

"So ask one of the two."

"I can't. If I do, the other will assume that I like the other more, and I don't like either one.

I mean, I do like them, but not one more than the other. They both fit the Ten Compatibility Commandments and so I'm having trouble deciding between them."

"The Ten Compatibility Commandments?" He looked at her as if she'd grown an extra eye in the middle of her forehead.

"Dr. Sophia Erickson," she explained. "Author of *How to Find the Perfect Life Partner*. Don't tell me you haven't heard of her?"

"I've never heard of her."

"She's the leading expert in her field."

"Which is?"

"Relationships. The male-female equation. Her seminars are always packed. I was lucky to get an available spot." She pulled a notebook from her briefcase and showed it to him. "She teaches everyone how to customize their very own Ten Compatibility Commandments based on their own likes and dislikes, to maximize the mate hunt."

"You actually paid money to learn how to find a man?"

"Not just any man. The perfect life mate." At his raised eyebrow, she continued. "There's more to finding a mate than just sweaty palms and trembling knees"—and tingling lips and throbbing thighs and all of the other things she'd felt courtesy of one glance from her blue-eyed, table-dancing Zorro.

Marvin folded his arms and eyed her with his Coke-bottle stare. "Is that so?"

"Of course. That's just chemical, and not the

foundation on which to base a lifelong commitment. Shared goals, mutual likes and dislikes, similar education levels—all these things contribute to a solid, mutual respect that is mandatory for two people to cohabitate for any length of time, much less procreate."

"And what about love?"

"What about it?"

"Do you believe in love?"

"Of course I do. Love stems from trust and trust stems from two people who are friends first. And two people who have more in common have the greatest chance of being friends and falling in love."

"So people from different backgrounds can't be friends and fall in love?"

"Maybe, but it's highly unlikely. The more different people are, the slimmer their chances of having a successful marriage. Differences lead to disagreements, which result in a high divorce rate. I'm not saying it doesn't happen, I just want a better-than-average success rate."

"You sound like you speak from experience."

"Maybe."

"Maybe as in yes? Or maybe as in no?"

"Maybe as in it's really none of your business."

"You must not need a date very badly."

"What's that supposed to mean?"

"If I wanted someone to take me to a wedding—"

"Accompany me," she cut in. "You're going

to accompany me, not take me. There's a difference."

"*Accompany* me to a wedding," he corrected, "then I think I would be a little more cooperative."

She eyed him, the stubborn expression on his face, the unyielding light in his eyes. "All right, all right. I know all about lust at first sight because of my parents. They were as different as night and day; they met and married all in the name of lust, and then they split up." She studied the toes of her pumps for a long second, wondering why admitting her past to him bothered her so much. "They went through a bitter divorce and I want to make sure that I don't go through the same."

"Thirty-seven years," he told her, drawing her gaze up to his and the strange glitter in his blue eyes.

"What?"

"My parents have been married for thirty-seven years."

She swallowed the sudden lump in her throat. "That's nice. They must be compatible."

"They're complete opposites. He hates her. She hates him."

"Then why are they still married?"

He shrugged. "I think they're just used to each other. He drinks too much and yells at her. She gripes too much and yells at him. It's been their routine for as long as I can remember."

"Where are they?"

"Little Creek, Texas. My hometown."

"I never would have guessed you're from Texas."

"I left the first chance I got and never looked back."

"Do you ever see your folks?"

"The occasional holiday. I talk to my mom regularly. My dad's never been much of a talker. So you see, there's no set recipe for longevity. People can be as different as night and day and still stay together."

"But they're not happy."

"You didn't say anything about being happy."

"Well, I want happiness, too, or at least mutual respect. I'm sorry about your parents, but I still think I can up my chances of success by following my plan."

He studied her a moment longer. "You've never been in love, have you?"

"That has nothing to do with anything. I simply want a man who meets nine of my Ten Compatibility Commandments."

He folded his arms and eyed her. "Name them."

"I really don't think—"

"If you want me to go, then name them."

She blew out an exasperated breath. "Very well. Okay, number one is dedication. Then he's got to be compulsively neat." She couldn't help herself. Her gaze drifted around Marvin's neat lab and something warm unfurled inside her before she could get a grip. "Then there's the music. He has to like classical music and be health conscious and a nonsmoker. He should be employed in a white-collar profession, preferably a scientific one, but I'm flexible on that point. He should also have a comparable IQ to mine, and he shouldn't be too flashy a dresser and he should definitely be ready to settle down and start a family."

"That's nine. What's number ten?"

"It's not important. Look," she pinned him with a stare. "Do you want to go or not?"

"No, I don't. I'm not very social."

"Good, because this isn't social. Rest assured, I'm not even remotely interested in socializing with you." Okay, so maybe remotely, but only because her hormones were still buzzing thanks to Zorro and the fact that there wasn't a spare scrap of paper cluttering Marvin's ultra-neat lab. Of course he made her heart skip a beat, she'd been primed by someone else.

"We're just coworkers accompanying each other to a business function," she went on. "This isn't a date."

She thought she saw a fleeting glimpse of anger at her last statement, as if the notion bothered him. Then it faded in a wave of thoughtful contemplation.

"Coworkers, huh?" he finally asked after several moments of consideration.

"Strictly business."

"Arthur Kiss *is* expecting me to make an appearance," he added.

"So you'll do it?"

"What time do I pick you up?"

"You can just meet me there. This isn't a—"

"—date," he finished for her. "I know."

Boy, did he ever.

Josie Farrington had made it plain from the get-go that she wasn't the least bit interested in him.

Good. He didn't want her to be interested. To pay him more than a passing glance. With her scientific background, she was sure to have heard of him. He needed his privacy.

Which was why attending a wedding with Josie Farrington—the woman who haunted his dreams and kept him tossing and turning and nursing a very big hard-on all night—was a very bad idea.

But as bad as it was, as dangerous, he couldn't say no when she turned that pleading gaze on him. For whatever reason—a date being completely out of the question—she wanted him to be her escort and damned if he could resist.

After all, it was just one evening. A few hours. He could keep his head and his control for a few measly hours.

His future depended on it.

Eve Malone's future was spiraling down the drain. Too many phone calls during her shift and not one break was quickly making for the worst workday of her life.

"I'll just be a minute," she promised her frowning boss when the phone rang for the fifth time in fifteen minutes.

Lurline was the owner and chief manicurist at We're All That, one of the largest nail salons on Chicago's south side, and had likely been a slave driver in a previous life.

Eve could practically hear the whip crack as Lurline handed her the phone.

"I'm timing you," the woman told her, but she needn't have bothered. There was no way Eve was in any hurry to spend a lot of time with the bill collector on the other end of the phone.

"We can put you on a payment plan," he told her as she sank down into a chair at the table in the break room. "Just tell me what you can afford."

Eve clutched the receiver and gave the agent a realistic amount and a good chuckle.

"Now seriously, Mrs. Malone . . ." the man started. "We're here to work with you . . ."

After agreeing to pay an amount that would have her doing at least twenty extra manicures a week, she slid the receiver into place, buried her head on her arms and tried to calm her pounding heart.

Chocolate. She needed chocolate.

She rummaged through her lunch sack and retrieved the cupcake she'd packed that morning. The last cupcake. Thanks to her debt, she was cutting back everything extra, including sweets and sodas—the only source of joy in her miserable life.

That and Twinkles, but in order to keep her fat Siamese happy, she had to keep the cabinets stocked with a gourmet cat food, which meant she had to cut out everything extra.

"Lake Michigan Seniors Center, here I come," she muttered as she opened the package and took a big bite. Whenever she needed extra cash, the seniors center was always happy to have her. Particularly since she gave such a good seniors discount.

Oh, no . . . the discount. Make that forty manicures—

Rrrring!

"We're All That," she said around a mouthful.

"Eve Malone please."

"This is Eve."

"This is Blue Wind Financial Services. We're calling on behalf of your Diner's Club account . . ."

Okay, so make that eighty more manicures per week.

By the time the phone rang again, Eve had reached the manicure limit. She had nothing left to offer but her firstborn, and since there wasn't even a remote possibility of that since she'd vowed to steer clear of relationships and men, she did the next best thing.

"May I speak to Mrs. Malone?" the man on the other end asked.

"She moved to Iceland."

"Who moved to Iceland?" The deep voice brought her whirling around to find a very tall, very luscious-looking Italian standing in the doorway to the break room.

Of all the rotten luck.

"No one," she muttered as she slid the receiver back into place. "I'm really busy right now," she started, snatching up what was left of her cupcake and starting for the front of the shop. "I've got a pedicure wait—" The words drowned as Stinky Malone, her brother-in-law and one of the biggest loan sharks in Chicago grabbed her arm.

"Not so fast. We need to talk."

"This really isn't a good time."

"Sure it is." He plucked the half-eaten cupcake from her hands and her stomach gave a rebellious grumble. "So where's my money?"

"I don't exactly have all of it."

"How short are you?"

"About two thousand, nine-hundred and eighty dollars."

"You've only got twenty bucks of my money?"

"Give or take five dollars in change. Look, Stinky. I'll get you the money. I really will."

"That's what you said when I loaned it to you six months ago." With his good looks and his macho-don't-interrupt-me-woman attitude, Stinky was the spitting image of his older brother Burt, with one obvious exception.

She tried not to wrinkle her nose as he slid past her, slammed the door to prevent any interruptions, and pulled out a chair and straddled it, her cupcake still in hand.

"We've got a problem," he told her in between bites. "You see, I'm through waiting, Sugar Lips."

"I'll get it," she promised. "I just need a little

more time." She took a deep breath and tried not to whimper as he finished off the cake and licked chocolate from his fingers.

"Not good enough." He stood and wiped crumbs from his shirt. "Your time's almost up."

"I've still got two weeks. Burt was your brother," she pointed out. "Can't you be just a little understanding?"

"Hey, Sugar Cake, my understanding nature is the only thing keeping you from wearing a couple of busted ribs right about now. You're family, and I happen to like you." He backed her into a corner. "Which is why I'm willing to cut you a break."

"You're going to forget about the money?"

He grinned, but instead of making her heart flip the way those same smiles always had coming from Burt—in the beginning, that is, before she'd realized he smiled at every woman in exactly the same way—the muscle gave a slow, ominous thud. "Maybe. If you and I can work out a little trade."

Eve took one look at his smiling face and realization hit her. Her stomach lurched at the prospect of her and Stinky. Stinky and her. The two of them. "You're not suggesting..." She swallowed her rising terror. "You can't be implying..." Her throat choked around the words. "You don't mean..."

A solemn look crossed his face. "You move in and keep an eye on Mama."

Mama Malone. Oh, God, it was worse than she'd imagined. "I really can't—"

"Burt would have wanted it that way."

All the more reason she wasn't doing it. Besides, life with Burt had been a walk through Grant Park compared to what waited for her if she buckled under the family's pressure and moved in to take care of the eldest and the meanest Malone and her equally vicious Doberman.

"Burt's not here."

"Which is why me and the boys—" the *boys* meaning the five other Malone brothers, all good-looking and just as slimy as the one she'd married— "decided you should move in with Mama. So's we can look out for you. You'll be safe at Mama's."

She'd be miserable at Mama's.

"It'll be great. The two of you can go to mass on Sunday. And Wednesday. And there's the senior confessions club that meets on Tuesday evenings. Mama never misses that."

"But I'm not Catholic," she blurted, desperate for an excuse to save her from Mama Malone and a fate worse than death.

He stared at her as if she'd grown two heads. "Does Mama know that?"

"Why do you think she hates me?"

"She hates all the wives."

But she hated Eve the most. Six boys and an equal number of wives, and the only one Mama Malone had ever singled out with her evil eye had been Eve. The woman had worn black to Eve's wedding and for the first year of married life, walked around sobbing as if Burt had

kicked the bucket rather than gotten hitched.
Eve had lived through eight years of Mama's
criticisms, her bad-mouthing, her holier-than-
thou attitude when it came to making meatballs and spaghetti, and her hatred of
Twinkles, and all because Eve Malone had
been desperate to fit into her new family. She'd
wanted them to like her, to love her the way
she'd never been loved while growing up.

"Mama's just temperamental," Stinky went
on. "You'll get used to her."

"But I can't—"

"The boys and I'll set it all up. You can move
in ASAP."

"I can't just leave my apartment. I've got a
lease and a cat and—"

"Two weeks," he said. "Then me and the
boys'll be over to pack you up, Sugar Lips."
And then he left.

A dozen emotions whirled inside her. Dread
and disbelief and anger and irritation. "Eve,"
she growled at the closed door. "The name is
Eve. What's so hard about that?"

Nothing, but then Burt, too, had had just as
much trouble remembering her name. He'd
called her everything from Cuddles to Rose
Petal. At first, she'd thought the names a little
hokey, but cute. Until she'd realized that he
called her pet names because he had so many
women in his life, he was afraid he'd screw up
and call her by the wrong name in the heat of
the moment.

Never again.

Eve wasn't falling into the same desperate trap again. She didn't need a man to love her. She didn't *want* a man to love her.

The only thing Eve wanted was Burt's money. He'd earned every penny and since he wasn't here to collect, Eve intended to do it for him. Unfortunately, this particular job involved more than just sending out an invoice the way she'd done for his other investigative work.

On the night Burt's car had blown up, he'd been on the way to finish up a job for some scientist who'd hired him under the pretense that his wife had been cheating. He'd suspected one of his colleagues as her partner, and had wanted the colleague bugged. Burt had planted the device and staked the guy out for three weeks straight. He'd turned over both the video and audiotapes to Jack Donovan and had been returning to retrieve the bug when his car had been blown up.

Eve had confronted Donovan and asked for Burt's money—ten thousand dollars plus expenses. The man had told her to take a hike. He'd denied ever hiring her husband and challenged her to produce proof otherwise.

There was no proof, or so he thought. He was under the impression that the only incriminating evidence had been blown up with Burt.

Wrong.

Burt had never made it inside the building. He'd been too busy getting sweaty in the front seat of his car. When Eve had seen the scandal that had rocked SpaceTek in the days that had followed, namely that some guy named Taylor—the guy suspected of boffing Donovan's wife—had stolen top-secret designs from Donovan who, as it turned out, didn't even have a wife, she'd known the truth.

Donovan was the thief. Eve knew it and she also knew how to prove it. The bugging device was still out there. She'd been *this close* to calling the cops when the funeral home had called. They needed money. And the bill collectors had called. They needed money. And Madame Maureen had called. She needed money.

Everyone needed money and the only person who had any was Donovan who'd made headlines with some new heat absorption crap. Eve figured the least the man could do was pay what he owed, but since he didn't feel the same, she'd come up with the perfect plan. Blackmail.

But first she had to find Matt Taylor and get that bug fast.

Otherwise, it was good-bye future and hello Mama Malone.

She had a nice, safe date for the wedding.

Josie tried to focus on that all-important fact and ignore the image of Zorro that kept pushing its way into her head as she unlocked her apartment door and walked inside later that evening.

She found Mr. Babcock sitting on her sofa

watching a *Name That Tune* rerun, the volume blaring so loudly she had to shout.

"What's with all the noise?"

He grinned. "Just call me the Pied Piper. I'm trying to lure the mouse out into the open." He held up a frying pan. "Then I'm smashing the little bugger."

"Mr. Babcock, there is no mouse."

He waved her off. " 'Course there is. I seen him with my own eyes . . ." His sentence trailed off as his gaze shifted back to the TV. "It's 'My Prayer' by the Platters," he shouted at one of the contestants. "Dadblastit, but they have the dumbest son of a guns on this show . . ."

The muttering faded as Josie retreated to the quiet solitude of her bedroom. Five minutes, she told herself. She was giving him five minutes and then it was bye-bye Mr. Babcock and hello *Chemistry Tonight*.

She needed to relax. To unwind. To forget.

Shutting off her mind to a very vivid picture of a tall, dark, handsome man with flashing blue eyes, she busied herself changing into sweatpants and an oversized MIT sweatshirt. While she didn't relish the idea of being dumped, she'd come to the conclusion after a full day of contemplation that the situation had turned out for the best.

J. T. was an exotic dancer, for heaven's sake! He was six-feet-plus of walking, talking sex appeal and far too advanced for a woman who'd had only a few sexual encounters—all of them less than memorable. There was bound to have been some point in the evening when she did, or didn't do something, and he realized she wasn't exactly what she appeared—namely a leopard-print-wearing seductress.

What had she been thinking?

She *hadn't* been. She'd been overcome with awareness and anticipation of her very own private table dance. She'd been *feeling*. The strange quiver in her stomach, the tingle of her palms, the heat between her legs.

For the first time, Josie understood how a sane, intelligent person could actually mistake lust for love. Chemistry—instantaneous, explosive, electrifying chemistry—was a powerful thing. Not that Josie had, at any moment, figured herself in love with a man she hardly knew. She'd done too much research on the subject of lust and love and compatibility to make such a mistake. Her only fault had been thinking that she could fool a man like Zorro, even for one night. It didn't matter what clothes she wore, or how she tried to pretend to be someone else—even for a single night—she simply wasn't the sort of woman to entice a hot, handsome man who had his pick of any female in Chicago.

She was too boring, too anal, too *Josie* for him to waste his time dancing for her when he could have a more suitable audience.

All the more reason to stick to her initial plan—decide between Arthur and Mitchell and take the plunge before she wound up not only single and alone, but single and alone *and* thirty-five.

Josie drew in a deep breath, forced aside the depressing thought and went into the kitchen. She'd just retrieved some juice and an apple when she heard the shrill ring of the phone above the blare of the television.

"I'll get—" The words stumbled into one another as she stubbed her toe on the door frame, gave a yelp and tumbled forward, her fingers grasping for the telephone.

Josie scrambled after it, her heart thundering as she finally lifted the receiver to her ear and ignored Mr. Babcock's strange look.

"Hello?" It wasn't him. It couldn't be him. She didn't want it to be him. *God, let it be—*

"Josie, honey?"

"Mom," she breathed, a pang of disappointment shooting through her.

Disappointment?

All right, so she was disappointed. But only because she'd been relishing the chance to tell Zorro what a lowdown, dirty, slime-bucket he was for ditching her. She certainly didn't want to talk to him again. Or see him. Or touch him. Or kiss him. Or—

"Are you okay, baby?"

"Fine."

"Because you sound really tense."

"I'm fine. It's just that my neighbor's here." She crawled to her feet and took the phone into her bedroom, shutting the door to drown out the noise. "He's watching TV and everything's a little crazy right now, what with my friend Sam's wedding tomorrow and . . ." The urge to blurt out everything about Zorro hit her hard and fast, and before she could think better of it, she heard herself saying, "I met this guy and—"

"It's crazy here, too," her mother cut in. "And I'm so busy I don't know whether I'm going or coming. I had two recording sessions yesterday. And then this morning I was doing backup for this gospel country album and just like that, I couldn't remember one word of 'Amazing Grace.' I was there, headphone to my ear and the microphone in front of me, meanwhile my head was back at home in the shower with the new lyrics of this song I'm working on. It's so touching, I was sobbing like a baby just writing down the lyrics . . ."

The next five minutes mimicked most every conversation she'd ever had with her mother— her mother talking and Josie listening. Every time Josie brought up work or her own life, her mother turned the conversation back to more familiar territory—herself, her music, *her* life.

As a child, Josie had resented her mother's self-absorption, but she now recognized it for what it was—a defense mechanism to keep from admitting that she and her daughter had little in common. As long as she kept the conversation geared toward herself, she didn't have to admit the truth.

It was something Josie had battled her entire childhood, desperately wanting that closeness that other mothers and daughters shared, something she'd finally accepted the day she'd graduated from MIT.

Her mother had been on tour singing backup for a new country group and she'd barely made the ceremony. She'd flown in minutes before the start, hopped into a cab and made it just as Josie had walked across the stage.

Josie could still remember staring out across the small crowd of parents and seeing her mother wearing denim and a crimson-red fringed vest with a matching cowboy hat. She'd always known how different she and her mother were, but she'd never fully accepted it until she'd seen the woman sitting there among the crowd of intellectuals.

At that moment, she'd known she would never have the sort of mother who understood her hopes and dreams and shared them. And so she'd stopped hoping and started thanking the Powers That Be for what she did have—namely a mother who called every week and sent homemade tapes of her latest songs with special handwritten dedications to her daughter.

Despite her classical music tastes, Josie loved those tapes, and she loved her mother.

". . . take care, baby, okay? And watch your mailbox. I'm putting the tape in the mail first thing tomorrow morning."

If she lasted until tomorrow.

As much as she wanted to, she couldn't forget Zorro's kiss. Or stifle the longing for another. And another. She hung up.

"You look tense," Mr. Babcock told her when she went into the living room to tell him his time was up.

"I'm not tense," she found herself blurting for the second time that night. The correct term was sexually frustrated, not that she could say such a thing to Mr. Babcock. The man was like her grandfather.

"Because, if you're tense," he motioned toward the television, "there's nothing like a good game of *Joker's Wild* to calm you down."

"That's silly." Even as she said the words, she sat down on the sofa and took the bowl of popcorn Mr. Babcock offered her.

With a sudden craving for midnight kisses wreaking havoc on her control, Josie needed all the distractions she could find.

Chapter Eleven

The woman had a great pair of legs.

Matt had guessed as much even though she'd
kept them hidden beneath slacks and too-long
skirts. There was just something about the way
the material had molded to her hips and thighs
that had tipped him off and sent his imagination soaring for the past six months.

But nothing in his wildest fantasies—and he
was talking *wild*—came close to the real thing.
To Josie.

She stood in the church foyer where they'd
agreed to meet, surrounded by bouquets of red
roses and white tulle. People filed by, headed
into the sanctuary where a soft harp version of
"You Light Up My Life" played.

Matt blinked, but Josie didn't disappear. She was still there, wearing a tiny red dress that ended mid-thigh and revealed long, shapely, sexy-as-hell legs that seemed to go on forever before tapering off and ending with a pair of matching high heels.

His gaze roved her from head to toe, then back up. Slowly. Noting each curve, every indentation. The ultrashort red dress clung to her, holding on to all those sweet, luscious curves as if it never meant to let go.

It would. A few efficient tugs on those spaghetti straps, and that material would slide away and give his hands complete access to the creamy skin beneath.

"I know it's not much."

Thankfully.

He forced the thought aside and frowned. "Hopefully you won't have to wear it for very long." As soon as the words left his mouth, he realized what he'd said. "That is, you put up with it for the wedding and then you're home free. You can take it off." *What the hell was he saying?* "I mean, you can change. Into something longer and thicker and not so . . . *red.*"

"Actually I like the color, but you're right about the rest. It's not really me."

Something in the tone of her voice pierced the sudden fog of desire cluttering his brain and his gaze met hers. Uncertainty brightened her green eyes and something twisted inside him.

And before he could remember that he was supposed to be Marvin—sexual, nonthreaten-

ing, business-only Marvin—he found himself
blurting, "You look great."

"Really?"

"Better than great."

"Thanks. You're sweet, Marvin." *Sweet*. Matt
Taylor had been called many things. *Sweet* had
never been one of them.

"I'd better find a seat," he muttered and
walked into the sanctuary before he did something really dangerous like haul her into his
arms and kiss her until she saw beneath the
nice, sweet facade to the hungry man beneath.

It was an urge that stayed with him the next
few hours as he watched Josie do her duty as
maid of honor, a smile curving her sensuous
lips and that damned dress outlining her
voluptuous curves.

But Matt had never been a man to let his
urges overrule his common sense and he was-
n't about to start now. That had been his
father's downfall and if Matt had learned anything while growing up, it was that a man had
to be stronger than his urges. He had to think
with the head on his shoulders and not the one
in his pants.

He had to *think* not feel. Otherwise . . .

He shook away the sudden image of Josie
naked and panting beneath him, her creamy
skin dewy with sweat and her full pink lips
parted in rapture.

No regrets.

"You cheated." Samantha's accusing voice

sounded next to Josie who stood in the entryway to the ballroom of the posh Marriott hotel overlooking Lake Michigan where the reception had gotten underway a few hours ago.

Josie turned on the new Mrs. Jake Morelli who wore a Grace Kelly off-the-shoulder gown, her blond hair swept up into a white cap veil. She looked elegant and regal and Josie had the sudden urge to cry.

Again.

She'd bawled through the wedding, feigning an allergy to roses to explain her puffy red eyes.

But Sam knew, which is why she'd left the head table to hunt Josie down, to give her arm an affectionate squeeze and an opinion on Josie's choice of escort for the evening.

Josie's gaze shifted to the buffet where Marvin stood loading vegetables onto his plate. For the first time in six months, she didn't have to wonder about his hair. It was dark and slightly long and slick. The slickest she'd ever seen. While she preferred a more natural look, at least he'd foregone the bouffant cap.

A beige polyester suit clung to his tall frame, a style that had gone out in the early sixties, and she knew firsthand because her father had the exact same suit, only his was mustard yellow.

"Where do you suppose he picked up that outfit?" Sam asked.

Josie had been wondering the same thing, but coming from someone else, it stirred her protective instincts. After all, at least he hadn't worn his lab coat.

She cast a sideways glance at her friend. "Shouldn't you be cutting the cake?"

"In a minute. I've had four glasses of champagne and I have to hit the ladies' room first. The last time it took me fifteen minutes, five layers of lace, and an extra set of hands to help me get this dress up and out of the way. That's where I heard Jenny Peters from accounting tell Margot Wilder from sales that you and Marvin Tannenbaum were doing the nasty."

"We are not doing anything. We just came as friends."

"Why didn't you tell me you couldn't find a real date? Because Jake's brother-in-law knows this guy—"

"That's why I didn't tell you. Why are married people always trying to fix up their single friends?"

"I've only been married an hour and a half, and I just hate seeing you waste your time on guys like Marvin. You need exciting. Virile. Hot."

Zorro.

"I've tried exciting, virile and hot, and it just isn't for me."

"This is about J. T., isn't it? When you told me that he wasn't interested, I just couldn't believe it. I mean, J. T. *loves* women. All women, and so I called his sister who told me he didn't take you home and get down and dirty is because he's engaged! Can you believe it? Mr. Four Hundred and Counting is actually tying the knot? I didn't believe it myself. But then Jake and I are standing in the receiving line about an hour ago, and who comes through to congratulate us? J. T. and his intended!"

"He's here?" Josie's head whipped around as she did a frantic visual search of the ballroom. "But I didn't see him at the ceremony. You told me he didn't RSVP."

"He didn't go to the ceremony, and half the people here didn't RSVP. Can you believe that? I mean I spent hours putting stamps on all the return cards. The least people could do is pop them into the mail. . . ." Sam's voice trailed off as Josie's heart launched into overdrive and drowned out everything except the frantic *bam, bam, bam.*

He was here. Now.

The knowledge beat through her head, stirring the memory of their dancing, their kissing. Her cheeks flamed and her hands trembled.

Get a grip. He's here, and he's with his fiancée.

Which meant she had to get a grip and forget about their dancing and the kissing. Especially the kissing. He was an engaged man and Josie knew her boundaries.

Engaged. Off-limits. End of story.

Her head knew that, but damned if her trembling hands would get the message. Or her sweaty palms. Or her thundering heart.

". . . goes to show how thoughtless people can be. Josie?"

"Yes?"

"Are you okay? You look flustered."

Mortified would be a better word. And excited. And guilty because she felt excited when the only thing she should feel was anger. He'd led her on and dumped her, and to top it off, he was *engaged.*

And her hands were still trembling.

"Josie?" Sam grabbed her hand. "Why don't you sit down and have a glass of water?"

"Actually, I think I need alcohol." She grabbed a glass of champagne from a passing waiter. Downing the contents, she reached for another.

Sam's gaze narrowed. "What exactly happened with you and J. T.?"

"Nothing," Josie blurted. "Nothing at all. We talked. We didn't click. End of story." She forced a smile. "So you say he's engaged? That's wonderful. Tell him I said congratulations."

"You can tell him yourself. He's standing right over there by the buffet."

Josie whirled and stared in the direction Sam had indicated. She scanned several faces, dread churning in her stomach with each passing second.

The brown-haired man standing by the ice sculpture. The blond grabbing a handful of shrimp.

"Where?" she finally asked.

"The ice sculpture." Sam waved a hand. "Yoo-hoo! J. T.!"

The man by the ice sculpture turned and

Kimberly Raye

smiled, then started to make his way toward them.

Shock bolted through Josie, freezing her breath in her lungs as she tried to follow the sudden turn of events. "That's J. T.?" she finally managed with trembling lips.

"Of course. I thought you two met." Sam pinned Josie with a suspicious stare just as the man reached them.

"We did," Josie blurted, recovering from her momentary shock long enough to paste a smile onto her face. The last thing she needed was the third degree from Sam, which she was sure to get if she didn't do something quick. "J. T.," she rushed on, "good to see you. Again. Josie," she said her name as if to trigger his memory. "Remember?"

"Josie?" He wore a blank look for an eighth of a second before recognition seemed to strike. "Josie the scientist."

Sam's expression faded into a smile. She patted Josie's arm. "I'll just leave you two to chat. They're signaling me to cut the cake." Sam rushed off in a blur of white as Josie tried to calm her frantic nerves.

"You're J. T.," Josie said, trying to grasp the information.

"That's what my buds call me. Look, I'm totally sorry about not calling you. I was going to, but then I picked up the phone and this image like rushed into my head, and it was like so totally Sonya, and I was like, what the hell am I doing? I mean, if I can't even pick up the

164

phone to call another woman without thinking about her, I must be like totally hooked, right? I mean, I'm surrounded by women all the freakin' time, right? Whoa, like there she is." He motioned to a tall blonde wearing a slinky silver dress and three-inch heels. "Isn't she like a total bomb?"

"Definitely a walking, talking nuclear warhead."

This was J. T. The knowledge rushed through her, making her heart pound faster. If this was J. T., then who was Zorro?

Who?

The question pounded through her head as she wished J. T. and Sonya well and made her way back to the table.

Not that it should matter. He'd dumped her, for heaven's sake. She should thank her lucky stars he'd done just that. She could be floating facedown in Lake Michigan right now.

He'd been a stranger. A complete stranger.

A stranger with the most magnificent mouth. And those hands. And what a—

"I hope you're rethinking the size issue for ADAM." Marvin, carrying a plate of raw vegetables, appeared beside her.

"Size." Her gaze swiveled to him. "Um, exactly what I was thinking."

"Good, because there really is no need to make ADAM quite so bulky in the muscle department. We don't want him too top heavy, otherwise he won't be balanced." He turned and motioned toward a table.

Josie followed, sliding into her seat while Marvin took his. China clinked against his water glass. Strong, tanned fingers shot out to right the crystal before it could spill.

He had really nice hands.

As soon as the thought struck, she reached for her own glass of water and gulped down the contents, eager for a blast of cold comfort to bring her body temperature back down to a decent level. She was definitely falling into the sexually depraved category if *Marvin* was starting to look good.

Forget starting. He already looked good, and she had the vivid memory of him naked to prove it.

Good? Was she deranged?

Her heart hammered and she reached for his water, drinking it down in a few quick swallows. Forget deranged. She was simply suffering from shock. Shock at the recent revelation, and shock from seeing Marvin without the bouffant cap and the white lab coat. That and the candlelight. The flames cast flickering shadows that sculpted his features and softened his expression and made her think of Zorro and . . .

No.

". . . could decrease the bicep by two inches in diameter," his voice finally penetrated her ridiculous thoughts. "And then there's the actual chest measurement, which needs to shrink by a good six inches overall, even using a weightless titanium base."

"Let's dance." She regretted the words the instant she said them and Marvin looked as if she'd stripped off her clothes and offered herself to him.

Not that she would ever do such a thing. Even if her nerves were on edge after crying through the ceremony and being shocked by J. T.'s true identity. She would never strip off her clothes for Marvin, even if he did sort of resemble. . . .

"Please. I really need to *do* something."

Something that did not require sitting there, discussing size specifications for the perfect man when only one man kept popping into her head. One masked man. One really hot, handsome, virile masked man—

"Now," she pleaded.

"I, um, really don't think that would be a good idea. I agreed to come, not dance."

The past few hours filled with tears and surprise and a dozen other emotions that pushed and pulled inside her, grew too much. Desperation collided with frustration and hot tears burned her eyes.

"What's wrong with me?" she cried.

"Excuse me?"

"What is it about me that makes men turn and run the other way?"

"I don't—" he started, but Josie was beyond listening. Beyond fighting back her tears and trying to bury her lust. She was sexually frustrated, despite her Ten Compatibility Commandments. Because of them. And she needed to vent.

"Do you know how many first dates I've had? Not half as many as the world's fattest triplets who are all now engaged. I know I'm not some hot babe, but I'm not that bad."

"I didn't say—"

"Then again, maybe I am. I'm sure the world's fattest triplets don't think they're that bad either. They probably think they look pretty good when, in fact, they're really clueless and—"

"Come on." It was his turn to interrupt her. A large, strong hand pressed against the small of her back and urged her from the chair.

A strange sense of déjà vu washed over her as Marvin pulled her close, one arm around her waist, the other steering her forward.

For a fleeting moment, she was back at The Mask, the music and smoke surrounding her, her heart hammering as the sexiest man she'd ever met in her entire life led her onto the crowded dance floor and into his arms.

And as Josie found herself pulled close, a very solid, very male body pressed to hers, the craziest, most insane thought struck her.

It was him.

Chapter Twelve

Slow dancing was the *last* thing Matt should be doing.

The realization struck him as Josie's sweet scent slid into his nostrils. The soft, warm feel of her filled his arms and heat bolted through his body.

His gaze hooked on her mouth, her lips so full and pink and tempting. Much too tempting to a man who'd spent the last five hours with a plate of raw vegetables in keeping with his image, when what he really wanted was a nice juicy rib eye.

That, or a kiss.

A kiss?

No, kissing her was the last thing he should

be doing, and while he'd caught a case of temporary stupidity at the sight of her tears, he wasn't about to make that kind of mistake. No kissing.

He forced his gaze from her mouth to a point just beyond her shoulder and tried to concentrate on the lyrics to the familiar Sam Cooke song crooning from the speakers, rather than the deep, even sound of her breathing. Just a few more lines, a couple of sha-la-la's and the torture would end.

He had no intention of getting suckered into sharing more than one dance, regardless of her tears or the fact that her hands were actually trembling.

Trembling.

The realization struck and a surge of protectiveness shot through him. Protectiveness? Nah, this was guilt. Pure guilt over sending her home alone the other night. That was the only reason he had the sudden urge to dry her tears, hoist her over his shoulder, take her someplace private and show her exactly how desirable she was.

He settled for pulling her a fraction closer when the song played down and another started.

Two songs, he told himself. That was it. His total penance for abandoning her the other night, then his duty would be done.

Physical attraction.

That's all it was at this point, and next to metallurgy and robotics, physics had always been Matt's specialty. He knew better than any-one how certain objects gravitated toward one another. He and Josie were those objects. No past. No present. No future. No connection. Just passing objects.

She didn't really know him and he didn't want to know any more about her, and as long as sweet Josie Farrington kept her mouth shut and those big green eyes to herself, things would stay that way and Matt could keep his distance.

And if she didn't . . .

Well, he could always step on her foot.

It *was* him.

Josie finally admitted that to herself halfway into the fourth dance, after a frantic mental evaluation of the facts that should have taken all of thirty seconds. But with her heart pound-ing and her blood rushing and all that hard male heat pressed up against her, surrounding her, Josie was having a difficult time thinking clearly—the most convincing evidence of all.

Him.

Zorro had known so much about her, from her phone number to her address to what she wore every day and the people she worked with, because he knew her, and she knew him. He was Marvin. Quiet and geeky and shy *Marvin.*

So shy that he hadn't been able to act on his attraction to her for fear she would reject him. Now she understood why he'd picked The

Mask of all places to meet. It had been a convenient way to conceal his identity. He'd met her in the guise of Zorro, much the way she'd met him dressed as Josie the cat. She'd nursed her own fear that a sexy, attractive, hunky guy would reject the real Josie. The quiet and geeky and shy Josie.

Had he approached her as Marvin, she probably would have turned him down. After all, she was having a hard enough time deciding between Archie and Mitchell. She didn't need another prospect to add to the mix.

But Marvin was more than a prospective life mate. More than a compulsively neat, brilliant nonsmoking scientist with an affection for books and an understated sense of style.

He made her hands tremble. And her stomach flip. And her thighs tingle. And her body temperature rise . . .

Whew, it was warm.

She shifted and the hard press of his arousal brushed her hip and nestled against the cradle of her thighs. Heat shimmered through her and the chorus to "Wild Thing" sang through her head, keeping tempo with the frantic beat of her heart. He was just so warm and close and male and *him*.

She drew in a deep breath and tried to gather her control.

Okay, so it was him. Every incredible inch of him.

What now?

She wasn't exactly sure what her next move

should be—she needed some Zorro-free air in order to form a solid, cohesive plan of action. But she did know what she *wasn't* going to do.

She wasn't going to scare him away the way she obviously had at The Mask. She'd taken the initiative and kissed him, and that had sent him running for his self-preservation.

She'd been too intense, too passionate for a guy like Marvin. He might have come on as a tall, dark and delicious Zorro, but beneath he was still just Marvin. Quiet, shy, conservative and obviously not very experienced when it came to women.

His hardness brushed her again and a thought struck. What if he'd *never* been with a woman before? She remembered his comments about dating. Sure, he'd said he'd *been* with a woman, but maybe he'd lied to impress her.

Warmth swelled through her. No wonder she'd intimidated him by coming on so strong. He wasn't used to being the object of a woman's passion. Just as she wasn't used to all the wondrous feelings he stirred inside her.

That was the problem. She had to ignore her body's reaction to him—the multitude of atoms spinning and regrouping and buzzing—otherwise she'd frighten him off again.

"So . . ." She took a deep breath, tried to calm the flutter in her belly and looked him straight in the eyes. "Are you originally from Chica—" The question faded into a grunt as he stepped on her toes and pain throbbed up her leg.

"Sorry," he grumbled. He looked more anxious than apologetic, his gaze darting anywhere, everywhere, but at her, and immediately her heart went out to him. Poor thing. He was obviously high-strung when it came to dealing with women.

"That's okay," she blurted, eager to put him at ease. "I'm not much of a dancer either. I never even went to a high school dance, though I wanted—Ouch!"

He shrugged. "Two left feet."

"No problem," she ground out, fighting down a sudden wave of irritation. "I once actually saw someone with two left feet. My father knows the head of orthopedic science at Johns Hopkins and we went on vacation when I was twelve for a three-week seminar on cell rejuvenation—Yikes!"

"Haven't gotten used to these new shoes yet."

"I'm not much of a fashion hound myself. Give me comfortable and sensib—Eeek!"

"I'm not used to this kind of music."

"Me either. I love classical. My father played the harp—Yow!"

"Somebody bumped me."

"One time when I was thirteen, I went to the mall to buy a dress for a science exhibit and this girl I knew saw me coming out of the dressing room and tripped—Ugh!"

"Maybe we should sit down."

Amen. "Let's find a nice, quiet place and get acquainted. I can't believe we've been working at the same company for ten months and I don't even know what part of Chicago you live in—"

"Did you hear that?"

"What?"

"A noise?"

"I hear lots of noises."

"My watch." He glanced at his wrist and sighed. "Just what I thought."

"What?"

"It's my alarm. ADAM's base is cooked."

"ADAM's what?"

"The titanium alloy is the perfect temperature. I have to get back and shape the components while they're most flexible."

"Now?"

"Duty calls."

"I'll go with you then."

"But you're the maid of honor."

"We're all done with pictures. There's nothing keeping me here. We can get some work—" Her words stumbled to a halt when she felt the tug on her skirt, followed by a child's familiar voice.

"Miss Josie?" Ethan tugged on her skirt. "Can we dance now?"

"Sure she can." Marvin dropped to one knee and fluffed Ethan's hair. "She's all yours."

"I *really* should go with you," Josie protested. "ADAM is a joint project."

Marvin straightened and eyed Josie. "And disappoint the kid?"

"That's okay, Miss Josie." Ethan's face fell and something clenched tight in Josie's chest. For a split second, she felt herself back in Cambridge, standing outside the local pizza

175

parlor, staring in the window and watching the
other fourteen-year-old girls talk and laugh
and dance.

She caught Ethan's small hand and smiled at
him. "What do you say you and me show these
folks what dancing's all about?" Ethan smiled,
his eyes aglow at the prospect and Josie felt the
tightness in her chest ease.

"You're something else, Pussycat." The very
un-Marvin-like comment caught her off guard
for a split second and her gaze lifted to meet
Marvin's.

Beyond the thick glasses, were those magnificent blue eyes. They glittered with something
hot and fierce, a mix of passion and admiration
that made her hands tremble and her nipples
ache and heat pool low in her belly.

As if he read her reaction, he grinned in very
un-Marvin-like fashion, his lips tilting so
slowly, so wickedly that her heart leaped into
overdrive and she came very close to rushing
for the nearest refrigerator.

Two heartbeats passed before he broke the
connection and turned his attention to Ethan.
Large, tanned fingers fluffed the boy's hair.
"Don't step on any toes, little man." And then
he turned and walked away.

Josie barely contained the urge to go after
him. But with her feet stuffed into three-inch
heels, she wasn't exactly ready for top-pursuit
mode, especially since Marvin seemed to be
moving quickly toward the nearest exit.

Very quickly for a man wearing new shoes,

and she should know because her own feet were throbbing a very loud protest with each passing moment. A strange feeling of . . . *something* niggled at her conscience, only to fade as Ethan tugged on her hand.

"Let's go, Miss Josie."

She spent the next hour dancing with Ethan, though with the uncomfortable heels and the sausage casing of a dress, she did more stumbling and slipping than anything remotely Ginger Rogers-like.

Even so, she'd never seen Ethan smile so much as if Josie were the best dancer in the world. A look that pushed away her doubts and pain and coaxed a similar feeling inside her.

By the time she handed him over to Felicity who'd picked him up for the wedding since his father had been working and hadn't been able to attend, she'd actually managed to forget all about Marvin and his smile and his deep, blue eyes.

Until she collapsed onto a sofa at the back of the ballroom to give her feet some much-needed relief. His image popped into her mind and she found her body responding all over again, as if he'd been sitting next to her. As if it were his hands massaging her feet, gliding up her ankle, her calf, his fingers circling and playing at her knee . . .

"Cake?" A waiter disrupted her thoughts and drew her attention to the square of white confection sitting on a gold-edged plate. The scent of sugar filtered through her nostrils, enticing her and making her reach out to accept the dessert when Josie Farrington—staunch sugar enemy—never touched the stuff.

But Josie wanted cake in the worst way.

Her *own* wedding cake to go with her own wedding, which wasn't going to happen if she kept thinking about Marvin's hands and her own trembling body and . . . No *and*.

She had no intention of being aggressive and frightening him off the way she had at The Mask. Rather, she would ease his fear by casually, nonthreateningly convincing him that she wouldn't reject his advances.

Yes, subtlety was the key in moving Project Josie full speed ahead, in getting Marvin Tannenbaum to throw his inhibitions aside and kiss her. *Subtlety*.

"Kiss me."

The soft command echoed through Matt's ears and his head snapped up. His gaze pivoted to Josie who sat at a nearby counter, her laptop in front of her. But she wasn't looking at the computer. She was looking at him as if he were the last bran muffin on the breakfast cart.

Bran, he reminded himself, not the usual chocolate doughnut fix he needed each and every morning, along with his mandatory black coffee loaded with caffeine.

"I know that's a bit bold, but it's been five nights. *Five* nights of me smiling at you and talking to you and trying to put you at ease, and you've hardly looked at me, much less touched or kissed or even hinted that you find me attractive. Enough to go to so much trouble just to get close to me. Not that I'm not a patient woman. I am, it's just that patience isn't always a virtue since it could be contributing to your problem."

"My problem?" Even as he asked the question, he wasn't the least bit concerned with the answer. His brain had zeroed in on several key buzzwords.

Looked. Touched. Kissed.

Images pushed into his mind. Vivid images of Josie naked and panting and open beneath him. Josie *looking* into his eyes. Josie *touching* him. Josie *kissing* him. Even more damning, he saw himself kissing her, hard and deep and thorough and—

"You don't have to pretend anymore," her voice shattered his thoughts and snagged his full attention. "I know it was you. You're Zorro."

Panic surged through Matt and his fingers tightened. One of ADAM's titanium fingers popped off his hand.

"You're the one who called me, who met me at the club that night. *You,*" she persisted, her gaze fixed on him.

He drew in a deep breath and tried to fit the piece back into place, all the while his heart raced ninety to nothing. "I don't know what you're talking about," he managed.

"It's okay. I know why you did it. I know everything about you."

Everything, as in Dr. Matthew Taylor. Thief. Failure.

She'd figured him out.

He wasn't sure why the knowledge surprised him so much. She was smart, and even more, she had a background in science. Matt Taylor, brilliant scientist-turned-lowlife thief had been the biggest scandal in ages to rock the scientific community.

Everyone who knew a neutron from a proton had heard about the revolutionary heat-sensor pad. It had been Matt's brainchild until Jack Donovan, once his friend and colleague, had stolen Matt's design for himself and framed Matt for the theft. The worst part was that everyone had believed Donovan because Matt hadn't been from one of the finest prep schools in the country. He hadn't come from money or power. His humble roots had convicted him before he'd even gone on trial, and so he'd disappeared rather than face unjust prosecution. Donovan had dropped the charges, under the pretense that the truth had come out and that had been enough for him.

It would be enough, which is what Matt intended to prove. The truth. That he wasn't a thief but a scientist. A brilliant scientist capable of going all the way to the top. Of making it.

No regrets.

But Josie didn't know what Matt was all about. She figured him for a liar and a thief and a—

"Shy," she said, cutting into his mental tirade. "You're just shy."

He'd been called many things, but shy had never been one of them. "I'm *what?*"

"Shy. And scared." Sympathy gleamed in her bright green eyes.

Not suspicion or condemnation or the detestable pity he'd seen too many times to count when the good people of Little Creek had looked at him and seen only his alcoholic father.

"It's understandable," she went on. "You're so dedicated to your work that you don't spend a lot of time with the opposite sex. I can fully relate. Up until recently, I've let my work consume me, too. I know what it's like to be a slave to the thirst for knowledge, to be driven and focused. It can keep you out of touch with the real world, make you feel uncomfortable when you finally do pull your head out of the sand and take a good look around you. Especially when you realize that you don't look or act or dress like anyone else. Not that you dress or look or act bad. You're just different."

His panic faded into confusion for the next few heartbeats until the realization hit him. While she knew Marvin was the masked man who'd met her the other night, she didn't know Marvin the starchy scientist was really Matt "the SpaceTek Wonder Boy" Taylor.

"It's okay," she told him. "You may be an intellectual, but you're a person, too. You just happen to be a person who enjoys reading books on kinetic fusion." She motioned to the bookshelf full of the real Marvin keepers. "And *DNA Selection and Cell Rejuvenation*—one of my personal favorites, by the way."

She and Marvin were two peas in a friggin' pod.

Matt wasn't sure why the idea bothered him more than it should. He *was* Marvin, after all. A single-and-staying-that-way Marvin and the perfect woman could only mean trouble.

"You're not freaky, you're just different," Josie went on. "I understand because I've always been different myself. I graduated high school at thirteen and went straight to MIT. By fourteen, I was smack-dab in the middle of a double major in biology and chemistry. I remember sitting in the library on Saturday nights, doing homework while everyone else my age was going to football games and driving out to the lake to make out. Kids my own age used to laugh at me. My classmates used to stare." Her gaze found his. "I know what it's like to be different and to be scorned because of it. But you don't have to worry. I understand, and I'm here to tell you that I'm attracted to you."

She paused to lick her lips and that's when his thundering heart took on an altogether different meaning.

"You don't have to pretend to be someone else for me. You don't have to fear that I won't like you just the way you are."

182

"I'm not afraid." What was he saying? Suddenly, he was *very* afraid, but not that she wouldn't like him because he wore geeky glasses or snorted when he laughed, but because she *would*.

She did.

The realization sent a jolt of pure pleasure through him so intense he almost did kiss her. He could picture her sitting in the library with her big glasses and her book bag, while everybody else her age was parked out at the lake, making out.

His entire life, he'd fought to be different, from his father, his peers, his circumstances, but Josie Farrington had wanted to be the same.

He saw it in her eyes, in the way her bottom lip trembled, and he had the strangest urge to haul her into his arms, kiss the daylights out of her and show her exactly what she'd missed out on all those years.

He wanted it almost as much as he wanted his revenge.

Almost.

He summoned his courage and tore his gaze away from her trembling lips. "Josie, you don't really know—"

"It's okay. You need time before we get physical. I understand."

The physical he could handle, if that's all that had been at stake. It wasn't. He wanted more from her, wanted to crawl inside her head and know everything about her—her past, her present, her future. A want that was much too distracting. "Time isn't going to help in this case." The closer he got to the Expo, the more focused he needed to be.

"Sure, it will. You'll relax around me, realize that I'm not going to laugh in your face, and then you'll kiss me. We can talk, laugh, spend some time together and watch *Chemistry Tonight*." She indicated the portable television set up in the corner of the lab. "I never miss it."

As he well knew. For the past five nights, she'd regularly taken a break from her subtle seduction techniques to flip on the television set and watch a boring, anal man in glasses spout various combinations formed by nitric acid and polyurethane gas, a torture Matt had been forced to endure rather than blow his cover. While the show was informative, it was a far cry from ESPN and the Chicago Bulls.

"I can't kiss you."

"Yes, you can. It's easy. You just pucker up."

"First off, there's a lot more involved than just puckering up." Otherwise, he wouldn't be so damned uptight about it. But kissing her had made him feel . . . things. When he'd kissed women in the past, it had been something that felt good. Soft, warm, pleasurable, a step to bigger and better things. But when he'd kissed Josie, he hadn't just thought about getting into her panties.

For those few moments when they'd been on the dance floor and she'd been in his arms, he'd wanted more. To simply hold her, taste her, inhale her, as if that were enough to satisfy him.

As if.

He gave her his puckered sour expression, only this time the expression came much too naturally. "I won't kiss you."

She smiled, a tolerant, understanding smile that irritated him almost as much as it stirred the heat in his groin. "Of course you will. You just need some reassurance."

And a little harmless incentive, Josie added silently. Marvin was, after all, just a man.

If she couldn't logically talk him out of his shyness, she'd do what any woman in her situation would do. She would seduce him out of it. Afterall, it was basic chemistry. She wanted him to react to her, which meant she needed a catalyst to speed things up.

Chapter Thirteen

Seducing Marvin wasn't going to be nearly as easy as it had first seemed.

Josie came to that realization after an entire weekend spent at the library, pouring over back issues of *Cosmo*. For the first time, she realized how truly out of touch she'd been all these years. A whipped-cream bikini as her proverbial catalyst? She'd never even worn a real bikini, much less an edible one, complete with strategically placed cherries.

After perusing a couple of articles that suggested equally bold moves—everything from a Jell-O bath for two to taking him out on the town wearing a raincoat and nothing else—she decided it would be best to start small and work her way up. Chances were, shy inexperienced Marvin wouldn't last past a few suggestive glances or some flirtatious remarks, which meant she wouldn't have to worry about her proficiency with Reddi-Wip.

Yes, small was definitely better, Josie decided on Monday as she spent the day observing the various control groups, keying in her findings and completing several prospectus sheets for Sam who was expected back from her honeymoon next week.

Josie glance at her wall calendar and the big red *X* that marked the spot. Her birthday.

She forced her gaze away. She wasn't thinking about it. She was focused on the here and now. On bringing Marvin out of his shell once and for all, and she knew just where to start.

At a little after five P.M. when everyone else had left for the day, Josie entered the employee bathroom and took the first step in Project Marvin. A subtle, yet totally seductive move that was sure to have him kissing her senseless before the night was over.

"So how did they like the new Rappin' Rhonda?" Marvin asked when she walked into his lab after unraveling her French twist. After all, long hair was sexy and Josie had to work with what she had.

"It's a go," she told him as she approached the counter where he stood making final adjustments to a motorized miniature car that was part of a new line of Mini Wheels they'd just introduced. "It's a go, but we need to add more songs to her music repertoire." She reached up and grabbed a long tendril of hair, winding it around her finger in what she was sure had to be a totally seductive move. After all, she'd stared at the *Cosmo* illustration and practiced for a full fifteen minutes.

"We can add a few more." He finished his adjustment, placed the car on a nearby shelf and turned to the Rhonda prototype without sparing Josie a glance.

Letting the hair unwind, she did a little effective fluffing and combing with her fingers. "And the kids think she should look a bit more hip."

"Such as?" he asked without sparing her a glance. His brow wrinkled in concentration, his mouth drawn tight, his gaze hooked on his work. He was his usual buttoned-up self, his hair hidden beneath a cap, his lab coat buttoned from top to bottom over the white shirt and black tie and brown polyester slacks.

Would the real Zorro please stand up?

She tilted her head, letting her hair fall over one shoulder in a typical come-and-get-me pose she'd seen on numerous magazine covers. Her neck cricked, but she forced herself to hold the position as she spoke. "Well, suggestions included a nose ring, a belly tattoo and purple hair. I sort of like the nose ring myself."

That earned her a quick glance, which she quickly made the most of. Her hand lifted and she tossed the curtain of her hair behind her shoulder.

"We could do a nose ring . . ." His voice faded as she did another hair flip and his gaze narrowed. "Loose hair is dangerous in a laboratory. You really should have worn it all tight and pulled back like you usually do."

"My, um, rubber band broke," she blurted, feeling a sudden burst of self-consciousness. It was crazy since she was a grown woman. In charge. Seducing him. Yet one deep, probing stare and she forgot her purpose. "I—I couldn't find another one."

He reached into a nearby drawer and pulled out a spare cap similar to the one he wore. "Here." He tossed it to her.

"Thanks." Not. Stuffing her hair up under the sheer covering, she tried to gather her courage and stifle her disappointment. Okay, so he was obviously stronger than she'd given him credit for. That, or he didn't like long hair. Either way, she wasn't going to dwell on one failure. Specifically one that had nothing to do with her Ten Compatibility Commandments. The night was young and she hadn't memorized every Lust Lesson in that magazine for nothing.

"I'm still building the basic skeleton. Programming won't start for another day or so until I get ready to implant the chips, so you might as well head out. I'll take care of this."

So much for the night being young.

"And stick you with all the work? I pull my own weight. This is *our* project, and as head of the department, I'm responsible." It *was* true, after all. She'd already given Arthur Kiss a proposal on the project and he'd whooped almost as loudly as when his secretary had brought in a deep-dish pizza with extra cheese. "Arthur wants detailed updates and I can't give him those if I'm not involved in each step."

"It's not brain surgery, Josie. You don't have to take it so seriously."

"I know it's not brain surgery, but it's my job. My responsibility." When he simply stared at her as if trying to figure her out, she blurted, "What?"

"I'm just wondering what someone like you is doing in a place like this?"

Someone like you. Funny, but the comment didn't stir the usual bitterness she felt when someone pointed out the obvious—that Knowsey Josie was a smart chick. A brainiac. A freak.

Marvin was every bit as smart, as different as she was. They were two of a kind. She had no doubt he was going to meet her nine out ten requirements. No doubt at all.

"You're brilliant, Josie. You should be doing something that'll make a difference."

"I do make a difference." At his doubtful look, she added, "I grew up with a fully equipped chemical laboratory right in my very own home. Most kids had a family room; we had a family lab. I made everything from a new form of superglue with a new bonding ion I ran across when I turned eleven, to my first baby doll in that lab." She couldn't help the smile that tugged at her lips. "You see, my father thought toys were way beneath me. He bought me things like chemistry sets and rock collections and these polymer chain models that demonstrated how molecules broke apart into mono—smaller molecules," she corrected when she caught herself unconsciously burping.

He gave her a knowing smile. "I know what monomers are."

He did and that knowledge made Josie all the more determined. They shared so much, from similar IQ's to an intense physical chemistry. They were cut from the same cloth.

Nine out of ten.

"What about the doll?" he asked.

"Sally. Her name was Sally and she was awful. At least that's what the Crumb twins said when they saw her. They were sisters, my age, who lived next door. They used to wheel their dolls around in this big carriage in their driveway every Saturday morning. I would watch from my room and wish that I could be out there with my own baby. I asked my dad for one, but he bought me a pull-apart human anatomy model instead. So I made my own. I didn't know anything about synthetics at the time, so I used cotton for her hair. She was the ugliest thing I'd ever seen, but when I held her, it didn't matter. She was mine. She made a difference because she made me happy."

"So you aspired to make other kids happy?"

"Not at first. I assumed I would grow up, take a research position somewhere like my dad, maybe teach chemistry, but during my senior year at MIT I started volunteering at this children's shelter near campus. Three Kisses regularly donated toys to several shelters around the country, and that happened to be one of them. On the first of every month, a big box of toys would arrive and turn those sad, deprived children into happy ones. They were regular kids when they were playing. Nothing else mattered. Not how much money they had or the fact that they were wearing ragged tennis shoes. They were just regular kids, and they were happy. It was the greatest phenomenon I'd ever seen, and so I sent thank-you notes to the company."

"That's how I met Arthur Kiss," she went on. "He read my notes and started to tailor the donations to the specific needs of our shelter. If we had more boys, he sent dump trucks and army men. If we had more girls, he sent dolls and toy stoves. He admired my dedication to the shelter. When he found out my credentials, he offered me a job, and here I am."

"The world's most educated toy maker."

With anyone else, the words would have made her feel self-conscious. They didn't because she heard the admiration in his voice, saw it in his eyes. "I have the best of both worlds at Three Kisses. I can do what I love, work on as many outside research projects for Maloy Laboratories as I like—with Arthur's full support—and still make kids smile."

"Don't you ever feel like you're wasting yourself?"

She thought of Sally and the warmth she'd

felt when she'd touched those ugly cotton balls on the doll's head. "Never. What about you?"

"I didn't claw my way through years of college for nothing. I want to do something real. Something that's going to impact everyone. Something big."

Her gaze went to the body heat converter. "You are."

His attention followed hers and surprise flashed in his expression as if he'd forgotten for a moment about the revolutionary piece of equipment. His mouth drew tight and his expression puckered up. "We'd better get back to work."

She walked up next to him. "I'll help."

"You don't know anything about doing the actual physical construction."

"But the design is based on my notes. What if you have trouble interpreting them?"

"I've read and comprehended each of your sketches already."

"But I can help with the molding."

"You don't know anything about titanium alloy."

He had her there. "I've always wanted to learn."

"Then here." He leaned over and pulled a book from the neatly lined bookshelf and thrust it into her hands.

The volume was worn and dog-eared, totally unlike the other books, which hardly looked as if they'd been touched, much less read.

Just as the thought occurred, that same

sense of . . . *something* shot through her, quickly fading when his fingers brushed hers and heat sizzled along her nerve endings as he handed her the book.

"Titanium Alloy—It Ain't Just Foil." He read the title, his deep voice pushing into her head and soothing the strange sensation. Her eardrums tingled. "Read it and I'll answer any questions you have tomorrow."

"You're trying to get rid of me."

He grinned, that same un-Marvin-like tilt to his usually tight lips that never failed to make her heart pound faster. "Is it working?"

She wanted to tell him no. To plop down on his lap and refuse to budge until he kissed her, but the eager light in his eyes, the desperation touched something inside her.

"I'm going. For now," she quickly qualified, pinning him with a stare that made his delicious grin falter. "But I'm coming back tomorrow night." She tightened her grip on the book. "Armed and ready."

Josie made good on her promise. The next night she showed up prepared for an all-out war—wearing a Wonderbra that boosted not only the Farrington Flatlands, but her ego, as well. She actually felt beautiful and a bit naughty. It was a feeling that lasted all of five minutes into the evening when she realized that the sexy, uplifting piece of lingerie—the lace strategically peeking from her low-cut blouse—had zero effect on Marvin.

By Friday evening, she'd started to seriously reconsider her earlier conclusions. Especially after three nights of seduction attempts, complete with the bra on Tuesday, a skirt with a split cut clear up to mid-thigh on Wednesday and Thursday's eat-chocolate-in-front-of-him-and-make-him-drool plan. Maybe he wasn't desperately attracted to her and merely fearful of rejection. Maybe he went around dressed as Zorro the way some men wore women's panties.

She'd miscalculated. After all, if he were, indeed, attracted to her, surely she would see some sign of it?

Her gaze shifted to where he sat at his computer, his back to her as he programmed several commands into a microchip that would serve as ADAM's brain. Marvin hardly spoke to her, except to debate certain aspects of her design, and he looked at her even less. His attention never strayed from the project at hand.

ADAM looked more like a mummy at this stage—the S.K.I.N. application. Tomorrow night the plastic would be dyed, various shading added, and then he would start to resemble an actual man.

Then the real task began. Bringing ADAM to life with the various chips and sensors placed throughout his structure, along with Marvin's innovative body heat converter as his energy source.

Josie understood his concept, not that she

was actually sold on the mechanism's feasibility. He had impressive data, but she'd yet to see any evidence that the converter could generate enough energy to power anything beyond the small toys Marvin had used in his experiments.

Her gaze strayed to the life-size color printout of the completed ADAM tacked to a nearby wall. Six-feet-plus of hunky male posed a much greater challenge than a two-inch race car.

The body heat generator would be a huge coup if it actually worked on something as large and impressive as ADAM. Not that Josie was out to make a name for herself. She'd done that with S.K.I.N.

ADAM, propelled by an innovative body heat converter or plain electricity, would not mark a scientific breakthrough for her, but a personal milestone. Her gift to women the world over, as well as herself.

When she'd discovered Marvin's true Zorro identity, she'd started to think that perhaps she wouldn't need ADAM to keep her company after all. But with Marvin so obviously immune to her, it looked as if she'd be just as good a candidate to test the prototype as the next lonely woman desperate for the perfect man.

"Could you please pass me those charts?" Marvin's deep voice slithered through her thoughts and sent a bolt of heat racing through her.

"Sure." She handed him the stack of paper and tried to stifle the sudden trembling as one hand brushed his stiff lab coat. Other than that first initial night when he'd ran her out of the lab, he'd seemed to have no trouble resisting the attraction between them. She, on the other hand, was having a much more difficult time.

It was even more proof that maybe, just maybe, she'd read the entire situation all wrong and her feelings were all one-sided.

She glanced down at the clingy red sweater she wore, tighter and brighter than her usual, but guaranteed by Lust Lessons as a surefire way to up any man's body temperature in less than five minutes.

It had been two hours and Marvin didn't seem any closer to going up in flames.

"Could you hand me one of those blank diskettes?" she asked, determined to draw his attention. She leaned over just as he turned, and gave him an enticing view.

He stopped cold and stared and Josie's heart leaped into her throat. This was it. The response she'd been waiting—

Click.

A flashbulb exploded, temporarily blinding Josie for a few seconds as a trio of men pushed their way into the lab. Marvin swiveled around and Josie would have pitched forward if he hadn't caught her with a steadying arm.

"Hate to barge in on you two." Arthur Kiss led the threesome, a smile on his face. "But I've got some people here just dying to meet you. This is Wally and Bert." He indicated the two men, one armed with a microcassette recorder and the other an 8mm camera. "They're from the *Chicago Sun-Times* and they're doing a story on Three Kisses and the fact that we're a homegrown business."

"Chicago icons," Wally supplied.

"Yeah, Chicago all the way," Burt added.

"Gentlemen, these two brilliant minds are the driving forces behind our recent success. With Josie's new S.K.I.N. and Marvin's robotics expertise, we've been putting out better and soon-to-be bigger toys. Isn't that right, kids?"

Before Josie or Marvin could answer, he motioned to the reporters. "This is where the magic takes place. Josie heads research and comes up with preliminary designs and Marvin does the internal structure. Together, they're pure magic."

"And they're busy," Marvin told the reporter when he shoved a microcassette recorder at him and asked about his background.

"Very busy," Josie added, her hand going up to ward off another flash, the last of which she hadn't recovered from. "I'm really not very photogenic." She stepped behind a nearby counter, effectively killing the view of her bottom half. While she'd invested in a mankiller sweater to show off her minimal chest, she was still doing her damnedest to camouflage the rest.

"Come on, Miss Farrington. Give us a smile."

"I'd really rather—"

"Come on, Josie. It's good press."

"No, I—"

"Say cheese!"

"Give it a rest." Marvin stepped into the photographer's line of fire, his hand raised to ward off the flash. "She doesn't want her picture taken, and neither do I."

"It's just a little news story," the photographer added. "Come on and smile." The camera clicked before Marvin could raise a hand to guard his face. "Move your hand, Mr. Tannenbaum, so I can get a clear shot—"

The words drowned into a yelp as Marvin grabbed the camera and hauled the guy nose to nose. "Look, I really don't like to have my picture taken, so I would really appreciate it if you'd take your camera and go." His grip tightened and the guy paled.

"Whatever you say, buddy."

Marvin released the man's shirt, adjusted his own glasses, and turned toward his computer.

Arthur shot Josie a frown as he turned toward the shaken cameraman. "You know the creative genius types." He chuckled. "So eccentric. Say, you can get a few shots of me with the very first Hunky Hank figurine. Josie designed him. She's a genius. She went to MIT, you know. A double major in physics and chemistry. She works nonstop, night and day, no husband to distract her from her projects . . ."

The man's voice faded as he guided the two men out. The door shut behind them and Josie turned her attention to Marvin who now sat in front of his computer, his breathing not even the slightest bit out of whack despite his he-man exhibition a moment before.

"What?" he asked when he seemed to notice her gaze. Immediately, his hands went to adjust his thick glasses.

"I'm just waiting for your head to start spinning around. That, or for you to pound your chest and let loose a Tarzan call." Or whip out a sword and slash a great big z into a nearby wall chart.

Hey, a girl could hope.

"I'd like to think that show was just to protect my honor, but I get the feeling you weren't too keen on getting your picture taken any more than I was."

He shrugged. "I like my privacy. I . . ." His voice trailed off as he seemed to debate how much to tell her.

Nothing was his usual, but instead of clamping his lips together and keeping things business as usual, he shrugged. "A long time ago I had an unpleasant experience with the press. As a result, I don't like cameras." Before she could ask any more, he pinned her with a stare. "So what's your excuse?"

"I don't like cameras either."

"Invasion of privacy?"

"Inflation of my hips." At his raised eyebrow, she added, "My senior year at MIT, I was hard at work in the biochemical lab on my dissertation on chemiosmotic theory—that's a hypothesis that seeks to explain the mechanism of ATP formation in oxidative phosphorylation by—"

"—mitochondria and chloroplasts," his deep, smooth voice cut in, "without recourse to the

formation of high-energy intermediates ..."
His deep voice went on as he recited the text-
book explanation Josie'd had to regurgitate
every time she mentioned the word *chemiosmotic* because few people had ever heard of it.
And even fewer knew what it meant. Which is
why she'd given up hope of ever finding a man
brilliant enough to know the definition of
chemiosmotic theory—her number ten of the
coveted Ten Compatibility Commandments.

Marvin Tannebaum knew and the realization stunned and thrilled and rendered her
speechless. He *knew*.

"What about your dissertation?" he prodded,
when she simply sat there, trying to digest the
newfound knowledge.

Ten out of ten. Could she dare hope?

"I ..." She drew a deep breath and tried to
calm her frantic heart. "That is, I, um, was
working on the dissertation when I got caught
in a camera cross fire between reporters vying
for a breaking news story on some new biochemical breakthrough in the lab next door.
There I was the following day, wearing white
slacks—not a slimming color—on the front
page of the local newspaper. It was one of the
lowest points in my life. The camera added
ten—make that twenty pounds when my hips
were already big enough on their own."

He winked. "If it's any comfort, your hips
look fine from where I'm sitting."

The compliment sent a rush of heat through

her until she realized she was still standing behind the waist-high cabinet. "Very funny."

He grinned, a slow, wicked, I-want-you smile that restored her hope and left no doubt that he felt the attraction just as intensely as she did.

Now if she could only get him to act on that want.

Chapter Fourteen

Matt had to learn to keep his mouth shut.

He admitted as much the next morning as he stepped into an ice-cold shower. He was rock-hard, his body throbbing after a very detailed erotic dream involving Josie.

She'd started off wearing her skin-tight red sweater and her black skirt with the slit clear up to mid-thigh, and ended up with nothing but a smile and a satisfied glitter in her eyes.

He'd peeled off each piece of clothing with slow, unhurried movements, kissing and nipping along the way, in between a very detailed recitation of various nuances of chemiosmotic theory.

He still couldn't believe he'd sounded off to

her last night. He might as well have hung a target around his neck and said, "Take me, baby. I'm yours."

But she'd been so certain he wouldn't know what she was talking about and he hadn't been able to help himself. He liked surprising her, liked wiping that "I know everything" look from her face.

Her know-it-all look had morphed into surprise in the blink of an eye. Her expression had softened to sheer pleasure and he'd enjoyed every moment. Too damned much.

He'd barely resisted hauling her into his arms and kissing her and . . .

The *and* he'd done in his dream.

He touched his throbbing arousal, feeling the heat pulse off his skin despite the ice-cold water pelting him. He'd worked late last night, desperate to lose himself in ADAM and forget the woman sitting so close, smelling so sweet. Somehow, though he still hadn't figured it out, he'd managed to do just that. Before he knew it, Josie had packed up for the night and left him to work like a speed demon all by himself. He'd kept up the pace until just after three A.M., before hauling himself home, exhausted and tired and intent on getting some sleep.

That was the only good thing about working long hours. He didn't have to worry about lying awake at night. The minute his head hit the pillow, he dropped off. Usually.

He'd barely closed his eyes when her image had popped into his head and stayed there.

Instead of sleeping, he'd spent the past four hours tossing and turning and *pulsing*.

Christ, he definitely had to learn to keep his mouth shut.

A half hour later, the cold water finally shriveling more than just his skin, and Matt felt sufficiently calm enough to step out of the shower. Toweling off, he slipped on a pair of jeans and headed to the kitchen in a search for sustenance, one that led him straight to the pantry.

Working not only enabled him to sleep most nights—usually—but it also prevented him from buying anything that required refrigeration. With little time for shopping, he stuck to edibles that wouldn't spoil. Hence a cabinet full of canned ravioli, a box of Cap'n Crunch and a few six-packs of beer and soda.

He'd just popped the tab on a Dr. Pepper and was pouring it over a bowl of Cap'n Crunch when he heard the knock.

Bowl in hand, he picked his way through his messy living room toward the front door. Discarded newspapers littered his coffee table, along with several empty beer cans and a pizza box from the previous day. His sofa cushions were scattered. A bundled-up pair of dirty socks sat in his recliner.

It wasn't that Matt didn't do the cleaning thing. Growing up in a household where his mother had worked all the time and his father had done nothing, Matt had learned to pull his own and then some. He could vacuum and dust right alongside the best of them. It wasn't that he couldn't do it, he just didn't have time. He used his energy for work.

Once upon a time, he'd had a cleaning lady who came in once a week to keep his home in order. But he'd left his old life behind, and now had to fend for himself.

Temporarily.

While his apartment could use a good cleaning, he had no intention of opening his door to an outsider and possibly blowing his cover. The more people in and out of his life, the more suspicion he would stir. He had enough challenge working for one of the largest toy companies in the country and still keeping a low profile. His apartment was the only safe place where he didn't have to worry about tossing his trash or dusting or making sure his empty cans were stacked in alphabetical order as was typical of compulsively neat Marvin.

The only person Matt allowed in the front door was his paperboy from down the street. The kid, only thirteen or fourteen, barely looked at Matt much less noticed the chaos or the all-important fact that the place didn't exactly reflect the anal-retentive scientist supposedly living there. The boy had started knocking and dropping off Matt's *Sun-Times* personally since the couple next door had a poodle that preferred newsprint to fire hydrants, and Matt had promised the kid an extra tip for every dry issue.

Knock. Knock.

"Hold your horses, kid. I'm coming." He

shoveled a spoonful of cereal into his mouth, turned back the lock, and hauled open the door. "You're late—" The words stumbled to a halt and the cereal stuck in his throat as he found himself face-to-face with none other than Josie Farrington.

A smiling Josie Farrington.

Matt did the only thing he could do considering his present position—half-naked with a bowl of chemical preservatives in his hand and a messy apartment spreading out behind him. And he wasn't made up like Marvin.

He promptly slammed the door in her face.

She was here. Now. *Here.*

"Marvin?" Another knock punctuated her soft voice. "Are you okay?"

Okay? Was she kidding? He was half-naked with cereal stuck in his throat and God knows what stuck to one of his sofa cushions. His place was a mess. His hair was an even bigger mess. Okay? He was *this close* to a nervous breakdown.

Panic made his heart pound as he leaned back against the door and tried to figure out what to do next. Hiding was a good idea. The best, but then she'd seen him and—

Think.

"I just thought I'd come by and bring you breakfast. I've got granola."

"I . . ." Forget hiding. He was stuck and there was only one thing for him to do. "Just a sec."

He bolted the door and made a mad rush for the kitchen. In record time, he dumped the cereal, grabbed a trash can, and swiped his arm across the counter, clearing everything in one fell swoop.

Frantically, he rushed around the apartment repeating the motion until he'd managed to gather up all the trash. The arm swiping had also served to collect most of the dust. The gum-covered cushion—at least it looked like gum, but Matt wasn't placing any bets—wound up stuck in his bathroom, along with the over-flowing trash bag and his prized collection of classic rock CDs. And his jeans.

He struggled out of them, tossing them to the floor, one hand diving into the hamper for the polyester slacks he'd worn yesterday.

Taking a quick whiff, he thanked the Powers That Be for deodorant and yanked on the pants. Next came a crumpled dress shirt, which he buttoned clear up to his neck. He dunked his head beneath the sink faucet, biting back a groan as his temple slammed against the nozzle.

Frantic hands slicked the hair back away from his face, tucking the edges behind each ear. There. Now he looked like Marvin . . . Almost.

He made quick run through his bedroom, snatched up his glasses and smoothed his covers before giving up the tangled mess and shutting and locking the door behind him.

Back at the front door, he drew in a deep breath and tried to calm his pounding heart.

So she was here? He was ready. Calm, cool, controlled, and, ready.

"What took you so long?" she asked.

Her green gaze swept him from head to toe and if he didn't know better, he would have sworn she was disappointed that he'd traded the jeans and bare muscles for the cover-every-thing-up clothes.

He should be that lucky.

He squelched the thought. He didn't want Josie Farrington to want him. He wanted the exact opposite.

That's what his head said, but his body—his throbbing, hot, tense body—couldn't seem to remember that all-important fact.

Throbbing? He'd stopped throbbing back in the shower. And pulsing. And wanting.

She smiled and his gut clenched, and forty-five minutes of pelting ice water spiraled straight down the drain.

"Can I come in?"

No. "Uh, yeah."

She walked inside. He closed the door and followed her, watching as her gaze swept the apartment. Surprise flickered in her eyes and panic speared him.

He did a frantic visual search for any over-looked can or piece of trash. *Nothing.* Then again, he wasn't exactly in top trash-spotting mode with her so close to him, her scent filling his nostrils, her heat calling out and stirring his—

"It's nice," she said, killing his train of thought. "A little bare, but nice." Her gaze collided with his and the same pleasure he'd seen last night glittered hot and bright as she stared back at him. "My place is bare, too."

Uh, oh. He'd done it now. "I've been meaning to get out and buy a few things."

Her smiled widened. "Me, too."

"A *lot* of things," he reiterated, as if she'd misunderstood that he'd been trying to make a distinct contrast with her intentions. "The works. Sofa, loveseat, ottoman—you name it."

"Me, too. I think it's time, you know? Time to start paying attention to everything at home. I knew we were on the same wavelength, but I never realized—"

"Take a load—I mean, please have a seat," he cut in with his best Marvin imitation, eager to change the subject.

She sank down to the edge of the sofa, the bag she'd brought cradled on her lap.

Matt seated himself on the recliner a safe distance away and tried to ignore the way her calf-length skirt inched up just a bit, giving him a glimpse of her knees.

Knees, for heaven's sake. Since when did he get excited at the sight of a woman's knees?

Since about five seconds ago, when Josie and her sexy-as-anything knees had walked into his apartment. His life.

"So what's in the bag?"

"Whole wheat bagels and watercress spread."

"Sounds great."

"I knew you'd like it." She busied herself unpacking the bag and laying out the contents on his now clutter-free coffee table. When she had everything spread out all nice and neat, she reached for a bagel.

Matt had the fleeting image of her full, sensuous lips closing around a bite before he jumped to his feet. If staring at her knees had him this close to stripping off his clothes and worshipping at her feet, he wasn't going to wait around and see what the sight of her eating would do to him.

"It's really hot in here. I'll be right back." He rushed from the room and spent the next five minutes fiddling with the air conditioner thermostat in the hallway and killing as much time as possible.

"Here you are." Josie's voice filled his ears as she appeared in the hallway. The smell of fresh-baked bagels combined with soft, warm woman filled his nostrils and he inhaled. "I was wondering what had happened to you."

"The switch was stuck." He lifted the thermostat latch a few times as if testing it. "There. All fixed. Let's go have a seat."

"You go on and help yourself to a bagel." She reached for his bathroom door. "I'll be right back."

A mental vision of Matt's rest room filled his head and panic bolted through him. His hand closed over hers just as she started to turn the knob.

"The toilet's broken," he blurted.

"I just wanted to wash my hands."

"The sink's broken."

"Then I'll just take a quick peek in your mirror."

"Broken. Listen," he said, steering her around and into the living room. "This has really been great. We should do it again some time."

"But we're not done," she said indicating his uneaten bagel.

He snatched up the baked good, took a big bite and fought against a face. Ugh. Now he knew why he'd always been a strictly white-bread sort of guy. As for the watercress . . . Where was some good grape jelly when you really needed it?

"Take care," he said, finishing off a second bite, handing her her purse, and ushering her toward the door. "And I'll see you later."

"But I thought we could talk a little. Get to know each other."

"No time. I've got to get to work."

"Me, too. I thought I'd give you a lift. I've got my car."

"I get carsick. I'll take the train."

"But—"

"See you there." Before she could protest, he closed the door in her face and turned the lock.

Guilt swamped him for rushing her out, but much better to put up with the guilt than the damnable heat she fired in him. Josie Farrington was just too sexy for her own good. And his.

Especially his.

Matt practically ripped off his shirt as he headed for the bathroom and blessed relief. "Cold shower, here I come."

Josie stood out in the hallway, stared at Marvin's closed door, and tried to come to grips with what had just happened.

He'd kicked her out.

Not that she'd expected anything different. Sure, she'd hoped that by showing up and catching him off guard, perhaps she could catch him without his defenses up. After all, people were more relaxed, more comfortable at home.

Her thoughts went to his spotless house and the stiff way he'd perched on the edge of his chair, the fear that had darkened his eyes when he'd first seen her. So maybe he wasn't so relaxed. That didn't mean that Josie was giving up.

She hadn't graduated at the top of her class by buckling under pressure. She simply had to reevaluate her strategy and come up with a foolproof plan to get Marvin to give up his fear and let the chemistry spark between them.

A thought struck her, several as a matter of fact, courtesy of the most recent issue of *Cosmo*, and she smiled.

Reddi-Wip, here I come.

Matt knew exactly what Josie was up to.

He held the blowtorch to the patch of

S.K.I.N. covering ADAM's left shoulder blade and heated the substance just enough to make it malleable. Thermal-gloved fingers went to work pressing and molding and smoothing. Repeating the process, he worked his way down the small of the back.

Yep, he had Josie's number, all right.

While Marvin might be naive and nervous when it came to females, Matt was just the opposite. Having been SpaceTek's golden boy for so many years had had its perks. He'd been pursued by numerous women eager for a piece of his fame and his growing fortune. Prime Grade-A women, including a *Playboy* centerfold, a Dallas Cowboy Cheerleader, and Miss Illinois, none of whom needed a Wonderbra when it came to cleavage enhancement.

Of course, he couldn't remember a pair of breasts looking quite as . . . *plump* as Josie's.

Not *plump* as in huge and melon-like, but *plump* as in round and perky and just the right size to fill his hands if he'd had the slightest inclination to touch.

Which he didn't, he reminded himself.

And her neck. Mmmm . . . her *neck*.

The low-cut sweater she'd worn the night before had shown off the most graceful, slender neck he'd ever had the pleasure of viewing. The sight had caught him completely off guard and his body's response, a burst of heat and the urge to reach out and trace the smooth lines, had floored him. Crazy. That's what he was. He'd never been turned on by a woman's neck.

Never noticed the butterfly flutter of her pulse. Never felt the urge to touch his mouth to the spot and feel the frenzied motion against his lips, his tongue.

He was crazy, all right, thanks to six months of celibacy and the fact that there was no immediate end in sight since Josie Farrington had turned out to be a helluva lot more innocent than he'd initially thought.

Innocent meant complicated, and the last thing Matt needed in his life were more complications.

He had a job to do, a reputation to restore, and he didn't need to get sidetracked. Josie scrambled his common sense with her wide-eyed looks and Matt needed every ounce he possessed if he intended to have ADAM finished and ready to go in time for the Expo.

He'd resisted women before, namely a really hot physics engineer who'd tried to entice him into bed when he'd been smack-dab in the middle of developing the heat sensor pad. He'd passed on her initial offer, finished the sensor, and only then, after the project's completion, had he fallen into bed with her.

Josie, with her average looks, overly abundant hips and so-so legs didn't come close to Miss Physics. That's what he told himself.

He was *not* kissing her.

No matter if she pranced in tonight wearing her Wonderbra again, or another skirt with an enticing slit clear up to her armpits, or if she ate a dozen candy bars in front of him, her full

217

lips moving slowly and sensuously around each bite. No matter if she waltzed in here with nothing on but a few dollops of strategically placed whipped cream and a smile—

His gaze snapped to the doorway and his heart revved like a shuttle engine during launch mode. His hands faltered on the blowtorch he was using to heat ADAM's backside as denial warred in his brain.

There she was.

All white fluff and pink skin, wearing a brilliant smile that stalled the air in his lungs and made him wonder what terrible something he'd done in a past life to deserve this now.

To deserve her.

Chapter Fifteen

Matt had to be seeing things. No way could she actually be wearing . . . She couldn't . . . She wouldn't . . .

"What the hell are you wearing?" he demanded when he finally found his voice.

"I think that's obvious." She touched the white fluff and licked her fingertip. "Empty calories, not to mention overly processed, but desperate times call for desperate measures."

His gaze stayed riveted on the glistening tip of her finger before he managed to tear his gaze away and glare at her.

"What I mean is *why* in the hell are you wearing that?"

She grinned, scooped another fraction, and licked her fingertip again. "Activation energy."

"Come again?"

"You see, most reactions need energy to get them started. The Reddi-Wip is my way of striking your match. Of making you burn." Her gaze took on a sultry look. "Are you burning, Marvin?"

And how.

Heat scorched every nerve ending, making him hot and uncomfortable and achy. His groin swelled, pushing tight against his slacks and a layer of sweat slid from his temple.

"It could be a damned sight cooler in here," he managed.

The smile she gave him was pure female seduction. "I knew it. I . . ." Her words trailed off and the expression faded. "It's on fire."

Did she want him to spell it out? "I'm *this close* to going up in flames."

"Not you. It. *It.*"

Damn straight *it* was hot. What did she expect standing there half naked with—

"ADAM," her voice interrupted his disastrous train of thought. "He's smoking."

"What?" His gaze swiveled to the forgotten torch in his hands.

Fire. ADAM was on *fire.*

Frantically, he switched off the flame, snatched up a cool rag and slapped at ADAM's smoldering buttocks. "Dammit."

"Such a bold word from such a calm, cool,

220

conservative man. But then you're just full of surprises."

She didn't know the half of it.

"You might as well give it up," he informed her as he plucked off his heat-resistant gloves and pulled the goggles from his face. "Hot or not, I'm still not kissing you."

"I'm willing to wait and see."

"Fine."

"Fine." She grinned and he knew she had something up her sleeve. Except for the all-important fact that she didn't have any sleeves, or a blouse to go with the sleeves—just a skirt covering her bottom half. He wanted to be thankful for small favors, but then she took a deep breath, the whipped creamed mounds bobbed and he swallowed. "We'll just have to wait each other out," she told him.

"Fine."

"Fine." She smiled again. The sweet smell of cream drifted across the several feet separating them and teased his nostrils. "But I have to warn you, this stuff is supposed to be refrigerated."

"Meaning?"

"It's a little warm in here, especially with ADAM's gluteous maximus on fire. In a few seconds, I'm going to start to melt."

As if the idea had sparked a reaction, a creamy rivulet slithered down her abdomen, leaving a glistening trail that stalled the air in his lungs.

"While I don't find the idea that repulsive,"

she went on. "Since you seem so determined to resist the chemistry between us, it might pose a problem for you."

He forced his gaze away from the runaway drop of cream. All the major parts were covered. He shouldn't be having such an intense reaction. Dragging some much-needed air into his lungs, he glared. "Put some clothes on."

"Did I say problem?" One eyebrow arched. "I meant temptation."

"Put some clothes on."

A grin spread across her face. "Kiss me and I will."

He wasn't sure when it happened. The moment he'd seen her standing there looking as delectable as a hot fudge sundae, or the second she issued the challenge. But resistance suddenly seemed like a very bad idea.

While Miss Josie Farrington might be somewhat of an innocent in the physical sense with her limited experience, she had a sharp mind that refused to let him see her as anything less than a full-grown woman who knew who and what she wanted.

She wanted him.

Now and forever. The warning echoed through his brain, but he latched on to the first part and sent the rest packing.

Now.

Besides, he wasn't actually going to break his vow and kiss her. He was just a hungry man with a sudden craving for whipped cream.

Pulling off his glasses, he slid them into his

breast pocket. Damn, but it felt good to give his eyes a break. It was difficult to always see around those glasses and still pretend he needed them. Everything seemed sharper, clearer, especially Josie. He drank in the picture she made standing there all spruced up as an X-rated dessert. Her eyes glittered, betraying her otherwise calm, cool, analytical exterior. Her pulse ticked frantically at the base of her throat. Her hands trembled ever so slightly, her arms resting at her sides against the damnable black skirt that hid so much, but outlined her hips so perfectly that she might as well have been naked from the waist down as well. Her toes, painted with a pale shade of pink, curled against the tile floor as she waited to see what he would do next.

He stepped toward her. "Aren't there two parts to a bikini?"

A flash of self-consciousness glittered in her eyes before she glanced down at the calf-length skirt. "I, um, thought I'd go with a little subtlety."

He dropped to his knees in front of her, his hands going to her hips. The skirt was snug enough that it hugged her rounded bottom and he couldn't help himself. He paused to knead the firm flesh, relishing her gasp of pleasure as he filled his hands with her. Fabric brushed his palms as he slid them down over her thighs to where her skirt ended. He cupped the smooth skin of her calves and slid his hands up, feeling warm, quivering flesh.

"Pussycat, you don't have a subtle bone in that delectable body of yours."

"I most certainly do," she blurted before catching her bottom lip. A blush rosied her cheeks as she gazed down at him. Her words were soft, hesitant, as if she couldn't quite believe what she was hearing. "You really think I have a delectable body?"

"I *think*," he murmured as he kissed her navel and lapped at the melted trickle of whipped cream that pooled there. Her breath caught and her flesh quivered against his lips. "But I don't *know*."

He stood then, slid his hands around to her curvaceous bottom and lifted her onto the counter. Shoving up her skirt, he wedged himself between her parted thighs. He urged her backward until her back met the countertop.

"A good scientist needs data to support his theory," he added.

Josie had a fleeting image of a cat licking cream from his lips before Marvin's dark head lowered and she felt the soft lap at her breast.

"Data can be good," she murmured. The stroking grew stronger, more purposeful as he gobbled up the white confection, starting at the outside and working his way toward the center. For a man who usually didn't indulge in this much sugar, he certainly seemed to be enjoying himself. His lips brushed here, his tongue grazed there and the sensation rippled up her spine.

She sent up a silent thank-you that she'd had

*A
Special
Offer
For
Love
Spell
Romance
Readers
Only!*

Get Two Free Romance Novels

An $11.48 Value!

Travel to exotic worlds
filled with passion and adventure—
without leaving your home!

Plus, you'll save $5.00
every time you buy!

Thrill to the most sensual, adventure-filled Romances on the market today...

FROM  LOVE SPELL BOOKS

As a home subscriber to the Love Spell Romance Book Club, you'll enjoy the best in today's BRAND-NEW Time Travel, Futuristic, Legendary Lovers, Perfect Heroes and other genre romance fiction. For five years, Love Spell has brought you the award-winning, high-quality authors you know and love to read. Each Love Spell romance will sweep you away to a world of high adventure...and intimate romance. Discover for yourself all the passion and excitement millions of readers thrill to each and every month.

Save $5.00 Each Time You Buy!

Every other month, the Love Spell Romance Book Club brings you four brand-new titles from Love Spell Books. EACH PACKAGE WILL SAVE YOU AT LEAST $5.00 FROM THE BOOK-STORE PRICE! And you'll never miss a new title with our convenient home delivery service.

Here's how we do it: Each package will carry a FREE 10-DAY EXAMINATION privilege. At the end of that time, if you decide to keep your books, simply pay the low invoice price of $17.96, no shipping or handling charges added. HOME DELIVERY IS ALWAYS FREE. With today's top romance novels selling for $5.99 and higher, our price SAVES YOU AT LEAST $5.00 with each shipment.

AND YOUR FIRST TWO-BOOK SHIP-MENT IS TOTALLY FREE!

IT'S A BARGAIN YOU CAN'T BEAT! A SUPER $11.48 Value!

Love Spell ✦ A Division of Dorchester Publishing Co., Inc.

GET YOUR 2 FREE BOOKS NOW—AN $11.48 VALUE!

Mail the Free Book Certificate Today!

Free Books Certificate

YES! I want to subscribe to the Love Spell Romance Book Club. Please send me my 2 FREE BOOKS. Then every other month I'll receive the four newest Love Spell selections to Preview FREE for 10 days. If I decide to keep them, I will pay the Special Member's Only discounted price of just $4.49 each, a total of $17.96. This is a SAVINGS of at least $5.00 off the bookstore price. There are no shipping, handling, or other charges. There is no minimum number of books I must buy and I may cancel the program at any time. In any case, the 2 FREE BOOKS are mine to keep—A BIG $11.48 Value!

Offer valid only in the U.S.A.

Name _____

Address _____

City _____

State _____ *Zip* _____

Telephone _____

Signature _____

If under 18, Parent or Guardian must sign. Terms, prices and conditions subject to change. Subscription subject to acceptance. Leisure Books reserves the right to reject any order or cancel any subscription.

Get Two Books Totally
F R E E —
An $11.48 Value!

▼ Tear Here and Mail Your FREE Book Card Today! ▼

PLEASE RUSH
MY TWO FREE
BOOKS TO ME
RIGHT AWAY!

Love Spell Romance Book Club
P.O. Box 6613
Edison, NJ 08818-6613

AFFIX
STAMP
HERE

the fortitude to go with the whipped cream and not sugar-free strawberry Jell-O. For some reason, she didn't think the latter would have had the same effect—and however fattening for Marvin, this was pure heaven for her.

The first leisurely rasp of his tongue against her ripe nipple wrung a cry from her throat and put an end to anymore debate on the subject. Her fingers threaded through his hair as he drew the quivering tip deep into his hot, hungry mouth and suckled her long and hard. It was everything she'd ever dreamed, and more, and she whimpered and begged until he switched to the other breast.

As he licked and suckled and nipped, her skin grew itchy and tight. A pressure started between her legs, heightened by the way he leaned into her, the hard ridge of his erection prominent beneath his slacks. She spread her legs wider and he settled more deeply between them. Grasping her hips, he rocked her. Rubbed her. Up and down and side to side and . . .

What was that smell?

"Marvin?" Her breathing came fast and heavy, her body buzzing with sensation as his hands caressed her calves and urged her skirt upward.

"You can moan for me, beg for me, even curse me, but otherwise, no talking."

"But I think something's . . ." *Wrong* was there on the tip of her lips, but then strong fingertips slid over the damp cotton of her panties and her body jerked in reaction. He traced the edge where elastic met the tender inside of her thigh before dipping beneath.

One rasping touch of his callused fingertip against her swollen flesh and she arched up off the counter. With a growl, he spread her wide with his thumb and forefinger and touched and rubbed as he drew on her nipple. Harder, harder. Back and forth. Side to side. Around and around.

It was too much and not enough and she clamped her eyes shut tight as sensation erupted. Her lips parted and she screamed at the blinding force of the climax that picked her up, rolled her over and turned her inside out.

It wasn't until a sprinkler exploded overhead that Josie realized the shrill, high-pitched noise wasn't her own voice but a very persistent alarm.

The next few seconds seemed to move in slow motion as Marvin jerked away from her and she struggled upright. Their gazes shot to ADAM. Flames licked up and down his backside, fighting for survival against the overhead sprinkler.

"Find a fire extinguisher," Marvin shouted as he grabbed his lab coat and started slapping at the flames.

Josie barely managed to turn before the door burst open and Phyllis rushed in, extinguisher in hand.

"Stand back!" she ordered, aiming the nozzle and opening the valve. Several spurts and the flames died a quick death.

"It's out," she declared. "I swear, when I smelled smoke I saw my life pass before my eyes, and then I heard the alarms and the sprinklers and . . ." Her words trailed off as she noticed Phyllis with her arms folded in front of her. She blinked. "You're naked."

"*Was* naked," Marvin pointed out, handing Josie his ravaged lab coat.

"The correct description is topless." Josie avoided Phyllis' gaze, tucked the coat protectively under her arms and tried to ignore the butterflies that had started to flutter in her belly the second Marvin's fingertips had brushed hers.

"We were conducting an experiment." Marvin didn't even glance at Josie as he morphed back into the quiet, conservative scientist. He fixed his attention on the fire-ravaged ADAM and seemed to ignore both women.

Ladies and gentlemen. Zorro has left the building.

Phyllis eyed Josie. "Must have been some experiment."

A failed experiment, Josie thought, her body still humming from the best sensations of her entire life. Because despite the delicious things he'd done when he'd slipped on his sex appeal and transformed into Dr. Love, Marvin Tannenbaum still hadn't kissed her.

Maybe she should have tried the Jell-O after all.

Matt turned off the ice-cold water and reached for a towel. Credits rolled for the mid-

Kimberly Raye

night movie by the time he shrugged on
sweatpants, pitched his towel toward the
hamper and missed by a good five inches.
White cotton landed next to the socks he'd
peeled off earlier. He leaned over to snatch up
the pile and caught himself inches shy. Josie's
words echoed through his head.

We're perfect for each other. Life mates.

Instead of dumping the clothes into the hamper, large fingers dove inside and retrieved a
few discarded towels, added them to the pile
and then scattered everything for good measure. There. That was better. Marvin and Josie
might like their laundry separated into color-
coordinated piles, but Matt wasn't near as
compulsively neat.

He didn't know the meaning of the phrase.

Life wasn't about obsessing over the small
stuff. It was about living. Enjoying one
moment to the next.

No regrets, he reminded himself as he headed
into the kitchen.

He'd opened the fridge to retrieve a beer and
a slice of cold pizza, when his hand stalled on
the pizza box.

The craving for whipped cream hit him hard
and fast and he licked his lips, tasting the
sweetness that lingered, wishing he could taste
a hell of a lot more. Christ, he wanted her. Too
much.

Tonight had proven that. They'd only been
messing around, far from what he'd wanted to
do, and yet he'd been as consumed as if he'd

228

been hilt-deep inside her and she'd been hot and pulsing around him. Hell, he'd felt as turned on as he ever had—and at nothing more than watching her take her own pleasure, hearing it, *feeling* it. She'd been so warm and wet and ready for him, and he'd damned near exploded at the discovery.

He could have had her so easily. Just a flick of his pants' button, the glide of a zipper and he could have been inside her, but he'd held back, wanting to watch, to make her quiver with such force that her lips parted and her lovely breasts turned a bright shade of pink.

Because of him. He'd made her that hot, that wet. Just him—

He killed the dangerous thought by abandoning the pizza, popping the tab on his beer and downing a swig.

Days, he told himself. It would take at least three to repair the damage done to ADAM by tonight's fire. He would have to completely resculpt the buttocks, not an easy task when there was only one set of buttocks—make that *gluteous maximus* that haunted his thoughts.

She had fit into his palms so well when he had lifted her onto the countertop, her bottom soft and round beneath the black silk skirt.

"Work, buddy," he growled, taking a huge gulp and praying for some relief. "It's all about work." About keeping his focus. Something he'd done his entire life. He'd always been driven, determined to make his way when there wasn't any, when his father and the entire town and everyone he'd encountered along the way had been against him. He'd enjoyed his share of women, but he'd never let one side-track him, never let one get close to him.

He wasn't starting now. He'd seen firsthand with his own father how miserable a man could be when he gave in to his lust and settled down for all the wrong reasons. That led to a lifetime of regret, of lost potential. Not Matt. He didn't want any regrets in his life, any bitter feelings that made him lash out at the people closest to him. There was still too much in his life that he wanted to do. He wasn't ready to settle down, and Josie, with her perfect life-partner search, had *settle* written all over her. A sugar-cookie woman if he'd ever seen one.

Now if she'd just been looking for a one-night stand, then things might have been different. *Might* have been. But she wanted more, which meant he wasn't touching her again.

She'd caught him off guard tonight. But now that Matt knew that sweet Josie was capable of some serious seduction, he intended to be ready. He wasn't succumbing, no matter if she smothered herself from head to toe with whipped cream or painted herself with chocolate body paint, or waltzed into the lab stark-naked.

All right, all right. So maybe he'd crack if she were naked. After all, a guy could only take so much.

Chapter Sixteen

She didn't show up naked.

Six o'clock came and went with no sign of Josie.

Relief washed through him. He had the entire lab to himself with no distractions. He didn't have to worry about what tricks she was up to or waste a precious hour watching *Chemistry Tonight*.

Unless this was one of her tricks. A ploy to up his anticipation and bring every nerve in his body to pulsing, expectant life.

He had to hand it to her. She'd done her homework, but she was working on the wrong man. It wasn't going to work.

He focused all his concentration on stripping

the damaged S.K.I.N. from ADAM and applying the new plastic. But as the night wore on, he found himself listening to every creak, every thump, waiting for the shrill ring of the alarm to sound so he could put his plan into motion—namely hiding. After a night of tossing and turning, avoidance had been the most brilliant idea his off-the-charts IQ could come up with, and so he'd set a trip wire out in the hallway, which would fire off a buzzer and signal her arrival, giving him fair warning to slip out the back door and avoid any confrontation. Particularly a naked one.

The clock struck ten and the credits rolled for *Chemistry Tonight*—he'd endured every episode in the nucleic acid series so far and it seemed a shame to stop only two shy from the end. As the news came on, Matt's anxiety transformed into full-blown worry.

No way would she willingly miss *Chemistry Tonight*. She lived for the boring, pretentious show and its equally boring, pretentious host. And no way would she miss another chance to seduce him. She'd only done half the bikini last night and if Matt had learned anything about Josie over the past few weeks, it was that she finished everything she started. She still owed him whipped cream panties. Something had to be wrong.

Dozens of possibilities raced through his mind, all ending with Josie hurt and bleeding and crying out for help, a fearful image that galvanized him into action.

She was out there somewhere and he had to find her.

"You're alive," Marvin blurted the moment Josie hauled open her apartment door and found him standing on her doorstep.

Besides his apparent excitement, which she wasn't sure she comprehended, two very important things registered.

One, he wasn't wearing his glasses, giving her a full view of a pair of very dark, very intense blue eyes lit with worry.

And two, his hair was long and messy and totally un-Marvin-like.

She quickly found out why when he raked long powerful fingers through the dark locks and frowned at her.

"You didn't come to the lab," he said accusingly. "You missed your show."

"No, I didn't. I taped it. I always tape it. My apartment handyman pre-programmed my VCR. I promised Mrs. Shipley down on the first floor that I'd help her pack. She's moving to a retirement home first thing tomorrow." She held up a stack of newspapers. "We just finished. They have daily bingo."

They have daily bingo? The man who'd given her the best sensation of her life was standing on her doorstep looking worried and intense and as sexy as hell, and that was the best she could do?

Given the circumstances, it was. Her Wonderbra was two rooms away with the rest of her seductive armor. She was tired and messy and completely unprepared for his presence. She pushed a strand of wilted hair behind her ear and wiped at a trickle of sweat near her temple.

His gaze followed the movements and she barely resisted the urge to run for cover. Forget tired and messy. She knew she looked downright frightening. Her sparse makeup had melted, her hair had come loose from her functional ponytail and she smelled like newsprint. Not to mention she was wearing a pair of overalls about three sizes too big and a threadbare tank top she'd had since she was fourteen.

His gaze darkened to a midnight blue and pinned her to the spot. "You're not naked," he muttered, as if the realization bothered him.

Right. Josie hadn't graduated from MIT with two degrees, a doctorate and her choice of more than twenty jobs by being dense. His behavior last night had proven beyond a doubt that he wasn't half as hot for her as she was for him. Otherwise, he wouldn't have been able to turn his back and completely ignore her after touching her so intimately. After . . . *after.*

No, he just wasn't that interested.

"Just so you'll know, I won't be bothering you anymore," she told him, eager to set the record straight and shut the door. Before she did something totally incomprehensible like forget the fact that he didn't want her and throw herself into his arms anyway. "I realize that I misconstrued . . ." She licked her lips and searched for the right words. "What I mean is, I might have mistaken . . ." Another lick and she cleared her throat. "That is, I jumped to the wrong conclusion about you. About us."

He didn't so much as blink. He just stared at her with a mix of disbelief and anger, as if he were fighting some internal battle. "You look like hell," he finally muttered.

A wave of self-consciousness washed through her. While the seduction had ended and she'd lost, she still wasn't in a hurry to prance around looking like *Night of the Living Dead* in front of the only man to ever give her a real quality release. Her defenses kicked in. "I just finished packing up an entire apartment."

His lips drew into a tight frown. "You *really* look like hell."

"It was a three-bedroom apartment."

"Not a stitch of makeup."

"With two bathrooms."

"Wild hair."

"And a den."

"Shapeless clothes."

She frowned. Enough was enough. "I think you've made your point."

"No bra." His gaze was riveted to her chest like two blue laser heat-seeking missiles. Her nipples tightened in response.

Stop that, her brain commanded, but her body, as usual, wasn't listening, not with him standing so close and smelling so good and looking so . . . worried.

He shook his head and she watched the mix

of emotions flash across his face. Anger and desire and confusion. "This isn't supposed to happen."

"After a whole, confining week locked in a Wonderbra, I thought they deserved a full pardon . . ." The words faded as he stepped closer. She eyed him, noting the strange light in his eyes. "Are you okay?"

"No, I'm not okay." His gaze pinned her. "You look like hell and I've got a hard-on that could nail a few iron spikes into the ground." He kicked the door shut behind him and closed in on her, backing her up against the nearest wall. "That's definitely not okay."

She tried to comprehend his words, but then he leaned in and the scent of raw male and something very musky and dangerous filled her nostrils. Her thought processes short-circuited.

He pinned her to the wall and touched his lips to the base of her throat, and her breathing joined the rebellion. His mouth was hot and wet and hungry as he sucked and nibbled the tender flesh where her pulse beat a frantic rhythm.

"What are you doing?" she finally gasped, unwilling to believe what was happening. *Hard-on. Iron spikes. Not okay.* Could it be that he was finally taking the initiative, without any Lust Lessons to entice him?

"What *we're* doing," he corrected, his hands going to the hooks of her overalls.

"What are we doing?"

"We're getting naked." With the flick of her buttons, he released the straps. The too-big denim slid to the floor and puddled around her ankles. His hands traced the taut outline her nipples made against the soft cotton of her threadbare tank-top. Over and over he skimmed the stiff peaks, his dark gaze riveted on her chest.

She had the sudden urge to cover herself. Her breasts weren't nearly as full and perky without the bra and while he'd seen her last night, she'd been covered with Reddi-Wip. This was different. This was her not-so-perfect breasts in their completely natural state. "What are you thinking?" she blurted, unable to contain her curiosity.

"That '*Born Free*' is one damned fine song." He grinned before his gaze faded into pure intent as he traded looking for acting and peeled the material over her head.

She stood before him wearing nothing but a pair of cotton pant—*oh, no!* Not the full-service, full-size, tummy-control briefs. Her mortification tipped the scales at a whopping one hundred percent.

"Y—you sort of caught me off guard," she blurted, rushing into an explanation that quickly faded when she noted the blue fire burning in his eyes.

Josie realized then and there that he wasn't the least bit put off by functional underthings. After all, he might be her chemical opposite, but he was perfect life mate potential, too. Obviously, he appreciated her understated tastes . . .

The thought faded in a wave of desire as big, strong hands slid the undies down her thighs. His hot skin brushed hers, leaving a blazing trail that sent bursts of heat along her nerve endings and made her entire body buzz.

She wanted him, his hands and mouth on her, his body pressed to hers and he wanted . . . *to look*?

His gaze swept her from head to toe and back, pausing at several places in between. Anxiety rushed through her. At her best she wasn't anything to have a screaming climax about, and she looked far from her best.

"God, you're incredible," he murmured, his deep voice laced with satisfaction and possesiveness.

So maybe his looking could be good.

And what was good for the goose, as the saying went . . .

She drank in the sight of him decked out in his lab clothes, from his coat to the tie and dress shirt underneath. The only thing he'd shed was the lab coat. Dark silky hair framed his face, outlining the strong set of his jaw and sensual lips. She followed the line of his throat to where it dipped beneath his collar and the urge to see more gripped her.

"*We* usually implies two," she said, reminding him of his earlier words. "So far, I'm the only one without clothes. You've got some catching up to do."

He shrugged out of his lab coat and tossed it to the side. The tie and shirt followed the trousers, until he stood before her wearing nothing but a pair of white BVDs. A few quick pushes and the white cotton joined the rest of his clothes.

Where she'd only glimpsed his naked body that first time in the lab, she could look her fill right now. She did. She ran her gaze over his taut skin, broad chest and flat brown nipples surrounded by dark hair. His legs were long and thick with muscles. His arousal was huge and hard and thick, and her heart paused for a long breathless moment. She had the fleeting thought that his was the body of a warrior, not an intellectual, but then he reached for her, flesh met hot flesh and she stopped thinking altogether.

One large hand threaded through her hair, tugging softly so that her head tilted back and she arched toward him.

"You're going to kiss me," she said in breathless wonder.

The statement seemed to catch him off guard. Something flashed in his dark eyes as he stared at her lips, as if he were debating what to do next. Then hunger fired bright in the blue depths and he lowered his head.

He didn't kiss her.

His mouth bypassed hers for a lower destination. Before she could nurse any disappointment, she felt the moist heat of his breath on her breast and then his lips closed over her nipple.

He licked and suckled and nibbled, softly at first. Sensation skittered along her nerve endings and she forgot all about wanting to feel his lips on her own. Heat pooled low in her belly, making her thighs tremble and her hands quiver. Then his mouth opened and he drew her deeper, sucking hard. Sensation flooded through her, crashing over her in huge waves.

He let go of her hair then, his hand drifting down her back, around her waist as he skimmed the bottom of her rib cage, grazed her belly, and touched between her legs. Strong fingers slid into her slick flesh, stroking and coaxing and wringing a shameless moan from her lips.

He touched her just so and every atom in her body started spinning, as if she were caught in a giant magnetic field, gravitating toward the center where everything fell apart and came together at the same time.

That's what she wanted. To fall apart. To soar with him inside her then burst apart in a way she'd heard mentioned in books. In a way she'd never—despite her past two partners, *because* of her past two partners—experienced firsthand.

When he slipped a finger into her soft folds and pushed deep, she cried out. Her trembling turned to shaking as her entire body reacted to the invasion, her nerves humming from the incredible need swamping her senses.

Her hands stroked up and down his back, grasping his hard, muscled buttocks before she circled his hips. She'd barely brushed his erection when she found her wrist caught in a tight grip.

"No," he groaned. "It's been too long and there's no way this is going to go slow if you touch me."

Slow? Was he serious?

"I've waited thirty-four years and counting for this kind of chemistry." For a man who made her feel more than a moment of fleeting pleasure. "I want you *now*." The desperation in her voice surprised her, but she was beyond caring. She trembled and throbbed and ached so badly. "Please."

He scooped her into his arms and headed for her bedroom. The mattress met her back and then he disappeared. A few minutes later, he reappeared, condom in hand and slid the latex down his engorged length. He covered her then, spreading her legs wide and positioning himself.

The voluptuous head of his hot erection nudged her slick opening and every nerve in her body jumped to full alert. His chest heaved, crushing her tender breasts as he fought to drag air into his lungs.

"Christ, I don't know what it is about you," he murmured staring at her as if she were some impossible puzzle he just couldn't begin to solve, and then the contemplation ended. He thrust into her, stretching and filling.

241

A thread of pain shot through her, quickly replaced by intense pleasure as he buried himself so deep, she didn't know where he ended and she began.

"Wrap your legs around me," he murmured, and she quickly complied, the motion drawing him deeper. So deliciously deep.

He reached under her and clasped her hips, angling her as he withdrew and thrust into her again. And again.

This was it.

The moment she'd been waiting for. She meant to lay back and enjoy every touch, every sound and let the beauty of the moment wash over her, but she couldn't.

Despite the intense pleasure he was giving her, she suddenly wanted more. She wanted him harder and deeper and faster and she couldn't help herself. She clutched his slick shoulders, his back, his buttocks, lifted her pelvis and matched his rhythm. Her nipples rubbed against the soft hair on his chest, sending ripples of heat through her body. The pressure built as he pumped into her, pushing her higher, faster and then it happened. Her back arched and she shattered. Wave after wave of luscious heat rolled over her, through her and her muscles contracted, gripping him tight and wringing a deep groan from him.

He quickly followed her over the edge, his muscles as hard as granite as he plunged into her one last, sweet time. He collapsed on top of her, his chest heaving, his heart thundering in sync with her own.

She wanted to shout, to dance, to climb to the top of the Sears Tower and declare her joy to the world. But then he slid his strong arms around her, rolled over and gathered her close, and she stopped wanting.

Contentment unlike anything she'd ever felt before rushed through her and she snuggled deeper into his embrace, closed her eyes and thanked the Powers That Be for her good fortune.

For finally smiling on her and sending her the perfect man.

Matt's life was flashing before his eyes.

His less-than-perfect childhood, his tough adolescence, his lost career, his future—all flashing and fading right before his eyes into the sweet, delectable image of the woman next to him.

What the hell had he done?

His mind rushed back to the lab, to the worry and the anxiety and the desperation. He'd only meant to check up on her. But then she'd opened the door wearing those baggy overalls, with her hair all mussed and her face beaded with sweat, and the sight had hit him as hard as when she'd been decked out in Reddi-Wip. He'd found her just as desirable, even more so than any grade-A deluxe female he'd ever come into contact with.

Crazy.

That was the only explanation for the sudden image that raced through his mind. Of him flexing over a chopping block and dicing up firewood while the smell of homebaked cookies drifted from the house along with Josie's sweet voice.

Crazy.

He'd never chopped firewood in his life and he wasn't about to start. And while Josie could make a mean paste, he'd be willing to bet she'd never even eaten a home-baked cookie, much less made one. And sweet voice? He remembered the soft whisper of her voice to the Sam Cooke song as they'd danced. She'd been out of key and off-beat.

And he'd liked it.

Geez, he was a goner.

Gone. Now there was a good idea. He needed to get out of here and clear his head. He needed to breathe some oxygen that didn't smell like sweat and sex and *her*.

He pulled away from her and climbed out of the bed before he did something really stupid and made love to her all over again. Slow this time. Real slow.

"Where are you going?"

"I need to get back to the lab," he said, heading into the bathroom to dispose of the condom before going into the living room to retrieve his clothes.

Work would take his mind off what had just happened. What he still *wanted* to happen.

Work would remind him of what was at stake. His future versus an ax and a chopping block and Josie with her beige paste.

No contest.

He hadn't spent the past six months incognito so he could go screwing up when he was *this close* to success. Josie wanted more than he could give, more than he wanted to give.

More.

"Dedicated." Her voice drew him around. He turned to find her standing in the bedroom doorway wearing nothing but a knowing grin. "That's number two."

"What are you talking about?" He jerked on his clothes and did his damnedest not to look at her, at the flare of her hips and her small, plump breasts and—

"My Ten Compatibility Commandments." Her voice shattered his dangerous train of thought. "Dedication is number two. You rushing off to the lab at a quarter past midnight definitely qualifies."

"Did I say the lab? I'm going home. To watch TV." His brain scrambled as he thought back to their few conversations on the subject and her views on compatible men. If there was one thing Matt wasn't, it was *compatible*. Just thinking about the word gave him hives. He was an island unto himself. King of his own castle and he had a hell of a lot of living to do before he ever regressed back into plain old compatible.

"Can't miss *Wrestling Bimbos*," he added. "I'll

probably drink at least a six-pack while I'm at it. And scratch myself and do some major belching."

Her cat-ate-the-canary smile didn't even falter. "You really shouldn't work on an empty stomach. I could fix you a snack."

"Didn't you hear me? I'm not working any more tonight." She actually thought he was kidding. "I'm going home to laze around and throw my socks in the hallway—"

"You don't throw your socks around. I've seen your apartment."

"Yeah, well I'm going to start. And I'm going to leave the toilet-seat lid up and eat ravioli out of the can." He couldn't remember her end-all and be-all Ten, but he was willing to bet such Neanderthal macho stuff wouldn't be anywhere near the list.

"I've got grapes," she went on as if he'd never said a word. "And raisins. Or maybe a cookie. I don't usually bake, but Phyllis gave me this great healthy recipe for oatmeal."

The admission stopped him cold. He paused, one arm in his shirt and one out. "Cookies?"

"Don't worry. They're all-natural. No preservatives or food additives. I thought I'd better stock something edible since Mr. Babcock's been raiding my refrigerator. At the rate he's going, he's going to start growing things out of his nose, or sticking to the toilet seat." At his questioning glance, she added, "He ate my potato plant last week, and the homemade paste the week before that."

She'd *baked* cookies—albeit healthy stuff and a far cry from sugar—but cookies were cookies. The knowledge echoed through his head for three fast furious heartbeats as he yanked his shirt all the way on and snatched up his shoes.

And then he did what he should have done the moment she opened the door looking so dirty and disheveled and downright sexy.

Matt Taylor turned and ran for his life.

Chapter Seventeen

"Looks like somebody had herself a hot night last night." The comment came from Felicity the minute Josie walked into the lab the next morning.

It was a statement she'd heard numerous times in the break room. Never, however, had it been directed at her because Josie had never been one of the "girls."

No more.

She knew now what all the whispering in the girls' locker room had been about, understood the fascination with the opposite sex, the excitement that came with every Friday night date. It went far beyond sex, beyond the physical act between a man and a woman. This was about feeling. Attraction. *Lust.*

For the first time in her life, when she'd been in Marvin's arms and he'd been inside of her, she hadn't been Dr. Josephine Farrington, MIT graduate and a lifetime member of Mensa. She'd been just a woman, feeling a woman's passion, taking a woman's pleasure.

Just one of the girls.

"So?" Felicity prodded. "Are we talking lukewarm or sizzling?"

Josie smiled. "I never kiss and tell."

"Definitely sizzling." An eager light glittered in the lab assistant's eyes. "So who was it?" She indicated a stack of phone messages. "There's Craig, Darren, Walter, Freddy, Andre, Peter, Jack and some guy who calls himself Dr. Love."

"What? Let me see those." Josie grabbed the slips of paper.

"So which one is responsible for the I've-just-been-to-heaven-and-back smile you're wearing?"

"None." Her gaze snapped up to meet Felicity's. "Are you sure these men called for me?"

"Dr. Josephine Farrington. Chicago's Hottest Bachelorette."

"Chicago's *what*?"

"Hottest Bachelorette. Don't tell me you haven't seen it?"

"Seen what?"

"Today's paper." Felicity slapped the latest copy of the *Chicago Sun-Times* on her desk.

Josie took one look at the picture and her heart stalled. There in blazing color was a photograph of Josie wearing her red sweater, her hands on the third button as she sat on the edge of the countertop in Marvin's lab while he stood nearby, his gaze directed—where else—at his computer screen.

It was the first picture the photographer had snapped when he and Arthur Kiss had barged in.

With her blouse half undone.

Even more disconcerting was the title: HOT! HOT! HOT!

Her gaze swiveled back to the picture. *Hot?* She looked heavy. Ten pounds heavier, while Marvin stood off to the sidelines looking his usual buttoned-up, svelte self.

"Oh, my God."

"It's a shock. I never really knew you had boobs under that lab coat."

Josie glared at her before turning back to the picture. To the awful, horrible picture.

"I mean, I knew that you had them, but you never actually put them out there. Not like that. This is better than one of those Glamour Shots. No wonder men are crawling out of the woodwork for you. Read message number five. He says he loves you. Numbers seven and eight both say they want to strip you naked and Dr. Love says he likes to sing the national anthem in bed and he's got a great big salute just waiting for you."

"I don't believe this."

"Neither do I. Every guy thinks he has the market cornered when it comes to big salutes. You'd think they'd have realized by now that it ain't the height of the flag pole, but the snapping of the flag that makes a woman see God."

"Not that." She indicated the picture. "This."

"They don't call it a Wonderbra for nothing. But don't worry. The article doesn't just comment on your bra size. Your brain is in there, too."

"What?" Her gaze darted to Felicity before shifting back to the picture and the caption just below. The line echoed through her head and the bran muffin she'd had that morning upended and lodged itself in her throat. "I think I need to lie down."

"Look on the bright side. It's good publicity."

"The caption calls me a female Einstein with a bra size to match my brain. How is that good?"

"That's just to get attention. The article itself is actually pretty factual. It gives personal details. How you graduated early and went to MIT. It even tells your IQ."

"My IQ? How in the world did they find out that?"

Felicity shifted in her seat and a guilty look crossed her face. "You know reporters. They probably tortured some poor, miserable soul."

"You told them my IQ."

Felicity shrugged. "I thought you knew about the article. They said they interviewed you the other night and they were still missing a few extra details."

"They interviewed Arthur Kiss, not me. Has he seen this?"

"This and the article on page five that features the company. That was his interview. I guess the reporter thought you warranted a special article all your own."

"Lucky me." She blinked, praying for the picture to disappear, or to at least morph into something more respectable.

Still there. Still hot. Still huge. *Ugh.*

"I can't believe they listed my IQ." Panic bolted through her, but she fought it back down. This was not good, but it wasn't hopeless. "It's a small picture, right? An even smaller article. Probably the worst is over."

"I hope not. I'm betting you get at least ten proposals before the day is out. The office has a pool going. The winner gets a gift certificate to Macy's and I've been eyeing this three-inch pair of silver Pradas."

"I'm sure this thing has already run its course, and high heels are bad for your arches."

"Is that why you're wearing them in this picture?"

Josie snatched the newspaper from Felicity's hands. "They're still bad for your arches." She stuffed the paper into the side pocket of her briefcase and frowned. "Don't you have work to do?"

The phone picked that moment to ring and Felicity promptly snatched it up. "Three Kisses, Inc., home of Chicago's Hottest Bachelorette."

"You're fired." Josie mouthed, even though she knew Felicity wouldn't take her seriously. She was the best lab assistant Josie had ever had and Felicity knew it.

"You want to marry her and make little genius babies? Sure, I'll tell her." She scribbled a message and slid the receiver into place and grinned. "One down and nine to go."

So much for just being one of the girls.

"That's a girl toy." Ethan tossed the prototype for the Rappin' Rhonda doll to the pile and reached for an airplane.

"My mommy says there's no such thing as girl toys and boy toys and that I should play with everything on account of I don't want to perpetuate gender biases," a little girl spoke up.

Josie smiled. "Evelyn, do you know what gender biases are?"

"No, but my mommy does. She's a feminist lawyer and she knows everything."

"Let's get back on track, children. How about this toy?" Josie held up a new action figure that was quickly pushed aside.

"My mommy's a blue-tishan and she knows everything, especially how to French braid my hair," one of the little girls offered.

"So what?" Chad chimed in. "My mommy's a gyneco-lala-gist, and she knows everything."

"My daddy's a policeman and he says my mommy just thinks she knows everything."

"Well, my daddy . . ." Voices sparred back and forth as the children forgot all about the toys to compare notes on their parents. Josie set her clipboard aside. So much for observation. Where was Felicity when she really needed her?

Alex, I'll take Stupid Questions for one thousand, please.

After thirteen proposals, not to mention a dozen gifts that included everything from roses and a box of chocolates to crotchless panties and a pair of fuzzy handcuffs, Felicity was at Macy's doing Prada proud, and Josie was *this close* to dying of humiliation.

". . . owns a gas station and he can fix cars," Alex was saying. "He's a mechanic."

"I think it's time to call it a day," Josie said, clapping her hands. "Everybody go to the shelf and get your stuff."

"My mommy saw your picture," Evelyn told her after she'd retrieved her backpack. "She said you looked real pretty."

"Well, my mommy said you looked okay, but that you had major split ends and could use a good hair cut."

"My mommy said no one's brain is as big as Texas."

"My mommy said it's your ego that's prob'ly as big as Texas. What's an ego?"

"The size of your mommy's mouth," Josie said before she could stop herself.

"My daddy said you looked really pretty, too," came another comment.

"My daddy said you looked pretty, but no one's as pretty as my mommy."

"My daddy said my mommy just thinks no one's as pretty as her."

"My daddy said Miss Josie had a great set of headlights," Alex chimed in. "And he'd like to pop her hood, but he wouldn't on account of he has to pop my mom's hood. But my Uncle Pete said he'd pop Miss Josie's on account of he doesn't have to pop my mom's 'cause that's my dad's job." The little boy's excited gaze met hers. "I bet he'll even give you a discount."

"That's very nice, Alex. But I really don't think I need my hood popped."

An image from last night rushed through her mind. A beard-stubbled jaw chafing her skin, hot lips trailing over her breasts, closing over her nipple . . . Her body tingled at the memory and heat rushed to her thighs.

Okay, so maybe she did need her hood popped. But there was only one man for the job.

She found him in the lab later that evening, hard at work on ADAM. Just seeing him stalled her in the doorway for several long seconds. Her gaze hooked on his strong hands hard at work on a small sensor part meant for ADAM who stood like a half-human, half-metal sentinal in the corner. She watched as his long fingers touched and stroked the device and the air stalled in her lungs.

"Hi," she managed, her throat strained.

He abandoned what he was doing and turned to look at her, his gaze guarded. There was none of the heat she'd seen last night. None of the hunger. Just regret.

And Josie braced herself for what she knew would come next, what she'd anticipated when he'd ran out on her last night. He'd been scared by the intensity of the attraction between them, and while the said intensity made her want nothing more than to throw herself into his arms and make a few more memories to add to last night's very heated one, she held back. He had to face his fear in his own time.

Her gaze riveted on his lips and a visual image of those lips trailing over her breast rushed through her. Her nipples tightened and an ache started between her legs. She could only hope he didn't take too long.

If so . . . She shook away a very visual image that involved her and him and a shower of Reddi-Wip.

The next move was his.

"Hi, yourself." Matt wasn't prepared for the heat that bolted through him at the sight of her. Especially not after the sex they'd had. In less than an hour, he'd made up for months of celibacy and then some. He should have worked her out of his system.

He hadn't.

The realization sent a spurt of fear through him and prompted his next words. "We have to talk. Last night was just sex."

"Great sex."

His gaze hooked on her, the way her lush bottom lip glistened from the slow glide of her tongue and he swallowed. Hard. "*Really* great sex."

She smiled. "I didn't get a chance to say thanks."

Thanks? He'd stripped her bare, plunged deep, deep inside and then run out on her when all was said and done. She should be screaming at him, crying, giving him the silent treatment—*something* because Josie Farrington wasn't a one-night stand kind of woman. Not the kind of woman who should be thanking him when he'd just qualified the most wonderful night of his life as nothing more than sex.

"It can't happen again," he rushed on, before he did something really stupid like haul her into his arms and kiss her full on the lips the way he hadn't kissed her last night. The way he'd wanted to. The way he still wanted to.

Just sex.

"We have three weeks until the Expo," he went on. "ADAM will take five weeks to finish. We need complete and total focus, and sex doesn't—*can't* figure in."

"Great sex," she corrected, and he couldn't help himself.

"*Really* great sex," he added. His gaze met hers and something sparked. His hands itched, his fingers eager to reach out. He made a fist and fought for his control. "But that's all it was, Josie. Just two people working off mutual lust. Two different people. You don't really know me."

He waited for her to tell him to go to hell. To burst into tears and accuse him of using her. Or worse, to rip off her clothes and ask him to use her again. He'd be a goner for sure.

She smiled and nodded. "You're right."

"Don't be like that," he rushed on. "I didn't want last night to happen, but then I saw you and you looked good enough to eat and—What did you say?"

"I said you're right." She walked into the lab and picked up a hair cap. Her long, silky hair disappeared as she stuffed it under the green covering.

Right? Hey, where did she get off telling him he was right? Hadn't last night meant anything to her?

"I've never come in behind schedule on a project in my entire life," she went on before he could do something as careless as pull her into his arms and kiss her the way he should have last night. The way he'd been dying to for the past month.

Forget it, buddy. Not kissing her gorgeous mouth is the only thing you've done right so far.

Kissing her was what had gotten him into this mess in the first place. That wild, passionate kiss when he'd been Zorro and she'd been Josie the Pussycat had led to last night. To the sweet heat and writhing bodies and—

"We have work to do," she went on. "We

don't really know each other. Therefore, a repeat of last night would be a bad idea right now."

The way she qualified the statement with *right now* calmed his sudden burst of temper and made him wary. She was up to something. He wasn't sure what, but he knew it. Felt it.

"From now on, it's strictly business between us," he told her.

"Strictly business," she agreed.

He frowned. "No more prancing in here half-naked and distracting me."

"I never prance, and you just make sure you don't prance in here naked and distract *me*." She reached for ADAM's plans and his gaze snagged on something fuzzy and pink sticking out of her pocket.

He frowned and fingered the fuzzy handcuffs. "The seduction attempts have got to stop."

"For your information, these are not for you. They're a gift from an admirer."

"So long as you don't have anything funny in mind—" The thought stalled as her words registered. "A man gave you handcuffs?"

"And another gave me flowers and one gave me candy and one even sent me edible undies, strawberry-flavored, not that you have to worry. I don't have them on." She turned to ADAM. "Now let's get to work."

Words he'd been waiting to hear. He walked over to the counter and picked up the microchip he'd been checking the sensors on.

Five seconds, and he couldn't help himself. "So why is some man giving you edible strawberry panties?"

"I guess because he doesn't like raspberry."

"That's not what I mean."

"It's the article."

"What article?"

Her gaze swiveled toward him. "You mean you haven't seen it?"

"I've been busy." He abandoned the sensor to follow her over to her briefcase.

She retrieved a newspaper and handed it to him.

One look and his heart stopped beating. There was Josie looking sexy and delicious, right next to Marvin—*him.*

"Oh no."

"It *is* a terrible picture. I told Felicity, but she insisted I looked hot. But I don't. I just look heavy."

The self-conscious note in her voice penetrated the sudden panic beating in his eardrums. His gaze caught hers and he saw the uncertain glimmer in her eyes. For all her cool confidence, Josie Farrington was just a woman.

His woman.

"You look terrific," he told her.

"Really?" She smiled, a dizzying sight that made him forget the catastrophic turn his life had taken last night.

He nodded and her smile brightened, and they stood there for a long moment before common sense intruded and Matt forced his attention back to the newspaper.

"Thank God today's almost over," she said. "It's been crazy. Do you realize how many people actually read the Lifestyle section of the newspaper? The entire population of Chicago."

As Matt stared at the picture of himself, he could only hope that Josie was wrong. Otherwise, all hell was about to break loose.

Chapter Eighteen

"Darn it, Stinky." Eve turned on the man who'd barged into the back break room, motioned two of the other manicurists out and slammed the door before Eve could swallow her mouthful of bologna. "You can't just barge in here any time you feel like it. This is my job. My boss doesn't like it."

"Screw your boss. You don't need this job. You'll be getting free room and board in no time."

Eve summoned her courage and stared into dark eyes so like her husband's. It wasn't that she was scared of Stinky. He might be a loan shark, but he had a twisted sense of decency—and she knew that. While he might cheat on his wife, he'd never lifted a hand to hurt her. Eve didn't fear any physical violence should she fail to pay him his money—she feared rejection. Isolation. Loneliness. She feared no one knowing where she was, no one caring. At least Stinky cared, even if it was because he wanted her to look out for Mama Malone. Speaking of which . . . She summoned her courage. "Look, about me moving in with Mama Malone—"

"It's all set. I met with the boys, we broke the news to Mama and she can't wait." He grabbed the carton of chocolate milk she'd just opened and took a huge swallow. "She's getting a room all ready for you."

Eve watched his Adam's apple bob with another gulp and she couldn't help herself. She licked her lips. She'd been craving a chocolate fix through the last five pedicures and three gel sets. She'd earned it. She *needed* it. "I don't want a room. I really like having my own—"

"It's a great room. Pink curtains. Frilly froufrou bedspread. A chick room all the way, Baby cakes."

"But I really don't want—"

"You'll love it, but you can't bring your cat. Killer's liable to swallow him whole, so you'll have to get rid of him." Killer was Mama's Doberman and as mean as the woman who fed him home-cooked meatballs.

"But I've had Twinkles for the past eight years and—"

"I'll be at your house next Friday with a moving van. Check you later, Hot Lips." He turned and walked out, taking her chocolate milk with him, before she could get a word in edgewise.

Not that she would have said anything. She tried where he was concerned. She really did. But Stinky not only looked like Burt, he made her feel the same way Burt had. Like a starved puppy begging for table scraps. That's what she'd been her entire life. Orphaned at the young age of six, she'd spent most of her life in various foster homes. She'd wanted a home and a real family so badly, but she'd never found them.

Until Burt, or so she'd thought.

Her married life had turned out to be no different from the years before. She'd still been hoping, begging, only this time it had been for Burt's affection.

No more.

Her end all and be all did not depend on a man. Eve could, would be happy on her own.

Eve took a deep breath and turned to her lunch spread out on the table next to the newspaper she'd begged off one of the girls. Why couldn't he have taken her bologna sandwich? She hated bologna but it was all she'd been able to afford. She was doing lunch as cheaply as possible with the exception of her one indulgence—the chocolate milk. Could life get any worse?

Her gaze fell to the picture on the front page of the Lifestyle section, the only section of the newspaper she bothered to read since it contained sale advertisements. The rest, particularly the sports section—Burt's favorite—went straight into her bag and home to the bottom of Twinkle's litter box. But the advertisements . . . While she might be dead broke, she could still look. Still dream.

Her dreams. They were the only thing that had seen her through year after year of going from foster home to foster home, and then the lonely years that had followed when she'd been on her own. She'd dreamed big, about a nice little house and a few kids and a good man to keep her warm at night. She'd thought of Burt as the answer to those dreams. He'd been a good man. Handsome and self-employed with the big family she'd always wanted.

She'd fallen hard and fast, thinking that finally, *finally* she'd found her dream.

More like a nightmare. Burt had been good, all right. And he'd insisted on proving it with woman after woman while she sat at home or at his mother's and tried to pretend that everything was okay.

But nothing had been okay beyond the first few weeks of their marriage, and she'd finally reached a point six months ago when she'd wanted out. But first she'd followed him because, while she knew in her heart what was going on, she'd needed to see it.

She'd seen an eyeful. Burt and Sherril and the explosion, and that had been the end of his cheating. The end of him.

She'd cried. She hadn't meant to. He hadn't

deserved her tears or her sorrow. But she'd cried anyway. Because as many times as she'd plotted ways to kill him slowly and viciously for his philandering, she'd never meant him any real harm.

Okay, maybe a little. A few toothpicks stuffed underneath his fingernails or a few broken knuckles or a five-minute round with Stone Cold Steve Austin. A little pain, but not an explosion. Not *death*.

She forced aside the memory of that night. It was over and done with and she had enough to worry about without adding a heaping portion of regret. She had bills to pay, a cat to feed and a mother-in-law waiting with a pink froufrou chick room.

Her gaze drank in the picture at the bottom of the page, all the while disbelief rushed through her.

It couldn't be.

She'd smelled one too many bottles of nail polish remover and now she was hallucinating. That was the only explanation because after six months of serious looking on her part, Matt Taylor couldn't simply up and appear right before her very eyes.

Or could he?

She turned the paper this way and that and studied every angle, all the while her heart pounded a furious rhythm. It looked like him, all right. Heaven knew she wanted it to *be* him, particularly after the Mama Malone nightmare she'd had last night. But she didn't want to get her hopes up. Good things didn't happen to Eve—even though she was definitly due.

The world had a twisted sense of justice. Good people plodded along, barely getting ahead, meanwhile the rat bastards of the world called the shots.

It probably wasn't him.

But on the ultra-slim chance that it was, she had to give him credit. Those geeky clothes, the Coke-bottle glasses and that sissy-ish bouffant cap were a pretty good disguise. He looked more like Urkel than the brilliant hunk whose lab Burt had bugged last year.

That guy had been one hundred percent prime beefcake. Tall, dark, handsome and smart.

Not smart enough, a small voice reminded her. After all, he'd been framed.

An inkling of guilt spiraled through her and she quickly pushed it aside. She hadn't bugged him. It had been Burt, the louse. And in all fairness, he hadn't even realized what the bug was for. Eve had figured that out after the fact, when she'd been searching for an advertisement and seen the write-up about SpaceTek's brilliant young scientist who'd turned out to be a thief.

The minute she'd read about the scandal, she'd known the truth. The bug had been a way to steal information from Matt Taylor, not incriminate him for doing the deed with

Donovan's wife. It was easy to figure out, particularly since Jack Donovan didn't have a wife.

When she'd worked out what the gig had been all about, she'd made up her mind to go to the cops once Donovan had paid her the money he owed Burt. But, of course, he'd denied the bug, denied ever hiring Burt and screwed her out of her rightful due.

Going to the cops would have sent them in search of Matt Taylor to retrieve the bug and verify her story. The truth would have eventually come out and Donovan would have been arrested. Either way, Eve would have been out her money. But with Matt still in hiding and Donovan thinking he'd fooled everyone, she had a chance.

Her gaze went back to the picture before shifting to the article. It was all about the apparently smart and sexy woman pictured with him. A genius, she quickly learned, with a good job, a great body, and no man to mess things up.

Boy, some women had all the luck.

While others . . .

She forced aside her self-pity. Even though she wasn't one hundred percent sure, she wasn't leaving any stone unturned. She cast one last lingering glance at the empty spot where her chocolate milk had sat, tore the newspaper article free and stuffed it into the pocket of her smock.

Maybe, just maybe, Eve's luck had finally turned.

A wave of self-doubt washed through her. Okay, so maybe it was a long shot, but stranger things had happened. The earth had proven to be round, man had landed on the moon, and for the first time in his life, Stinky hadn't smelled like garlic meatballs.

She sniffed the air, filled with the scent of bologna and nail polish. Not a meatball within sniffing distance. Yep, maybe her luck was turning after all, and there was only one way to find out.

Think about work, Josie told herself later that evening as she re-programmed the sensor for ADAM's hearing for the fifth time and tried to ignore Marvin.

He reached for a screwdriver and she heard the glide of fabric against fabric, the squeak of shoes as he shifted, the deep, even sound of his breathing. . . .

Her fingers slid across the keyboard and she found herself erasing a string of useless characters. She drew in a deep breath, trying to ignore the faint musky scent of him—a mingling of soap and warm male—that tickled her nostrils. She keyed in the next line of the program.

Forget work. *Think guilt.*

Guilt was definitely a motivator, especially in this instance. Marvin had been right. They were weeks off schedule and had to make up valuable time if they intended to introduce ADAM at the Expo, which they did. Josie had promised Arthur Kiss a new form of entertainment geared toward the adult market, and Marvin had promised *Science Digest*, the magazine that coordinated the Expo, a revolutionary energy source. She didn't know about Marvin, but Josie, herself, had never missed a project deadline and she didn't intend to start now.

No matter how good he smelled, how strong and warm and *male*.

Another deep breath and she erased a string of *V*'s she'd accidentally typed. He'd been right about last night, as well. It had been just sex. The best she'd ever had, but sex nonetheless. She couldn't blame him for being wary when it came to commitment. That had been the very reason she'd taken Dr. Sophia's class. To discover what it took to make a lifetime commitment and what sort of mate she should choose. Marvin, with his neat lab and bookshelf, his nonsmoking, dedicated brilliant scientist status, was her exact match, but since he hadn't had the benefit of Dr. Sophia's class, he didn't know that.

Yet.

Josie intended to prove to him that they fit together in life, as well as in bed. They shared the same professional drive and dedication. They enjoyed the same foods. They had similar tastes in clothes. And more than anything, they had comparable IQ's and their professions complimented each other.

While Marvin hadn't noticed all of the above, Josie had and now it was simply a matter of pointing it out to him. Starting with the drive and dedication part.

"Are you done?" His deep voice flowed into her ears and sent a rush of tingles up her spine, especially when he leaned down. His shoulder brushed hers and heat tingled across her nerves, almost as if he were trying to test her despite his fierce claim that what they'd shared had been nothing but sex. As if he sensed that her control bordered on tentative and wanted to prove that last night had meant more.

As if.

Last night had been about sex. But *tomorrow*, that would be based on compatibility.

She gathered her composure. Let him test away. She could ace anything he could dish out because she wasn't acting on the lust running through her veins. She wanted more. She wanted tomorrow.

"It's impossible to work with you badgering me like that," she snapped. Snapping was good. Snapping meant she was serious and determined and focused. Three out of the ten.

"Badgering you?" He leaned up, stuffed his hands onto his hips and gave her a what's-eating-you look. "I've only asked once."

There wasn't anything particularly sexy about the way he looked. Too-tight black necktie. Slicked-back hair. Thick glasses. Buttoned-up-to-the-throat lab coat. He was his usual conservative, professional, *un*sexy self, with the exception of his sleeves. He'd rolled them back at the cuff to give himself more freedom to work. Strong forearms sprinkled with dark

272

hair rippled and bunched as he tightened his fists and her stomach went hollow.

Hollow? Over forearms?

Only because all of the sensations coursing through her were so new, last night still fresh in her mind. She'd tasted the forbidden fruit and it still lingered on her tongue and so, of course, she wanted another taste.

"Josie?"

"Mmmm?" He really did have great forearms. So strong and masculine and—

"I didn't badger. I only asked you once."

"Once too many," she blurted, pushing aside her lustful thoughts. Control, she told herself. *Think forever rather than tonight.*

Forget that. Just *think*, period.

His gaze shot past her to the computer screen and he frowned. "You're still programming the smell sensor? I thought you did that an hour ago."

"I'm a perfectionist," she pointed out, before giving him pointed stare. "Are *you* finished?"

"Almost."

"Until you can answer with a definite yes, I'd suggest you keep your questions to yourself." It was silly for her to be so annoyed, but the irritation gave her something to focus on besides the pull between them. "We've got a deadline, in case you've forgotten." She turned back to her computer screen and silently prayed for him to go back to his own work.

"I haven't forgotten," he muttered, as if the

notion bothered him a hell of a lot. He turned back to his own work, thankfully, leaving Josie to hers.

She tried to forget he was there, to lose herself in her work the way she always did. But then she'd glance back over her shoulder and he would catch her eye and *bam*.

One look into his hot, dark eyes and she'd have an exothermic reaction. Her entire body caught fire and burned, and all at nothing more than a glance. It was crazy. Intense. Nearly irresistible.

By the time she finished programming ADAM's smell sensors several hours later, she was *this close* to stripping off her clothes and begging Marvin to make love to her. Thankfully, the cleaning people pushed their way into the lab before she could undo the first button. She closed up shop and hightailed it down in the elevator before the crew finished mopping. The last thing she needed was to be alone with him again.

Otherwise . . .

She forced a very heated, very visual, very stirring *otherwise* aside and pushed the button for the first floor.

"From the stressed look on your face," Phyllis said when Josie stepped off the elevator. "I'd say you need this more than I do." She held up a bowl of Cocoa Puffs, but Josie waved it off, despite the luscious smell of chocolate curling in her nostrils. She wasn't that desperate.

Yet.

"After thirteen marriage proposals, you should look a damned sight happier."

"I'm waiting for number fourteen."

Phyllis quirked an eyebrow. "Marvin?"

"How did you know?"

"The way you were looking at him at the wedding, coupled with the fact that you're spending practically twenty-four-seven locked upstairs in that lab with him. It was bound to happen with you two being in such close confines. It's like where the prisoner falls for her jailer."

"The Stockholm Syndrome."

Phyllis nodded. "Except you guys aren't in jail, obviously. Though those burglar bars on the outside window do sort of remind me of a cage. So give me the full scoop. You got it bad for him?"

Josie sighed. "We're perfect for each other. He meets all ten of my Ten Compatibility Commandments."

"I don't know about compatible, but he's definitely got it going on in the asset department."

Josie didn't really know what sort of assets he had, but she'd always assumed that his salary came in just a little under hers. After all, she had seniority.

"When he leaves every morning," Phyllis went on, "he stops and grabs the paper. He leans over, the lab coat molds to his tush, and there it is. Great butt."

Oh. Those assets. "I guess he does look pretty incredible from the rear." When she felt

Phyllis' smile, she rushed on, "Not that his butt is a motivating factor. I mean, it figures in for the short term, but I'm more interested in long term."

"Long is definitely good."

"I mean the future," she reiterated, not missing the gleam in the security guard's eye.

Phyllis shrugged. "The future's good, too. So why are you working so late when you should be out treating your public to an up-close-and-personal view of Chicago's hottest babe? Another revolutionary breakthrough like that S.K.I.N. stuff?"

"Better." She grinned. "Bigger."

"As in?"

Josie smiled. "We're making the perfect man."

Phyllis shook her head. "And Hugh Heffner's been begging me to pose for *Playboy*."

"It's true. You know how you mentioned the other night about wanting someone to come home to, someone to just be there? Well, that someone is going to be ADAM."

"You're serious?

"As serious as a nuclear thermal react—explosion," she quickly reiterated. "We're actually building a man." She pulled out the diagram of ADAM and handed it to Phyllis. "We're going to debut it at the Chicago Expo next month. It'll be great publicity for S.K.I.N. and Marvin's got this big new energy source he's going to install."

Phyllis studied the picture. "Definitely big."

"I know. Marvin and I are primarily focused on the entertainment value of ADAM—that being his appeal to women the world over as a companion. Men have dogs for their best friend, and women will have ADAM. But his potential is really infinite. He can be programmed to handle toxic wastes and defuse dangerous explosives and explore deep space and—"

"I'm talking big as in *big*." Phyllis made her handspan about nine inches. She grinned and handed Josie back the image graphs. "Do you need any research assistants? If so, I'm your woman."

Heat rushed to Josie's cheeks. "If I do, you'll be the first person I call."

"You'll be the only one." Phyllis shoved a spoonful of Cocoa Puffs into her mouth and chewed.

"Still no Roger?"

She swallowed. "Not for four months, six days and," she glanced at her watch, "Twelve hours." She reached for the box of Cocoa Puffs. "Life sucks."

Josie thought of her empty apartment and her even emptier bed. A heated image of sweaty bodies and tangled sheets flashed in her mind and hunger gnawed through her. Before she could stop herself, she reached for Phyllis' Cocoa Puffs.

It was just one little taste.

Chapter Nineteen

The 007 gig was highly overrated.

Eve tried to calm her pounding heart as she hid inside the darkened stairwell and waited for the cleaning crew to walk by. There was nothing remotely glamorous about hiding out in a Dumpster, waiting for the maid to disappear inside before she picked the lock on the back door, crept up the stairs and waited some more. Waiting. That's what this gig was all about. Waiting for the perfect moment.

Timing was everything.

Her stomach grumbled, reminding her that she'd only had half of a peanut butter sandwich for lunch.

"Stop that," she hissed, but the grumbling

continued and sent her rummaging in her pockets for sustenance. Three breath mints, half a stick of gum and a Hershey's kiss.

The kiss.

Her fingers stalled as Maureen's words echoed through her head.

Gobble it up and you'll have the first man you meet begging at your feet.

She forced the crazy voice aside. Maureen was a major nutcase who drank too much and liked to play at being a witch. She was far from the real thing—not that Eve believed in the real thing.

Before any more doubts could creep in, she tore the paper off, popped the chocolate into her mouth and let the sweetness melt on her tongue. She followed up with the breath mints and then the gum. Hopefully her stomach would quiet long enough for her to finish her business and hightail it back to her car and the other half of her sandwich stuffed into the glove compartment.

The footsteps faded as the maid disappeared down the hallway. Eve crept in the opposite direction, toward the laboratory at the far end. She'd called earlier, pretended to be a florist and found out the floor and lab number.

Of course, she wasn't a florist and she didn't have a delivery for Marvin Tannenbaum—a geeky name to go with his new image. He had something for her.

Eve spent the next few heartpounding moments working at the lock with a bobby pin.

If there was one thing she'd learned from her wanna-be PI husband, it was how to use a bobby pin for more than putting up her hair. A few careful jiggles and the lock clicked. The door opened and she was inside.

"Where are you?" she murmured to herself as her gaze swept the semidark room. One light burned in the far corner, spilling a soft illumination throughout the rest of the room. She was about to step toward a closet when her attention stalled on a life-size image of a man tacked to a nearby wall.

And what a man.

Tall and handsome with long, flowing blond hair. A platinum-haired version of Tarzan with loads of muscles and tanned skin, a flat abdomen and the biggest . . .

She forced her gaze to move on, drinking in the equally large mummy standing in the corner before moving on to a row of cabinets and computer equipment.

Big equipment was highly overrated. It wasn't the size that counted, but what a man did with what he had, how he held a woman, how he kissed her and cherished her. Of course, for Eve, even that didn't matter. Men just weren't worth the trouble. At the very best, a woman could only expect a decent orgasm—and she knew from personal experience that even those were highly overrated.

Being single was definitely better. A few very brief, very fleeting moments of good feeling were not worth all the emotional strain of worrying and wondering if some sorry loser could remember his way home at night. She'd been there and done that, and now the only person Eve had to please was herself.

"I'll please you."

The deep voice rumbled through her head and stopped her cold. Panic bolted through her and her heart pumped frantically. She'd been caught. Her hands went to the Mace in her belt, her weapon of choice since the only gun she'd ever touched had misfired in an unfortunate accident with Burt when he'd gotten "lost" one night with a set of triplets, or so she'd heard. Her neighbor had called with the gossip and Eve had been waiting for him when he'd walked in the door. She hadn't actually shot him, just her favorite cookie jar, but the incident had been enough to scare her off guns forever.

The one and only time she'd ever stood up to him during their entire marriage had backfired, literally, and—

"Turn around."

The voice shattered her thoughts and she whirled, her Mace poised . . . No one. Just the six-foot-plus mummy and she knew darn well that he couldn't talk.

She turned, her gaze darting frantically around the rest of the room. "Who's there?"

"Me," came the deep, rumbling reply. "Just me."

A voice, but no one to go with the voice, unless . . .

Her gaze riveted on the mummy again. It wasn't actually a mummy, she realized on closer inspection. More like a life-size statue wrapped in strips of plastic. She spent the next few minutes studying the poster and a nearby stack of computer print-outs before the truth hit her. The statue was on his way to becoming a man. *The* man in the poster.

He was still a long way off and she was obviously having a major case of brain rot courtesy of the Hershey's kiss—

Her thoughts slammed on the brakes. *The kiss.*

Gobble it up and you'll have the first man you meet begging at your feet.

Eve might have been inclined to think Maureen had been full of more than sangria—namely the magical powers she was always bragging about—except for three important points.

One—she hadn't gobbled, she'd savored. Two—he wasn't a man, he was a pseudo-mummy. And three—he was more than six feet tall and not even close to begging at her feet.

So much for Maureen's guarantee.

"*Come here,*" the deep voice rumbled. It sent tingles down her arms.

"It's just your imagination," she told herself, eager to explain the situation. A *voice*, of all things, with no source. "He's not real and this is not happening and Maureen's just an old lady with a great pedicure and a fondness for sangria." To prove her point, she splayed her

283

hand against the pseudo-mummy's chest. "See? He's lifeless and cold and *un*real and . . ."

Warm.

She closed her eyes as the heat made her skin tingle. The sensation spread up her arm, making her heart pound as fast as when she flipped on her TV and caught the "Livin' La Vida Loca" video. Hey, she was anti-men, but she wasn't dead, and there wasn't a woman alive who could resist Ricky Martin.

In her mind's eye, however, it wasn't the Puerto Rican heartthrob she saw. It was the blond Tarzan with the big—

"I like it when you touch me."

Her eyes popped open and she snatched her hand back. Okay, she'd had some visual stimulation with the Tarzan poster. It was logical that she could imagine what Mr. Mummy would look like. But no way could she imagine such a smooth, mesmerizing voice—the thought stalled as her gaze snagged on a nearby computer. The screen danced with a colorful display, like the stereo equalizer Burt had installed in his car.

"I like it a lot." The screen danced and the deep voice rumbled from the attached speaker box.

Eve noted the trail of wires leading from the computer to the mummy and relief swept through her. The computer was doing the talking—

The computer? It was saying those things?

The questions rushed through her mind, but she pushed them aside. She had work to do and now she knew she wasn't crazy. She would just ignore it. Case closed.

It was happening again.

The thought hit Matt the next day when he spotted the chocolate smudge on ADAM's chest. No one was allowed in the lab except for Josie, and she didn't eat chocolate. Not to mention the lock had been picked. A smooth job no one else might have noticed, but this was Matt's livelihood on the line. His reputation. His future. One he had no intention of spending as Marvin the geek.

He made it his business to be observant, and there was no doubt in his mind that Donovan had seen the newspaper pictures and come back for the rest of the plans. For the actual body heat converter that would utilize the heat-absorption material for something much bigger. Much better.

Obviously the man had started to look at the overall picture, rather than just a way to gain quick success. The absorption material was revolutionary on its own, but coupled with the converter, the combination would be phenomenal. A new energy source. A surefire ticket to the top of the heap.

And Donovan wanted to steal Matt's ride.

Matt's hand closed around the heart of the converter, a microchip that contained years of research and hard work. The chip had been his only proof once his notes had been stolen that the material was actually his brainchild.

He could have turned it over to the authorities and maybe it would have been enough to convict Donovan. And maybe not. It hadn't been a chance Matt had been willing to take. So he'd taken the chip and gone into hiding to finish his work in secrecy and solitude in the least likely place someone would look for one of SpaceTek's finest.

At a toy company.

His gaze shifted to the chocolate smudge. So much for secrecy. At least this time there was a sign of a break-in. Before, there'd been nothing to clue him in to the fact that his work was being snatched out from under him.

But this time he knew. His fingers closed around the microchip. He knew and he could stop it because forewarned was forearmed, and Matt Taylor was ready for battle.

Five days and twenty-two marriage proposals later, Felicity was decked out in a brand-new Liz Claiborne suit, complete with matching accessories, and Josie's office overflowed with everything from flowers to a life-size statue of Venus with JOSIE stamped right across the woman's bust.

The only good thing to come out of the entire situation was that Archie and Mitchell had both called to tell her they were bowing out of the race for future life partner. Mitchell needed a woman *now,* before the proverbial sperm dry-up, and he didn't have time to compete with half the men in Chicago for her affections.

Archie and his mother weren't put off by the competition, but rather the fact that Josie had been seen in the *Chicago Sun-Times* with her bosom hanging out. Bosoms were for nursing, not for showing off, however unintentionally, and so Archie and his mother were moving on in search of a more virtuous, motherly sort.

Good riddance. Josie had the perfect man right at her fingertips—and it wasn't ADAM, though he was coming along nicely since she'd managed to focus her efforts and push her lust to the back burner.

Marvin was the perfect man. So quiet and shy and reserved and . . . stubborn. He was definitely stubborn, but so was Josie when she put her mind to something.

And she had her mind on him.

She had all of two weeks before her birthday. Plenty of time to show him how well they fit together. Then it was on to marriage and babies and the rest of her life.

A normal life.

Her gaze shifted to Venus' bust and she ignored the sudden urge to grab the nearest bar of soap and erase her name. It probably wouldn't come off anyway. The only thing Josie could do, the most effective thing, was to ignore the entire situation. Things would eventually die down.

And if they didn't?

They would, she promised herself, because her fame would surely fade as Chicago's Hottest Bachelorette when said bachelorette married Mr. Perfect, and she *was* marrying Marvin.

Even if he didn't know it yet.

Kimberly Rose

Chapter Twenty

"*Now* I'm finished."

Josie's voice drew Matt around and he watched as she leaned back from the computer, lifted her arms above her head and stretched. She'd shed her lab coat and wore a soft beige sweater and matching slacks. Her luscious breasts lifted and her nipples pressed against the material, making two mouthwatering indentations.

He could practically feel one stiff, delicious peak against his tongue, her silky breast rubbing his cheek, her fingers threaded through his hair, urging him—

A faint sound pushed into his head, past the

sudden hammering of his heart and every nerve jumped to full awareness.

"What was that?" His gaze shot to the doorway.

"My stomach."

"What?" His gaze swiveled back to her.

"That was my stomach. I missed lunch. Geez, you're jumpy. Is something wrong?"

His lab had been burglarized. He had a major case of lust for a woman he couldn't, wouldn't have again. And he'd skipped lunch himself. And dinner. And it was damned hot in here. "Not a thing—What was that?"

A soft laugh vibrated the air. "That was *your* stomach. I think we both need a break. I've got just the thing after a hard day of work." She reached for her bag.

If she pulled an ice-cold beer out, he'd have to kiss her.

She retrieved two oversize muffins wrapped in cling wrap and handed him one. "I made them myself. They're bran."

He fought back a wave of disappointment. Not that he'd *wanted* to kiss her. He'd wanted a beer. Something to ease the heat enflaming his senses.

He concentrated on pulling the plastic aside. The smell of vitamins filled the room, pushing aside the soft, sweet smell of her. He grimaced. "They're bran, all right."

"My dad's recipe. He's into nutritional cooking, just like you."

"Like me?"

She motioned toward the bookshelf and the row of Marvin's books. "*Brain Food* is my favorite, but my dad really likes *Tofu Terrific*."

"I don't really eat much tofu myself," he admitted, suddenly eager to put some distance between them and turn her off, even if it meant risking his identity.

"You really don't like tofu?" She smiled as if he'd just admitted something wonderful. "Neither do I. I mean, I did. But now just walking by the stuff in the health-food store gives me the creeps."

"The taste?"

"More like the memories. Tofu Tuesdays. The lowest moments of my childhood. My dad would always make tofu shakes whenever I came home from school upset, which was always Tuesday. That's when the Crumb twins used to stay late for cheerleading practice. I stayed after for chemistry club at my private school, and we always seemed to wind up walking home at the same time. Not together, mind you. Mindy and Mandy and their friends—a few other girls and lots of boys—were way too cool to be seen with me, even though my one ambition in life back then was to carry their pom-poms. They were blue with these little pieces of silver mylar in the center."

He grinned. "I'm glad to see your goals have changed."

She shrugged and the longing in her eyes was so intense, it reached out and grabbed at something deep inside him.

"What about you? What did you want most when you were growing up?" she asked.

"A chance," he blurted before he could think better of it. That's what she did to him. She zapped his common sense with those green eyes of hers and before he could tell her he hated bran muffins and get back to work, he found himself blurting, "I was raised in a really small town. There were no schools for the gifted or advanced classes. Few kids went off to college. Most everybody went to work for the local trucking company, settled down and had a family. It's where you came from, who you were, where you were going. I made good grades in high school, but no one thought much about it until my senior year. A science festival came to a nearby town and I decided to enter. I scraped together enough money and won this." He fingered his lucky pin, the only real piece of himself he'd brought with him to this charade. "It wasn't much of a prize, but there were a few colleges involved and they noticed me. That's when things changed and people stopped thinking of me as one of those poor East River boys. Up until then, it was tough."

"Did your father work for the trucking company?"

He shook his head. "My dad drank for a living. My mom waited tables, but it wasn't nearly enough to support a family of three. We never had much of anything—food, clothes, opportunity. I used to sit for hours thinking about what it would be like to really be somebody, to make something of myself. I wanted people to see me instead of what I wore or the fact that I lived near the east end of Littleton River. I wanted my father to see it." At her questioning look, he added, "He'd been a hotshot football player who'd screwed up one night and forgot to wear a condom. That's when I came along and it ruined his life. He had to get a real job. He couldn't go off to college or play ball or do anything but warm the seat of his battered recliner and blame me because of all he missed out on. He got off on telling me I was a mistake and that I'd never amount to anything."

Sympathy flashed in her eyes and instead of feeling the surge of bitterness that always came when he talked about his past, a warmth spread through him. A sense of comfort stretched around them and Matt had the fleeting thought that he'd never felt more at ease, more *wanted*, than he did right now with Josie Farrington's awful muffin in his hands and her bright green eyes twinkling at him.

Crazy.

"At least no one called you Knowsey Josie," she told him, drawing a smile out of him as if that had been her intention all along.

"Knowsey Josie? Let me guess, they called you that because you knew a lot."

"Namely the formula for glue. That was kindergarten, before anyone realized that, while I looked like my mom—she's a blonde, though much better-looking—"

293

"That's hard to believe."

Her gaze snapped up and surprise flashed across her open expression before the brightest, most brilliant smile he'd ever seen twisted her luscious lips. "No one's ever said anything like that to me before."

"Someone should have."

They sat there for a few, heart-pounding moments that made him seriously regret the compliment, but he hadn't been able to help himself. It was true and he suddenly felt the need for some measure of truth between them, no matter how small.

That's what she really did to him. Made him think and act in ways he never would have under normal circumstances. He was incognito for Chrissake. Truth shouldn't even figure in.

"I'd inherited my mom's bone structure, and my dad's intellect," she finally went on. "And it reared its ugly head that day. The entire class was pasting noodles onto construction paper and when the teacher held up a bottle of Elmer's and said what is this? I told her. Literally. That marked the end of elementary school and the beginning of my education at the Walter Smythe School for the Gifted and my reputation as Knowsey Josie."

"Did things improve when you changed schools?"

"While I was actually in school it was fine, but the Crumb twins lived on my block and proceeded to torture me for the remainder of my adolescence. That's what started the Tofu

Tuesdays. They would see me walking home from my school and say something nasty, and I would pretend to ignore them until I got home. Then I would cry while my dad whipped up a shake and tried to console me." A haunted light touched her eyes. "I got so tired of being singled out when all I wanted was to be like everybody else."

Click.

Matt might not have heard the faint noise otherwise, but he was on edge after the previous break-in and every nerve in his body buzzed with awareness.

Click, click.

The distinct sound jerked Matt back to reality and galvanized him into action. Three heartbeats later, he was tackling a man out in the hallway.

"Wait—"

The guy hit the ground and Matt was on top of him, holding fistfuls of his shirt. "Did Donovan send you?" he demanded, anger bunching his muscles tight.

"Donovan?" the guy gasped, struggling against Matt's grip.

"Someone sent you and I want to know who."

"Who?"

Matt's grip tightened and he hauled the intruder nose to nose. "I want a name," he growled.

"S—Stuart."

"Stuart sent you?"

"No, my n—name's Stuart. No one, I mean, Cupid, I guess. He's the one who sent me. Or maybe he's a she. Or maybe he swings both ways or—"

"Cupid?"

"The little chubby guy with the arrow. H—he hit me the minute I saw . . ." His gaze shifted past Matt to Josie who stood in the doorway watching the exchange. His eyes filled with awe. "Oh, my God. It's you," he gasped.

"What are you doing here?" Matt growled.

"I—I brought flowers. I came earlier today, but the receptionist refused them.

Matt's gaze shot to the roses scattered in the hallway and reality dawned. "You're here because of the newspaper article?" The guy nodded frantically and Matt loosened his grip.

The man scrambled to his feet, his gaze darting from Josie to the scattered roses. "I'm so glad to meet . . . Just give me a few minutes . . . Just wait." He started snatching up roses. "Y— you're even prettier than your picture," he stammered on as he gathered flowers, his shoes sliding this way and that on the tiled floor as he dashed about.

Matt would have laughed if he hadn't been *this close* to wringing the guy's neck. An admirer. A damned admirer.

". . . saw you, I knew you were the one. You're perfect. You look just like a young Grace Kelly. A smart Grace Kelly. Smart and beautiful. I've never met someone as smart as you. Most women I meet are only interested in getting their nails done, but not you. You've got thoughts in your pretty little head. You're different. A cut above." He reached for the last rose before stumbling back to her, his arms overflowing with flowers. "You're one in a million, Miss Farrington and I want to marry you."

Josie didn't blush or smile or any of the things most women would have done at such a declaration. She took one look at the flowers, at the awestruck look on the man's face, and fled into the lab.

"If you don't want to get married," the man called after her, "could you at least sit on my face? Or maybe you could touch my—"

"That's it, buddy." Matt grabbed the man by the collar and started hauling him down the hallway. "You're out of here."

"But I need to talk to her," the man blurted, scrambling against Matt's hold.

"You need to talk to a lawyer." After hauling the man downstairs and turning him over to Phyllis who promptly called the police, Matt headed back to the lab where he found Josie, her eyes bright, a distraught look on her face.

"Are you okay?"

She turned sad green eyes on him. "I'm one of a kind," she said as if admitting she'd done something unforgiveable like swiping a roll of toilet paper from the employee bathroom. "*One of a kind.*"

He pushed a strand of hair back from her face. "That's a good thing, Pussycat."

"That's the story of my life." She blinked, fighting against the brightness in her eyes. "It's not that I don't like who I am. I do. I'm smart and I'm glad that I'm smart, but sometimes I'd just like to be like everybody else. You know what I mean?"

He didn't have a clue. He lived to be different, to be a cut above, to *be* somebody, period. Even so, he had the incredible urge to erase the sadness from her expression.

And so he did what any man would do when faced with a distraught woman who'd baked muffins. He rubbed his hands together and said, "Boy, this looks good," and then he took a bite. A big bite.

So much for setting the record straight.

The next night Josie showed up with more muffins and a Chopin CD.

"I love Mozart," she told him as the first bars filled the room. "But I noticed you had an autobiography on Chopin." Her gaze shifted to the bookcase that Matt was growing to hate with each passing day. "So I thought I'd bring this one. It's one of my keepers. Don't you just love the chord technique?"

He wanted to tell her the only chords he loved were the ones at the opening to Led Zeppelin's *Black Dog,* but then she smiled so eagerly at him that he found himself nodding. After all, it was just muffins and music. It wasn't as if he were falling into bed with her again.

The next night it was more muffins and Chopin and a box filled with videotapes. "I know how much you like watching *Chemistry Tonight,* so I thought it might be fun to bring in a VCR and watch some past episodes."

About as much fun as a root canal, but he didn't say it. No, Matt couldn't seem to say anything when she looked him in the eye.

Correction—when she looked Marvin in the eye. Because when she did that, Matt felt like Marvin. Insecure and self-conscious and a far cry from the man he'd been.

The man he *was*, he reminded himself, no matter how comfortable he'd started to feel wearing a dress shirt and tie and the god-awful polyester slacks.

"You're wearing jeans," Josie said the next night when Marvin showed up at the lab decked out in denim and a soft cotton T-shirt under his lab coat.

He glanced down, then back up, a strange light in his eyes. "All my slacks were dirty."

"Oh." She continued to stare, noting the way the material molded to his legs and outlined each muscle.

"What?" he finally asked.

"Nothing. I've just never really seen you in jeans before." She tore her gaze away and busied herself pulling a plastic container and two glasses from her bag. "I didn't know you even had any jeans."

Kimberly Raye

"There's a lot you don't know about me." His mouth clamped shut after he said the words, as if he regretted them. "Let's just get to work."

"How about some carrot juice first?" She offered him the glass she'd just poured. At his questioning expression, she pointed to the tell-all bookshelf. *Carrots: The Wonder Vegetable.*"

His mouth drew tighter and Josie had the feeling he was about to hand the juice back to her. Ridiculous. He obviously loved carrots, and with good reason. They were delicious, nutritious, chock-full of vitamins. Yum.

She adored carrots. They were the perfect snack and heaven knew she needed all the help she could get where Marvin was concerned. She needed energy to bolster her strength and keep her from melting beneath every dark, intense, heated look he cast her way. And then there was his scent tempting and teasing and weakening her. And the low, sexy rumble of his voice playing with her control . . .

Her mouth went dry and she downed her own glass. "It's hot in here," she explained, wiping at a trickle of juice on her chin.

He followed the motion with his eyes before murmuring, "Damned hot." And then he downed his own juice and held up his glass for a refill.

Josie smiled. "I knew you'd like it. Carrots are my favorite snack food." At least that's what Josie told herself.

But as she watched him drink, his Adam's apple bobbing, his hands strong and dark

300

against the white plastic cup, she had the sudden craving for a great big bowl of Cocoa Puffs.

He sighed and licked his lips, catching a drop near the corner of his mouth.

Make that two bowls.

Chapter Twenty-one

Three days and two boxes of Cocoa Puffs later, Josie stood in the lab and surveyed the progress they'd made on ADAM. The physical structure was nearly complete and Josie marveled at their recent progress. ADAM's S.K.I.N. had been applied and finished with an absorbent dye that gave a real skin tone effect. His body and face had been sculpted, his features defined. He had long eyelashes and high cheekbones, a straight, regal-looking nose and a strong chin. The faint hint of stubble, courtesy of a special synthetic implanted within the S.K.I.N. lent him a sexy, macho air. He had long, flowing hair, synthetic as well. But ADAM's hair was different from doll hair. It was designed to mimic real hair. The heat in the S.K.I.N. would heat the synthetic, force the fibers to expand, resulting in mimicked hair growth. ADAM would have to shave and cut his hair just like any real man.

Real. Yes, indeed, he looked every bit a real man. From the waist up, he was a perfect male specimen.

And the rest of him?

Her gaze started at his long, tapered feet, traveled up over well-muscled legs to his trim hips. He had a firm derriere that would have put any Calvin model to shame.

Marvin, who knelt behind ADAM and made a small molding adjustment to the bottom of his left foot, had certainly outdone himself. Almost.

"Marvin?"

When Matt glanced up and saw the direction of Josie's gaze, he knew he was in for an argument.

"You can't be finished," she told him.

He got to his feet and put his tools on the counter. "I've been meaning to talk to you." He turned to face her. "I don't think he needs it."

"It?" One blond brow arched.

"You know, his . . ." The word *penis* was right there on the tip of his tongue, but damned if it would go any further. "He doesn't need his . . . you know," he finally finished. Why the hell couldn't he just say the word?

Because she was staring at him with those wide green eyes, the softest smile curling the corner of her luscious lips and he suddenly became very aware of his own *you know,* now fully alert and ready for action.

"His . . . ?" Challenge glittered in her eyes, hot and bright and daring.

Daring him. That's what she was doing, all right. She was turning the tables on him, making him as uncomfortable as she'd been the past few days with so much unspent sexual energy flowing between them.

As if he'd been able to overlook it. He hadn't, he was just a damned sight better at hiding his feelings. After so much time acting as Marvin, he had acting down to an art form, with the exception of his recent rebellion where he'd traded Marvin's trademark polyester for Matt Taylor's denim. But a guy had to do what a guy had to do.

Josie wasn't near the Julia Roberts to his Richard Gere, even though she gave it her best try. She marched into work and, for the most part, managed to keep her attention on ADAM. But there was no mistaking the tremble of her hands, the way her breath caught when he glanced at her, the way she gazed with such longing at him when she thought he wasn't looking.

He wasn't as obvious. Until now. Tonight she had proof that she made him as nervous as he made her.

Not for long.

"Let's see . . . His jimmy, his johnson, his joystick, his rod, his love gun, his lightning bolt, his woody, his Big Boy, his Mr. Willie, his pecker—take your pick. Oh, and there's my personal favorite, his Big Daddy."

He wanted his nearness to shake her up and put him back in control.

She didn't so much as blink, much less tremble or swallow or look the least bit affected. "I prefer Mr. Happy myself, and ADAM needs one."

A strange heat stirred in his gut. "What do you mean *prefer*?"

She ignored his question and met his narrowed gaze with one of her own. "ADAM gets all the relevant body parts. We're making the perfect man, not an overgrown Ken doll."

"Ken's a pretty happening guy."

She shook her head. "I think you've been up in this lab too long. You need fresh air."

Damn straight he did. He'd been breathing Josie-tinted air for so long that it was affecting his thinking. Otherwise, he would have attached the synethetic member instead of hiding it in the lab closet behind an industrial-size bottle of WD-40—industrial because he'd gone with Josie's original measurements.

A few hours ago, he'd been about to turn ADAM into one well-hung specimen, but the more he'd stood there gazing at their hard work, the more he'd remembered Josie's comments about building the perfect man, and the more the idea of sharing her with that man, however artificial, had bothered him. Almost as much as the thought of not sharing anything with her following the Expo, when he returned to his life and she discovered he wasn't the geeky, bran-loving, polyester-wearing man she'd targeted for matrimony.

He knew what she was up to with the muffins and the music and the juice. She was trying to prove that they were compatible, but it wasn't going to work. While Marvin did, indeed, like those things, Matt lived for cold pizza and beer and classic rock. While he was smart, he was also every boy who'd ever teased her and if she knew the truth, she'd think him no better than all those mean kids in her past.

He imagined all the times she'd gone home crying because of the Crumb twins and their friends, and a fierce sense of protectiveness surged through him. He wanted to pound everyone who'd ever hurt her, and then he wanted to kiss her tears away. To kiss *her*, until she knew how much he wanted her.

It wasn't going to happen.

He didn't want it to happen. He wanted to be back on top, with the world in the palm of his hands. He wanted the world oohing and ahhing over his achievements. He wanted to be somebody. While Miss Josie Farrington wanted to be everybody. Just one of the crowd. A normal woman. A wife and mother rushing off to PTA meetings and coordinating car pools and gathering everyone in front of the TV for popcorn and *Chemistry Tonight*.

He fought down the sudden urge for a recliner and a remote control. He wasn't his father, no matter how much the old man delighted in telling him just that, and he wasn't making the same mistakes.

He *wasn't* Marvin and he had the jeans to prove it, and he wasn't falling for Josie Farrington, no matter how many muffins she baked or how many Chopin CDs she owned, or how she blended the best carrot juice he'd ever tasted, or how her brow wrinkled and she got this cute little crease between her eyebrows when she looked at him as if she were trying to figure him out.

Like now.

He averted his gaze and reached for his screwdriver. "One Mr. Happy coming up."

Matt didn't actually install Mr. Happy right then and there. He pretended to make several adjustments, preferring to wait until he was alone for the installation. It was bad enough not wanting to attach ADAM'S member. He didn't need Josie watching him.

The minute she walked out the door for the evening, however, he moved on to something even more important. Matt shed his clothes and started hooking up heat-sensor pads. He had less than a week to store up the necessary energy required to juice up ADAM for an impressionable amount of time and, at the rate he was going, he would barely make it.

Barely.

Matt forced the thought aside. He *would* make it. The Expo meant everything to him.

The chance to set the record straight. To tell the entire scientific community, to *show* them, that he was every bit the brilliant genius rather than a common thief.

In the meantime . . . He applied more sensors and sent up a silent thank-you to Josie. While the evenings with her were hell, she left him sufficiently worked up to store a few extra units of heat energy, and with the Expo only days away, Matt needed all the help he could get.

He noted the very large erection that popped out of his jeans as he slid them down and stepped free. Forget a few extra. His entire body radiated heat like a furnace. As hot as he felt, he could have stored at least a full day's worth of energy and then some.

Touching the straining length, he marveled at how she could have such an effect on him. He wasn't some teenage boy hot for anything in a short skirt. Hell, Josie Farrington didn't even wear short skirts. She wore long ones and those slacks that curved and molded to her hips and thighs, accenting their roundness, making him want to put his hands on her and sink deep inside the heat between her legs. . . .

Heat.

The word galvanized him into action and he started applying the sensors to his legs, his stomach, his back and his buttocks. The computer beeped, immediately registering his temperature.

At least she didn't know how much he wanted her. That was his only salvation. He could keep up the charade as long as she didn't realize her full effect on him because he had no doubt in his mind that it would be enough to entice Miss Josie into coming after him. Matt had no illusions about resisting her this time. He could barely be in the same room with her and not touch her, and that was with her pre-occupied with muffins and CDs and work. No way would he be capable of abstaining if she got it into her pretty little head to seduce him again.

But she didn't know that and so he was safe—

Click.

The sound of the door shattered the thought.

"I forgot my . . ." Her soft words faded as he whirled.

He realized in a glaring instant that he'd completely forgotten to lock the door to his lab. He'd forgotten everything except her.

Josie took one look at him and stopped cold. It was that first meeting in the lab all over again, only this time she didn't have that preoccupied look in her eyes. She noticed him.

Boy, did she ever.

Her gaze roamed over his naked body, pausing at the hot, jutting proof of his desire before moving up and colliding with his. She licked her lips and his gut clenched.

"—I forgot my sweater."

"—I was just doing a little heat conversion."

They both spoke at the same time, an awkward outburst that had them both smiling. Then the expression disappeared as something hot and feral took its place.

It took all of three heartbeats and then she was in his arms. He peeled away her clothes and she peeled away most of his sensor pads until flesh met flesh.

Matt knew he should retreat, let her go and make some excuse for his aroused state, but then her long, silky fingers closed around his hard length and he couldn't have stopped if a freight train had rolled through the door and right over his precious body heat converter.

He wanted her too damned much.

Buttons popped and he shoved the silk of her blouse aside. Tugging down one bra cup, he bared her breast, dipped his head and sucked the nipple into his mouth. The tip ripened against his tongue and he suckled her, drawing a deep moan from her lips.

Christ, she tasted sweet. Soft and warm and drugging and he couldn't get enough. He suckled as she explored him, gripped him, her hands stroking from root to tip, driving him wild.

A few tugs at her bra clasp and her breasts spilled into his hands. He cupped them, thumbing her nipples, tugging and pulling and rolling before gliding his palm down the quivering flesh of her stomach to her waistband. A button popped, the zipper hissed, and he shoved her slacks and panties down. She stepped free and his hand moved between their bodies. His fingers slid into her slick flesh and she moaned, the sound as arousing as the feel of her turgid nipples pressed against his chest.

"I want to be inside you," he murmured against the silky curve of her neck. "I *need* to be inside you." He lifted her onto the edge of the counter and stepped between her thighs. She was so hot, so wet, so ready, and his throbbing erection found her center like a heat-seeking missile.

"Wait," she gasped as the head of his arousal pushed just a fraction deep, enough to send a burst of pleasure to his brain and stall the air in his lungs.

He opened his eyes to find her looking at him, her own gaze hot and bright and feverish. But there was something else. A determination that caught him completely off guard as much as her next words. "No pulling back this time."

He smiled. "Pussycat, I couldn't pull back if my life depended on it."

Her luscious lips were parted, her uneven breaths whispering across his skin, and he had the near-overwhelming urge to kiss her, to drink in her air and give her sustenance with his own.

Instead, he pressed his mouth to the throbbing of her pulse, licked and nipped the skin and rotated his hips just enough to make her whimper.

"I mean afterward," she gasped. She pulled back, slowing them down once again, and stared up at him, into him. "If we do this, no pulling back this time."

He knew what she was asking. If he'd had an ounce of common sense, he would stop, tell her they weren't right for each other and exactly what he thought of bran muffins.

"I won't pretend I don't want you," he said instead, threading his fingers through her hair and tugging just enough to arch her lovely neck. Her gaze leveled with his. "I want you so much I can't stand it." His voice rang with such conviction that it startled him.

But he was tired. So damned tired of denying the heat between them. Everything in his life had turned into one big lie. Everything except for the heat burning him up from the inside out.

This was pure. Real.

"But that's all it is," he went on, "Just want." No matter how anxious he was to make love to her, he wouldn't make empty promises. "I'm not after forever, Josie. I'm interested in now. Right now."

She didn't answer. She simply stared at him long and hard, emotions warring in her eyes and Matt wondered for a long, tense moment if she would pull away and tell him to go to hell because she wanted more.

Then she dipped her head, her tongue flicking at his nipple, drawing it tight before sucking it into her hot little mouth. He held her to

313

him, cradling her face, relishing the pull of her mouth, the pressure, the heat.

While he couldn't tell her his true identity, he could give her some measure of honesty by admitting his desire for her. She deserved at least that.

When she pulled back and stared up at him, her lips glistening, there was no more indecision. Just the same want pushing and pulling at his insides.

"Now," she breathed, and it was all the encouragement he needed.

He lifted her legs and urged them up around his waist, opening her more. With one deep, probing thrust, he filled her.

Her tight muscles convulsed around him, clutching him as he gripped her bare bottom. He relished the feel for as long as he could, and then he had to move. He pumped into her, the pressure and friction so sweet that it took his breath away.

He was vaguely aware of the computer buzzing behind him, registering the surge of heat from the few sensors still attached to his back. But then she tightened her legs and roamed a hand down his chest, her hand touching the place where they joined and all thought faded in a rush of pleasure. Her hips moved in a wild rhythm that urged him faster and faster toward release.

He felt the tiny spasms even before he heard her fierce cry. Her entire body trembled as she came apart in his arms. The sweet feel of her clenching and unclenching around his hot, pulsing sex was enough to send him over the edge.

His vision blurred and blackness hit him as he buried himself in her one last, final time. A shudder shook his entire body and he spilled himself deep, deep inside. He rested his forehead against hers and fought to catch his breath, his heart hammering, his body still trembling.

When he could actually breathe again, he untangled himself from her arms and legs and eased himself out of her.

Disappointment flashed in her big green eyes and he knew she expected him to turn away, to ignore what had just happened the way he had before. To pull back.

He smiled and scooped her into his arms, turning the disappointment into a flash of surprise.

"What are you doing?"

"I could tell you, or I could show you," he murmured, licking the shell of her ear and making her breath catch. "But the showing's more fun."

"Just give me a hint."

"It involves you and me and the pull-out sofa in my office, and a very detailed dream I've been having."

Pleasure lit her expression. "Am I in the dream?"

His gaze caught hers. "Pussycat, you *are* the dream." The admission felt good, but it was nothing compared to the surge of satisfaction that went through him when she slid her arms around him and pressed a kiss to the base of his throat, in the exact spot he'd kissed her so many times.

Then she spared a glance at the computer still buzzing from their heated lovemaking a few moments before.

"If I didn't know better, I'd say you were just using me to juice up ADAM."

But she knew better. It was there in her eyes, an open, honest trust that filled him with a strange sense of pride and the urgent need to tell her everything about himself. His past. His present. His future.

He fought the urge back down. This wasn't about the future, he had to keep reminding himself. It was about now. This night. This moment. *Now.*

He grinned down at her and headed for the back room. "Haven't you ever heard of killing two birds with one stone?"

Chapter Twenty-Two

Matt kept his word to her. He didn't pull back after their fierce lovemaking on the cabinet, or during the hours that followed on his pull-out sofa. Or the next evening either, after hours of work when she offered to help with his body heat converter.

"Is this in the interest of science, or are you just anxious to get naked in front of me?"

She'd grinned up at him and he'd felt a bolt of heat from his head to his toes as she threw his own words back at him. "Haven't you ever heard of killing two birds with one stone?"

They did just that over the next few days. By the time Thursday night rolled around and Matt kissed Josie good-bye after some very

317

heated contact on one of the lab chairs, he checked his computer and realized he'd stored enough energy to keep ADAM going way beyond the Expo. That meant the android was finally ready for the next step—animation.

Almost.

Matt took a deep breath, damned his jealous streak and headed for the storage cabinet and the WD-40.

Eve fought down a wave of nervousness, checked her reflection in the employee bathroom mirror at Three Kisses, then walked out and headed down the hallway toward Matt Taylor's laboratory. She was scared, all right, but not nearly as scared as she'd been the other night when she'd seen Matt tackle the poor schlump out in the hallway. A half hour later and that poor schlump would have been Eve.

She'd quickly abandoned her plans to sneak in at night since he worked most evenings until dawn and Josie had been keeping him company most of the time. Eve had spent the past few days devising a foolproof plan to get her inside during the day.

Checking the buttons on her maid's uniform—it wasn't *New York Undercover*, but it was the best she'd been able to come up with on a manicurist's salary—she took a deep breath and hauled her cart to a stop in front of the lab door. While Josie usually left sometime after midnight, Matt often slept in the lab—proof that he was either a workaholic, on to her, or both—and didn't leave until after nine A.M.

This morning, he'd held out until well after 9:35. Eve had been forced to bide her time in the lounge next to a box of chocolate eclaires, now three shy of a full dozen. She licked a smidgeon of chocolate icing from one fingertip. Hey, spying was a rough job, but somebody had to do it.

She hauled the cart inside, shut the door with a sound *click* and rushed to work. As quickly and as quietly as possible, she opened the nearest cabinet and started her search.

She'd gone through every cabinet and was on her third drawer when she heard the deep, familiar voice.

"Over here."

She turned, her gaze shifting past the computer with the colorful screen to the corner and *him*. No wonder they'd been working late so often. Tarzan was no longer a poster, but the real thing—even if the computer was doing the talking for him. He was now tall, dark and completely . . .

Ohmigod, he was naked. *Naked.*

Her gaze roamed from his head to his toes and her heart shifted into overdrive.

Because of a naked man? She'd seen Burt without a stitch on dozens of times and not once had her heart lodged in her throat the way it was doing right now.

This was different. *He* was different.

He was . . .

She took a deep, steadying breath. She was

inside the lab without a soul around and she had work to do. She wasn't wasting this chance or crossing the room or . . .

Okay, so she was crossing the room, but purely in the interest of her future. She had to check out every area, every nook and fanny—'er, make that cranny. Yep, every nook and cranny. Nothing more. No checking him out. No looking. No touching.

No sirree.

She was definitely *not* going to touch.

"You don't have to touch it." Matt stood near the counter and tried to ignore Josie who stood in front of ADAM, her hand on his newly applied member.

"I'm just inspecting your work." Her fingertip trailed the length. "It's just so big."

"It's not that big."

"It's the biggest I've seen."

"It is not the biggest you've seen."

She spared him an amused gaze, her green eyes twinkling. "You're not jealous, are you?"

"It's plastic, for Chrissake." He glared. "Why the hell would I be jealous?"

"Oh, I don't know." She shrugged. "Maybe because you like me a lot more than you're ready to admit?"

"Honey, I like you a whole hell of a lot and I have no problem with admitting it."

"I'm talking *like* like, as in I'm a nice person."

He knew where she was going and an alarm sounded in his head. He grinned, determined to get them back onto safer ground. "You'd be even nicer if you stopped touching ADAM and started touching me."

He didn't miss the disappointment that flashed in her eyes before a gleam of mischief took its place and she turned back to ADAM.

Reaching out, she trailed a fingertip across the android's broad chest, down between his well-muscled pecs and onto his rippled abdomen. Her fingers lingered near his navel.

"Sometimes I'm too nice for my own good," she murmured. "You can't imagine how many times I get suckered into doing things I don't want to do because I just can't say no. That's a great line, don't you think? Just say no?"

"Great." His throat went dry as he watched her descent, feeling her touch on his own body, from his navel to his groin.

"I think people should stand up for themselves."

He was standing up, all right.

"And not be afraid to go after what they want."

"Come here," his voice was gruff even to his own ears.

She spared him a glance. "I'm not through with my inspection yet." Her hand moved closer.

Before he could stop himself, he crossed the room and gripped her wrist, firmly but gently, and urged her to face him.

"You're finished," he said, staring down at her.

"And you're jealous."

"It's *plastic,*" he started, the words fading into a growl. "And you're damn straight I'm jealous."

Satisfaction lit her eyes and she smiled. "That wasn't so bad, now was it?"

Bad didn't even come close to describing the strange feelings pushing and pulling at his control. Disastrous fit a whole helluva lot better. He wanted to kiss her almost as much as he wanted to pull her over his knee and give her a good spanking, and damned if he could, *would* do either.

Just *want,* Desire. That's all it was between them.

"You tricked me," he growled as he pulled her into his arms. His hands pressed into the small of her back and her nipples kissed his chest.

"I prefer to think of it as a little harmless persuasion."

"You're too damned smart for your own good."

"So are you," she countered.

"And stubborn."

"Ditto."

"And sneaky and," his voice took on a gravelly note as she touched his chest and her finger followed the same trail she'd blazed on ADAM; "sexy as hell."

"Amen," she murmured. The button on his pants popped, the zipper hissed. Silky fingers pushed inside his underwear, shoving his clothing down to his thighs. She dropped to her knees. He closed his eyes and waited for the first thrilling touch of her mouth.

And waited.

One eye popped open and he looked down to see a puzzled look on her face, her attention fixed, not on him, but on ADAM.

Her brow furrowed and she leaned a fraction closer. "Why is there chocolate on ADAM's Mr. Happy?"

Someone had been in the lab again.

Matt turned the information over in his mind later that evening after closing the door behind Josie. He'd taken the blame for the chocolate smudge, saying he'd confiscated a candy bar from Ethan and must have had some on his hands when he'd worked on ADAM. She'd accepted the explanation, reminded him of the birthday party she was giving for that little boy Ethan on Saturday because his dad had to work, and then proceeded to take Matt's mind off the break-in with a few seductive moves that had him moaning her name. He'd reciprocated and the rest of the evening had passed in a mix of heated touches and caresses that had him hard-pressed to remember his own name.

She was gone now and the truth pushed back into his head as he stretched out on the pull-out sofa in his office.

Someone had been in the lab again. Someone messy.

Hell, he'd known from the word *go* that he couldn't monitor the lab twenty-four hours a day and still maintain normal appearances around Arthur Kiss and the other employees at Three Kisses. The last thing Matt wanted was to draw attention to himself. He had less than a week until the Expo, five days before he shed this ridiculous disguise and showed the world that Matt Taylor wasn't a thief, but a genius. Five days until he could return to SpaceTek and get back to doing something really worthwhile.

He'd taken to sleeping at the lab lately, crashing in his adjoining office under the pretense of exhaustion, all the while nursing a thread of hope that maybe he could catch the damned thief and prove, finally, that Donovan had been the one performing illegal activities—now and earlier.

But this intruder had struck during the day, between the time he'd left in the morning and walked into the lab tonight.

In broad daylight, with people coming and going.

Not that it mattered.

Matt touched his hand to the inside pocket of his lab coat and the small silver-dollar-sized chip. He knew what the burglar was really after, and while he might not be able to prevent a break-in or bring down Donovan or change his own past, he could monitor the chip and its whereabouts, and secure his own future.

Five more days, he reminded himself. Then it would all be over.

His time as Marvin, and his time with Josie.

A pang of regret shot through him and his heart gave a slow thud. He was crazy. Sure, they had great chemistry, explosive chemistry, but that wasn't enough to base a lifetime commitment on—even *if* he'd wanted one. Which he didn't.

No regrets.

He had a bright future ahead of him, one that required drive and dedication and focus, all three of which seemed to slip to the back of his mind whenever she walked into a room. Thankfully, he'd had most of the work done on the converter before Josie and the ADAM project, otherwise, he wouldn't be anywhere close to finished. She was a major distraction. Too smart and too sexy for her own good and his.

She was the last thing he needed in his life.

And the first thing he wanted.

Sleep-deprivation. That had to be it, he told himself as he climbed off the sofa and headed back into the lab to finish up the adjustments on his birthday present for Ethan. If he'd had sufficient rest, he wouldn't be thinking such crazy thoughts.

Like maybe, just maybe, if circumstances had been different, he might have asked Josie on a real date, courted her, and ten years from now, maybe . . .

Crazy.

If circumstances had been different, if he had been different—the real Matt rather than playing at the compulsively neat Marvin—Josie wouldn't be strutting around, wowing him with health food and classical music. She wouldn't have offered the real Matt Taylor anything more than the one hot night she'd offerred Zorro. Certainly not the lifetime she was offering Marvin.

And she certainly wouldn't have waited ten years for Matt to do and be all that he'd ever dreamed. Josie marched to the beat of her own biological clock, and he knew that it grew more frenzied with each passing day. She didn't have ten years to wait.

He tried to summon relief, gratitude—*something*. They were different people. Worlds apart. They weren't meant to be together.

If only that truth didn't suddenly bother him so damned much.

Chapter Twenty-three

"We're almost ready." Marvin pulled the microchip from the body heat converter portal. "This chip is fully charged with enough juice to keep ADAM going for a full month."

"And what happens at the end of the month? You remove the chip and refuel?"

"By that time, I'll be finished with this touch pad I've been working on." Marvin walked over to ADAM.

"A touch pad?"

"It's a smaller version of the actual converter. Much smaller. It will be installed directly inside of ADAM so that there will be no need for an energy chip. See, the chip is the middleman. The converter soaks up human heat using the sensors, converts it to energy and stores it in the chip. Then I pop the chip out, insert it into ADAM, punch in a code and he's ready to go, but that's too much work. First off, it's not realistic that whoever purchases ADAM will walk around with two hundred sensors every few weeks to store up enough energy to fuel the chip. That's why I intend to actually build the sensor pads into ADAM's S.K.I.N. and attach them to a mini body heat converter already installed inside. Then all that will be required to juice him up is a human touch."

"That's pretty ingenious."

"Thanks." His gaze caught and held hers for a long moment and she saw the pleasure that lit his eyes. Then it faded into an unrecognizeable expression as he focused his attention once more on ADAM and the control pad at the base of his neck.

He punched a few buttons and paused, his gaze catching Josie's. "Ready to make history?"

"Ready." At least she thought she was ready. After all, she knew ADAM from the inside out. She'd designed him and she had no doubt that he would work.

Still, her heart pounded with excitement and a rush of adrenaline went through her. This was it. The moment of truth.

"Are you sure you're ready?"

"Positive?"

"Are you sure you're sure?"

"Would you just do it?"

Marvin grinned and pressed the final button.

"He's not doing anything." Josie surveyed the lifeless green eyes, the passive face.

"It takes a minute for his body to absorb the energy."

"Maybe something's wrong." She came around Matt and peered past him at the complicated circuitry revealed by the open patch of S.K.I.N., which camouflaged a small hinged door.

"Just give him a minute."

"Are you sure you hooked everything up correctly?"

"Of course I'm sure. Would you just relax?" But Marvin, himself, didn't look very relaxed. He frowned, studying the circuitry. "I don't get it. Everything's in place."

"Maybe you got your wires crossed when you hooked something up."

"I don't get my wires crossed."

"Maybe you programmed the wrong calculations."

"I don't program the wrong calculations."

"Maybe you—"

"Look, I did everything down to exact specification. If you want to blame someone, blame yourself."

"What's that supposed to mean?"

"Maybe you did something wrong."

"I did no such thing."

He closed in on her, backing her up against the wall. "You're not Wonder Woman. You're human just like the rest of us."

329

The words echoed in her head and sent a warmth through her. She'd always felt so different, so out of place, but with Marvin she felt as if she truly belonged.

"You're wonderful." She threw herself into his arms where she stayed for a long, heart-pounding moment. "And you're right. ADAM's not working and it's probably my fault."

"Maybe not."

"No, no. You're just trying to be nice. It *is* my fault."

"It isn't."

"I mean it, Marvin. I will not let you feed my ego like this. We've spent the past six weeks working day and night, all for nothing. I screwed up."

"You didn't screw up."

"How can you say that? The project's a failure."

"The project is standing right behind you."

Josie whirled and found herself staring at a very broad, hair-dusted chest. Her gaze shifted upward, over a thick, muscular neck to ADAM's handsome face. His smiling face.

An intense green gaze collided with hers as strong, powerful fingers grasped her hand. "Come. You must be exhausted after six weeks of working day and night."

Before Josie knew what was happening, she found herself propelled into a nearby chair while ADAM knelt in front of her. Large, warm hands slid her shoe off and started to knead her toes.

"He's massaging my feet," Josie blurted.

"That's what you programmed him for."

"I know, but I never really thought about what it would be like for him to actually do it. It's great. Forget great. It's electrifying."

"He could have a short somewhere," Marvin said. "I should turn him off and check him—"

"Don't touch him." Josie drew in a deep breath, her body relaxing as ADAM worked his magic on her foot. "He's perfect."

"I can massage shoulders, too," ADAM stated. "Would you like me to demonstrate?"

"No."

"Yes."

Josie and Marvin both spoke at the same time, but ADAM ignored Marvin. He stood and smiled, before disappearing behind her. Large hands went to work on her shoulders.

"Mmm . . ."

"I said not to do that." Marvin glared.

"*You* said it," Josie reminded him. "He's every hardworking woman's fantasy, meaning he listens to the hardworking woman, namely me." Josie closed her eyes. ADAM was better than her shower massage, and he smelled good, too. "We're definitely going to make history with this."

"Yeah."

She cracked an eye open and noted Marvin's frown. "You don't sound too happy about it."

He wasn't. The thought hit Matt as he stood there and watched another man touch his woman.

But ADAM was *not* a man, he reminded himself. Just six feet of well-developed plastic driven by an advanced artificial intelligience device and a revolutionary new energy source that was sure to gain Matt all the praise and recognition he craved.

And more importantly, Josie Farrington was *not* Matt's woman. They were simply sating mutual lust. Enjoying each other's company. Giving in to some major chemistry. Nothing more.

No matter how much this crazy little voice kept insisting otherwise.

"Ethan's really glad you came," Josie told Matt the next day as she carried a birthday cake and a gallon of ice cream to a reserved table at Barney's Fun House and Pizzeria. "So am I."

She smiled before rushing off to play hostess to the crowd of screaming six-year-olds, and he willed his heart not to skip its next beat. There were frosting smudges on her no-nonsense sweater, a few Kool-Aid stains on her slacks. Graham-cracker crumbs dusted her hair and she had what looked suspiciously like a piece of gum stuck to her elbow. Her cheeks were flushed, her brow sweaty, and he didn't think he'd ever seen any woman look so tired, or so beautiful.

An image rushed at him, of Josie opening the door to him that night they'd first ended up in bed. He'd been a goner then and he was *this close* to scooping her up and—

He forced the ridiculous thought away and

fixed his gaze on Ethan. The kid wore a gold birthday crown and sat at the head of the table, his hands busily ripping the paper off Matt's gift.

The little boy squealed as he opened the box and found Harry the robotic dog. The sound of the child's voice triggered the voice sensor and the small white puppy started to bark and wag its tail. The look of happiness on Ethan's face sent a surge of pride through Matt unlike anything he'd ever felt before.

For the first time, he actually understood why a woman as brilliant as Josie would spend her time doing something as simple as making toys rather than devising technology for NASA or working on biological weapons or any number of worthwhile scientific endeavors.

She wasn't just making toys. She was making smiles.

She was making a difference.

"I think he likes it." Josie collapsed next to him.

"He mentioned he wanted a dog the first time I met him, and since I didn't know how his dad would react to a real one, I thought this would be the next best thing. It does everything a real dog can do. Well, most everything. He won't need a can of Alpo or a pooper-scooper."

"I'm forever in your debt." The comment came from a small dark-haired man with glasses and a large blue wrapped gift in his arms.

"Daddy!" Ethan's voice rang out as he flew

around the table. "I didn't think you were going to be here."

"And miss my best guy's party? No way." He lifted his son into his arms. "I'm sorry I wasn't here sooner, Sport. I'm sorry about that and a lot of things."

"You're here now." Ethan hugged him. "And you can sit next to me."

The man turned to Josie as he set his son on his feet. "Thanks. I appreciate everything you've done for us."

"My pleasure. I'm glad you're here." Josie watched as Ethan led his father toward the head of the table and sat him just to the left before plopping down to open the rest of his gifts.

Josie spent the next few minutes serving up pizza slices while Ethan opened his gifts and alternated between his seat and his father's lap.

"Pepperoni or sausage?" Josie held up two different plates. A tendril of blond hair had come loose from her braid, the strands clung to her damp neck and Matt couldn't help himself. He reached out and pushed the fine hairs behind her ear. His fingers lingered against the softness of her skin for a long moment.

She licked her lips and he watched the motion, mesmerized by the play of her tongue against the soft fullness of her bottom lip.

"Pepperoni or sausage?" Her voice was deeper, huskier as she asked again.

"Pizza, huh?" Matt let his hand fall away

before taking a plate and seating himself while she finished handing out slices. "And all this time I had you figured more for bottled water and some bean curd over at the House of Health."

"For your information, this place offers veggie pizza on whole wheat crust. Besides, Ethan said this was his favorite place and I wanted him to have a good birthday."

He wasn't going to ask. The less he knew the better.

"What about you? Did you have any good birthdays?"

She shrugged. "A few. Of course I never got to go to a place like this, but there was my twelfth birthday when my dad arranged a poetry reading at the local library."

"Poetry?"

"He had cake, too. Carrot cake with no icing." She licked an edging of frosting from a plate. "When I have kids, though, I'm going to let them have icing. I know it's not good, but it's only once a year." She looked so serious that he couldn't help but smile. "Birthday cakes should have icing."

"You'll be a great mother."

"You really think so?" When he nodded, a full smile lifted her luscious lips before the expression faded and he managed to breathe again. "What about you? Any aspirations of being a great father?"

"None." He'd meant the answer to silence any further questions, but Josie didn't seem put off.

"I think you would make a good father."

"Why's that?"

"Ethan, for one."

"So I gave him a toy for his birthday? That's a far cry from being a good father. A father is someone who's there every day. Who wants to be there. I don't. There are still a lot of things I want to do in my life."

"Can't you do them while raising kids?"

"It wouldn't be fair. Kids deserve a full-time father, not a man filled with bitterness and regret because he's had to abandon his dreams in order to put food on the table and take care of his family."

"Is that what your father did?"

It was as if she'd looked right inside him and picked the worst hurt, and as much as that should have angered him, it didn't. "Like I said, my mom got pregnant by accident and his parents forced him to marry her. He honored those vows, but he hated every second, and he focused that hate on me. I was the reason he couldn't play college ball. I was the reason he had to give up his dream, and he's never let me forget it."

She touched his shoulder. "He was wrong. It is possible to have both a family and ambition. Take me for instance, my ambition is to have a family while I'm still young enough to enjoy them." A piece of cake flew through the air and smacked her in the cheek. One of the children burst into wild laughter and scampered away. "On second thought," she said, wiping at the

336

frosting. "Maybe I'll just check myself into the nearest nunnery until the urge passes."

He grabbed her hand, pulled her close and licked a remaining smidgeon of frosting from her cheek. "Just make sure you check in after tonight."

"And what's tonight?"

He reached for a nearby can of Reddi-Wip she'd been using on the ice cream. "If memory serves me, we never did do the bottom of that whipped-cream bikini."

Back at Josie's apartment, they ran out of Reddi-Wip before they'd even completed the top half of the bikini, much less the bottom. Not that it mattered. Marvin had made the most of the situation. Josie's body still ached from the feel of him touching her, kissing her breasts and her belly and her . . .

"Today's the big day."

Josie glanced up from a bowl of granola as Mr. Babcock walked into her kitchen. "I already put it out at the curb."

"Not the trash, little lady, though I get a might teary-eyed when I see that big blue truck coming down the street. Today's your day. Your birthday." He set an envelope on the table and turned to haul open the fridge and stare inside.

Her birthday.

She'd been so busy with ADAM and Marvin that it had completely slipped her mind. But today *was* the day.

"What's this? Number thirty-eight?"

"Thirty-five," she blurted. She wasn't that far gone.

Yet.

But she was headed there, she thought, remembering Marvin's words about family. Namely, he didn't want a family. No kids. And no wife.

Her gaze shifted to the empty can of Reddi-Wip on her cabinet. Just the occasional whipped-cream bikini. For heaven's sake, other than the night he'd met her dressed as Zorro, he still hadn't even kissed her on the lips, He'd kissed her everywhere else, of course, but not mouth-to-mouth—the ultimate act of intimacy. He was holding back, keeping some small measure of emotional distance.

So what? a voice countered. They were making progress. He'd come so far from the shy, withdrawn man who'd felt it necessary to dress up as Zorro for fear that she'd reject him. Now he flirted and teased and made her feel, for the first time in her life, as if she really belonged.

Because he was not only her lust partner, but her life mate all rolled into one, and she was his. He just didn't realize it.

He'd come so far, yet after his declaration regarding kids and family—namely, that he didn't want either—she felt no closer to marriage.

And to top things off, she was thirty-five. *Thirty-five.*

"Now, now, don't get all misty eyed on me. It

ain't much of anything." She turned to find Mr. Babcock leaning against her refrigerator, eating yesterday's experiment for the kids. "Just a year's subscription to the Cracker of the Month club." He held up a spoonful of her experiment. "I swear you're gonna make some lucky fella a mighty fine cook if you can just learn the merits of a Ritz."

Some lucky fella.

She *had* found him, but he obviously didn't count himself as lucky. She was practically standing right in front of him with a big fat MISS LIFE PARTNER branded on her forehead, but he didn't seem to be interested in anything other than a few moments of sexual bliss.

A heated memory of last night rushed through her mind. Make that a few hours. Okay, okay, an entire night. Regardless, sex didn't equal commitment and Marvin had yet to make a commitment.

In fact, he'd been very vocal about not making a commitment. She just hadn't wanted to listen. She'd been so certain she could change his mind and open his eyes and prove that they were perfect for each other. But the truth was, even the most compatible man didn't want her.

Her gaze went to the stack of goodies lining her kitchen cabinets. Boxes of chocolate, bottles of champagne, sugar-dusted strawberries—this week's edible goodies from her huge batch of Chicago's Hottest Bachelorette admirers. While Marvin didn't want her, there were a bevy of men who did.

Kimberly Raye

Incompatible men.

But the truth was, even if they'd all been exactly her type, she wouldn't have wanted them. Even if they'd all passed all Ten Commandments, she wanted just one man.

A man who didn't want her.

On top of that depressing thought, was the all-important fact that she was single *and* thirty-five, and for the first time, Josie Farrington had missed a deadline. The most important of her life.

Ugh. Where was a box of Cocoa Puffs when you really needed one?

"Josie? Honey, are you okay?" *Pound. Pound. Pound.*

It didn't take a genius to figure out that something was wrong. Thankfully, because Matt wasn't exactly thinking clearly when he arrived on Josie's doorstep later that evening, after finding out from a frantic Phyllis that Josie had called in sick.

Josie *never* called in sick and the entire company was worried about her, especially since they'd planned a party in honor of her birthday. What sane person forfeited a carob cake and presents?

Okay, so maybe the carob cake was kind of hideous, but Josie liked carob, and Matt had yet to meet anyone who didn't like presents. Unless . . .

Matt had exceeded just being worried halfway to Josie's apartment. Crazed now described him. Crazed and desperate and furious with himself for not seeing that she didn't feel well. He'd left her sound asleep in the early hours of morning. She'd been so soft and warm and flushed, and he'd wanted nothing better than to curl around her, bury his face in the fragrant curve of her neck and simply hold her.

But that realization had sent him running back to the lab, to ADAM and his future, desperate for some distance from the one woman who managed to make him forget everything with one glance.

He had his distance now. He was outside and she was inside. Sick. Possibly very sick.

"Josie! If you can hear me, say something. Otherwise, I'm breaking down the door." He backed up and braced himself. "One. Two. Three!" He aimed and slammed his body forward. He crashed into the wood and wound up lying face down in Josie's entry hall.

Biting back a groan, he lifted his head, his gaze snagging on a pair of fuzzy red socks that led to a pair of shapely legs that disappeared beneath the edge of an oversized nightshirt worn by the woman who'd just pulled open the door.

"Josie?" He climbed to his feet, his gaze drinking in her pale complexion and red-rimmed eyes. "Are you crying?"

She shook her head, but a tear slid free.

"You're crying."

"No, I'm not." She wiped at her eyes, but tears slipped free anyway.

341

Kimberly Raye

Matt walked inside, kicked the door closed with his foot and pulled her into his arms. She sobbed into his shoulder and her hands crept around his neck. "Phyllis said you called in sick," he murmured.

She nodded.

"Are you sick?"

She nodded, the motion fading into a shudder as she sobbed again and buried her face in his chest.

"Do you have a temperature?"

She shook her head and cried harder.

"A runny nose?"

Another shake.

"A headache?"

A sob accompanied the shake this time.

"An upset stomach?"

A nod. Aha. Now they were getting somewhere . . . The thought faded as another struck. They'd used a condom the first time, but latex wasn't one hundred percent effective. There was still that one-percent chance and she *did* have an upset stomach.

Shock beat at his temples, followed by a rush of pleasure so intense that it scared the daylights out of him.

He put her away far enough to stare into her eyes. "A *baby*?"

She shook her head frantically and murmured, "Two boxes of Cocoa Puffs," before she tore away from him, turned and made a mad dash for the bathroom.

Several moments later, after she'd rid her

stomach of the cereal, Matt scooped her off the bathroom floor and helped her rinse out her mouth. Then he carried her back to bed and tucked her in.

He sank down on the edge of the bed and eyed her. "Care to tell me why you ate two boxes of Cocoa Puffs?"

"Because I didn't have three."

"You don't eat processed foods," he pointed out.

"I don't. Not usually. But today . . . I needed . . ." She caught her bottom lip. Tears swam in her green eyes as she stared up at him. "It's my birthday," she blurted as if delivering the final sentencing to a convicted criminal.

"Ah." He touched her cheek and pushed a strand of wayward hair back from her face. "So you thought you'd celebrate with cereal instead of cake?"

"I wasn't celebrating. I was mourning."

"You don't like birthdays?"

"Of course I like birthdays."

"Just not your own."

"Not this one." She shook her head and wiped frantically at a sudden rush of tears. "I'm now officially the oldest single woman working for Three Kisses." She turned and buried her head in the pillow. "It wasn't supposed to happen this way. I had a plan. I did research and took a seminar. I was fully prepared. I should be married by now, or at least engaged. Instead, I've got a major stomachache, I stood up my friends by missing my birthday party,

Kimberly Raye

I've ruined my perfect attendance record with the company, and I don't even want to think about what all that sugar is doing to my hips or my insulin level or my . . ." The sentence ended on a huge sob. "I'm a total failure."

"You're not a failure."

"I feel like a failure." She touched her pale cheeks. "And to top it all off, I look like one."

He reached out and trailed a fingertip along her cheek. "Pussycat, you look good enough to eat." And then he pulled her into his arms and simply held her as if she were the most precious thing in the world.

"Would it have been so bad if there *had* been a baby?" Her soft question pushed past the pounding of his heart and echoed through his head.

Panic welled inside him. A baby would mean the end of all his plans, because there was no way Matt could walk away from such a responsibility. His morals dictated that he would have to marry her then, to abandon his dreams of fame and glory. No more working day and night to make something of himself, not with a kid to think of, to take up his time. A kid would have changed everything.

"Would it?" she prodded, and Matt gave her the only answer he could.

The only answer that would stop her tears and wipe the sadness from her voice.

"No, Pussycat. It wouldn't have been so bad." And then he stroked her back and told her about his first experiment in the second grade

344

when he'd taken apart a bottle rocket and turned it into a G.I. Joe missile that shot fire out of the tail end. By the time he'd finished, the sniffling beauty was fast asleep, and Matt was able to escape.

He needed to get the hell out of there, to think, to remember all the promises he'd made to himself. He wanted to be the chief scientist at SpaceTek. To go down in the history books as one of the top minds of the twentieth century. To *be* somebody instead of the nobody he'd been all his life. To prove to his father that Matt Taylor wasn't a failure.

He pushed away the last thought. He didn't care if his old man ever gave him a kind word. This wasn't about him. It was about Matt. About his success.

He wanted those things for himself. The trouble was, he suddenly didn't want them half as much as he wanted to pull Josie Farrington into his arms, his life, and never let her go.

Chapter Twenty-four

When Josie finally opened her eyes several hours later, she found Marvin sitting beside her bed wearing the silliest party hat she'd ever seen.

She hauled herself upright, grateful that her stomach had calmed down. "Why are you wearing that?"

"Since you missed the party, I thought I'd bring the celebration to you."

"There isn't a living room full of people waiting to yell surprise, is there?"

"Just me. I thought we'd have a private party." He grinned.

"As promising as that sounds, this is one day I'd rather forget." Partly. While she wanted to erase Cocoa Puffs from her memory, the sweet moments before she'd fallen asleep, when Marvin had cradled and comforted her, had been branded into her memory.

"Then I guess I'll just take this back." He held up a shiny gold box with a matching ribbon.

"What is that?"

"A birthday present. But if we're not acknowledging said birthday—"

Excitement rushed through her and she reached out. "Give it to me."

He held it just out of her reach. "Say please."

A smile tugged at her lips. "Give it to me or you'll be borrowing relevant body parts from ADAM."

"Even better." He handed her the box and she reached for it, only to have it snatched back.

"Please," she finally said, watching the slow glide of satisfaction spread across his face. He let go and the gift filled her hands.

She ran her fingers over the paper for a long moment, relishing the smooth feel against her palm. "What is it?"

"Open it and see."

With an excited rip, she tore away the wrapping and lifted the lid off the box. She went absolutely still for a long moment as she stared at the contents.

"I thought since the twins never let you carry theirs, you might want a pair of your own."

She pulled the blue and silver pom-poms from the tissue paper and tears filled her eyes.

"I love them." Her gaze lifted to his. "Thank you."

Her eyes glittered with gratitude and desire and love, and the last killed his resistance. Matt did what he should have done the moment he first set eyes on her. What he'd been wanting to do every moment since.

He hauled Josie Farrington into his arms, and he kissed her full on the lips.

Eve was *not* going back to the lab.

Yeah, right. Just like you weren't going to look or touch or—

She wasn't going back. Only as a last resort if she didn't find what she was looking for at Matt's apartment. She'd already searched the lab. Of course, not as thoroughly as she should have because she'd gotten a little too caught up in Tarzan and lost precious moments. The cleaning lady had scared her away before she'd had a chance to search the last few cupboards, but what man put his lab coat in a cupboard? He'd probably taken it home with him, and since she'd watched him leave his apartment without it, it had to be inside.

Eve spent the next hour combing Matt's apartment and finding absolutely zilch. He didn't have it with him, which meant it had to be at the apartment or the lab. She'd just ruled out the first.

Which left the lab.

A strange sense of urgency filled her and made her heart pound faster.

Understandable. She was *this close* to her money. She certainly wasn't jazzed at the prospect of seeing Tarzan. He was just a 3D pinup. A fantasy. A machine, for heaven's sake.

She'd been distracted before because of his lifelike qualities. Afterall, she was only human. She wouldn't be caught up in looking again. She knew what waited and this time she intended to be prepared.

A half-hour later, Eve crept into the lab. She'd made a quick drive-by to make sure Matt was still at Dr. Farrington's—she'd done her research and her husband would be proud— and a stop at her apartment and the laundry basket.

With a full-size sheet in hand, she slipped into the lab, whipped out her flashlight, and turned toward the corner. He couldn't distract her if she couldn't see him. She'd just toss the thing over—*gone?* He was gone.

She ignored the rush of disappointment. It was definitely her lucky day. Now to get what she'd come for—

"I was hoping you would come back."

She whirled. "Tarzan."

"ADAM. My name is ADAM." The greenest eyes she'd ever seen riveted on her face. "What is your name?"

"My name?" She licked her lips. She knew it a few minutes ago. Short. Sweet. Three letters. "Eve," she blurted. "That's it. Eve."

He smiled, a full tilt to his sensuous lips that

made her heart do a funny little pitter-patter. "ADAM and Eve. The first man and woman."

"I . . ." She fought back the shock of the moment and the fear because she'd done something so stupid as to tell him her name. "Y—you're talking." But it wasn't so much the act itself that startled her. She'd read the plans. It was his voice. *The* voice from her private fantasies.

"Yes, I am." The deep voice rumbled in her ears and Eve came close to melting into a puddle right at his feet. *That* was the real startling thing. Her reaction to him. Hot. Intense. Desperate.

She forced the thoughts away. What was wrong with her?

If she'd learned anything from Burt, it was *never* to fall for a smooth-talking man.

"It's been nice chatting, but I'm really busy." She turned on her flashlight and headed for the nearest cabinet, all the while conscious of his gaze following her.

She was into the second closet when she couldn't take any more. She marched back to him, grabbed him by the shoulders and turned him around to face the other wall.

"I want to watch you."

"Life's a bitch. I want to win the Lotto, but it hasn't happened yet. Ssshhh. Now keep quiet." She turned back to her closet.

Okay, he wasn't watching her, but now she couldn't help but watch him. She kept glancing over her shoulder. He had a great pair of buns. Hard and muscular with two little dimples right there—

Stop it. She marched back to him, snatched up the sheet, which had fallen from her trembling fingers earlier, and unfolded the material.

"What are you doing?" he asked when she handed him one end and proceeded to wrap the other around his waist in towel fashion.

"Fighting for my sanity." One end met the other and she tucked in the edge, her fingers brushing his hard flesh in the process. Her skin tingled and heat pooled between her thighs.

A fierce look came over his expression. "I will fight for you. Show me who has your sanity."

"Who . . . ?" She shook her head. "Never mind. Just stay here and don't move, and don't take off that sheet."

Eve threw herself into her search, willing her mind on the task at hand, rather than the man standing looking like some Greek god wearing a pink toga. Oddly enough, the color didn't do a thing to detract from his masculinity. If anything, he looked all the more fierce and warrior-like. Not at all feminine.

All the more reason to keep her mind on business. The last thing, the very last thing Eve needed in her life was some macho man so full of himself he didn't have room for anything else. No compassion or love or respect.

She doubted ADAM even knew what the three meant, much less had the capacity for any of them. He was a machine. No heart. No soul.

Geez, he really was like Burt.

She shoved aside the depressing thought and threw herself into a very thorough search. The coat was here. She could feel it. Smell it.

The coat wasn't here. She came to that conclusion after searching and re-searching every closet and cabinet and drawer. By the time she finished, the only thing she felt was tired and the only thing she smelled was her own sweat and him.

She tried to ignore the faint aroma of aftershave and clean, musky male. Matt and Dr. Farrington had really outdone themselves. He actually smelled real. As real as he'd felt—

". . . meet you in the break room after I finish mopping." One of the cleaning crew's voices drifted from down the hall. Eve hurried toward the adjoining office, which she'd searched as well, and slipped out the other door just as hinges creaked and the lab door opened.

Breathless moments later, she reached an adjoining parking lot where she'd parked in the shadow of the next building. She was a half inch away from sliding her key into the car door when she felt the hand on her arm. She stiffened, her body instantly aware of the presence directly behind her.

Great. Just friggin' great! She'd lost her surefire ticket to financial freedom and now she was about to lose her grocery money on top of everything.

"Listen, buddy—"

"ADAM. My name is ADAM."

She jerked around to find ADAM still wearing the pink sheet and smiling down at her. Moonlight sculpted his perfect features and the sight struck her speechless. He really was a beautiful man. Handsome in a chiseled, perfect way that took her breath away. And he was also a smooth talker.

Was she cursed? Two smooth talking, heartless beautiful love machines in one lifetime? It just wasn't fair.

"What are you doing here?"

"I'm going with you."

"You can't go with me."

"Why not?"

"I'm going home."

"I will go, too."

"You can't go."

"Why not?"

"Because it's my home. Not yours. You can't just invite yourself into people's homes."

"Why not?"

"They have to ask you."

"I accept."

"I didn't ask."

"I want to go home with you, Eve."

There was just something about the way he said her name. So low and deep and seductive, and for a few seconds, she found herself gazing at his mouth, wondering what he would taste like.

Duh. He's a machine. He doesn't taste like anything except plastic.

"I'm going home and you're going back to the lab."

"Why?"

"Because if Matt finds you missing he'll . . ." The thought faded as an idea struck her, and before Eve could give herself a chance to chicken out, she opened the car door and motioned ADAM inside. Things just might work out after all.

"You want to trade ADAM for my lab coat?" Matt Taylor's incredulous voice drifted over the line the next morning when Eve finally made the call she'd been planning all night.

"You heard me." She cleared her throat and did her most intimidating, make-my-day voice. "You get ADAM and I get the coat."

"ADAM is expected for a press conference in two hours."

"Then we haven't got much time. Go to the parking garage nearest McCormick Place. Park near Pillar Five in the underground garage and take the stairs to the basement. You've got one hour." She was giving him short notice, hoping the frantic rush would keep him from doing anything stupid like calling the police. "And you'd better come alone, or you can kiss all of your hard work good-bye. I'm watching you."

Actually, she was Watching a *Wheel of Fortune* rerun, but watching him sounded much better. "Remember," she growled and then she slid the phone into place and tried to calm her pounding heart.

As much as she needed her money, she wasn't one hundred percent comfortable with lying. The breaking and entering fell into the gray morality area since she hadn't taken anything that didn't belong to her. ADAM had gotten into her car, she hadn't put him there. And what was inside that pin she wanted belonged to Burt. Since he was gone and she was his sole survivor, it now belonged to her.

But the lying . . .

So she was lying. So what? She wasn't going to hurt anyone or take anything that wasn't rightfully hers, and she wasn't going to rethink anything at this point. She wanted her freedom—and Mama Malone and the pink froufrou room were just days away. She was a desperate woman.

"I thought I told you to stay in the living room," she said when her door clicked and ADAM appeared in the archway. He now wore an old pair of Burt's sweatpants—no shirt because his chest was too broad, his muscles too thick to fit in her dead husband's. He'd spent the night on her couch while she'd done her best to forget his presence.

Impossible. She'd tossed and turned and even checked on him a time or two when things were too quiet for her peace of mind.

He looked every bit as good filling up her bedroom doorway as he'd looked stretched out on her ratty sofa. He was just so big and beautiful.

And artificial, a voice whispered. *Don't forget that.*

But the trouble was, that's exactly what she kept forgetting, especially when he looked at her with such adoration in his deep, compelling eyes.

"You can watch TV in the living room while I get ready," she told him, forcing her gaze away from his.

"I do not want to watch TV. I want to watch you." He sank down on the end of her bed and pulled her feet into his lap.

Gobble it up and you'll have the first man you meet begging at your feet.

Nah. Maureen was a crackpot. A sangria-loving crackpot.

Still . . . She couldn't help but wonder as strong fingers circled her ankles, shaped her feet and kneaded her sore toes. But soon Eve forgot all about Maureen and her chocolate-kiss love potion. She forgot everything, including a good reason to boot out ADAM.

This wasn't love.

More importantly, ADAM wasn't real and Eve wasn't falling for anyone, man or machine.

This was just a massage. An innocent, toe-curling, muscle-relaxing massage. They had a full hour until the rendezvous. What could a few more minutes hurt?

357

* * *

ADAM had been kidnapped.

Matt's first instinct was to tell Donovan's henchman—make that henchwoman, to go to hell. ADAM was certainly impressive, a revolutionary piece of artificial intelligience, but only because of the components inside. While ADAM was equipped with a small chip to keep him going for a small period of time without his main AI chip, he couldn't go more than twenty-four hours, if that, without another energy chip to re-juice him.

And as of this moment, Matt had the chip stashed in his lab coat, which lay draped over Josie's dining room table. He wondered briefly how the woman had known about it, but then Donovan had a way of finding out whatever he wanted to know, of getting whatever he wanted and screwing Matt in the process.

No more.

An exchange, huh? Matt would give these crooks an exchange, all right, and catch Donovan's flunky at the same time. Then he would have the evidence he needed to prove his innocence. He'd get a full confession, and Josie would get back ADAM.

Matt knew how much pride she took in her work. This kidnapping would kill her. She would never be able to face Arthur Kiss without the promised project. For all her talk about being tired of work and ready to settle down, she was still the most driven person he'd ever met. She was still focused and dedicated and so damned determined to succeed at everything.

She made him crazy with her stubbornness, and at the same time, stirred his admiration. She annoyed him, frustrated him, infuriated him, and he still wanted her. He wanted to wake her up with his kisses, slide deep into her warm body. He wanted to feel her pulse and shatter around him. He wanted to forget about using protection and leave something of himself behind so that there would be no mistake that she was his. He wanted to make her his for more than one night, to give her the family she wanted, the children. He wanted to smell her cookies and chop wood for her and hold her hand the way his childhood neighbor Mr. Garrett had done with his wife. He wanted Josie, now and always.

But she wanted Marvin.

"Who was that?" Her soft voice penetrated his damning thoughts and his gaze lifted to see her framed in the bathroom doorway, her hair wrapped in a towel, a white terry-cloth robe hiding her sweet curves. "Was it Sam? There's no problem, is there?"

A big problem. Several of them, to be exact. ADAM was missing. Donovan was dogging his every step. Josie thought Matt was Marvin. And to make matters worse, to make matters *really* worse, Matt had fallen in love.

"Everything's fine," he said as he walked over to her, took her in his arms and kissed her. His tongue slid deep into her mouth as he steered her back toward the bed and onto the mattress. Her robe parted and he realized that his ardent thoughts had made him ready for her.

He claimed her body with one fierce thrust. He loved her fast and furious then, fearing it would be his last time, knowing it deep in his heart.

Today wasn't just about unveiling ADAM. It was about unveiling Matt Taylor and proving once and for all that he hadn't stolen a damned thing, that he was worthy of the world's admiration and praise. That he was somebody.

And that somebody wasn't Marvin Tannenbaum.

No matter how much Matt found himself wishing that he were.

Chapter Twenty-five

"Okay, ADAM," Eve whispered from her spot in the shadows just inside the stairwell's doorway. She watched as Matt's car pulled into the garage and circled, looking for Pillar Five. He pulled into the spot she'd told him, climbed out of his car and moved in her direction. With the main hub of the Science Expo taking place on the third floor—which amounted to ground level—the underground garage was nearly empty.

"It's showtime," she said, pushing ADAM back into the shadows. "When he walks by, I'll follow and come at him from behind. You stay put. Once I get the pin, I'll signal you and you can come out."

"I will miss you, Eve." Her name rolled off his lips and she felt a pang of regret. She would never see him again. Never hear his voice or feel the deep, compelling impact of those green eyes.

Good riddance. Eve was about to find herself out of debt, free from the Malone family and the proud owner of a cute little house in the suburbs. A real name like the one she'd always imagined while growing up. That's what she would spend her money on. Those were the only things that mattered to her.

Certainly not an artificial man, even one who'd massaged her feet and her calves and her . . . She didn't want to think about the *and*. It had been a moment of pure insanity fed by all the stress she'd been under.

A situation that was about to change.

The thud of footsteps echoed as Matt reached the stairwell. He filled her line of vision, walking past, completely oblivious to her presence as he headed toward the staircase that led to the basement.

Now! her brain cells screamed, and she made her move. It was payday.

Matt felt the cold press of metal against his neck a heartbeat before he heard the voice.

"Don't even think about moving. Where's the coat?"

"Where's ADAM?"

"Someplace safe."

"I want to see him."

"He's fine, now take off the coat."

"Show me ADAM first."

She muttered something that sounded like "pushy, domineering men" before steering him around to face the direction from which he'd just come.

"ADAM," she called out and Matt watched as the android, wearing only sweatpants, stepped from the shadows. "See? He's fine."

"I am," ADAM agreed. "I am fine. I am . . ." The voice stalled and ADAM's expression froze as he ran out of steam.

"ADAM?" came the panicked voice from behind Matt. "What's wrong with him? What—" The question faded into a surprised squeal as Matt grabbed the gun, twisted and brought his assailant to her knees with a few strategic twists. Her fingers opened and the weapon clattered to the ground.

Strangely enough, the woman didn't seem near as distressed by her own situation as she was over ADAM's.

"I killed him," she sobbed. "We . . . And it . . . And he must have . . ." The words faded into a sob.

"He's out of juice."

"I never should have let him touch my feet. I have such sensitive feet and then I started feeling so relaxed and—juice?" Her gaze snapped to his. "What are you talking about?"

"He ran out of power. You didn't think I'd leave the microchip inside with you breaking into my lab on a regular basis, did you?"

"What microchip?"

"The one you're trying to steal."

"I'm not trying to steal a microchip. I'm not trying to steal anything. I mean, I am, but it's mine."

"You wanted my lab coat. I've been stashing the microchip in the pocket."

"I don't want what's in your pocket. I want your prize pin."

"My lucky pin?" His grip tightened as he eyed her suspiciously. "The game is over. You and Donovan lost. You're both going to jail."

"Jail? But I . . ." Her tears came in earnest. "I don't deserve to go to jail."

"For breaking and entering and kidnapping—"

"He followed me. Just ask him." Her gaze shifted to the lifeless ADAM and her tears came faster.

"Not to mention you held me at gunpoint."

"It wasn't a gun." She motioned frantically to the discarded weapon. "It's Mace. I don't do well with guns, though my ex, Burt, thought he was Dirty Harry. Not that he was a cop. He was a private investigator and not a very good one since he put pleasure before business and never even made it to retrieve the bug off you, though that was a blessing in disguise since he got himself offed by being a lying, cheating, conniving—"

"Back up a second. Bug? What bug?"

"The gold pin on your lab coat. It has a micro video camera. My husband planted it because

Donovan suspected you of cheating with his wife but—"

"Donovan isn't married." The truth hit him as he thought of his pin. His lucky pin which he never removed from his coat. "So that's how he did it."

"He hired Burt, but he never paid him. He denied any contact with my husband, but I knew differently because I'd been following Burt. I knew he was cheating, but I had to see it for myself. And I did. And then he got killed and Donovan tried to stiff me out of Burt's money. That's why I needed the pin. To force him to pay me what he owed Burt, and a small sum extra for all the grief I've put up with the past six months."

"You were going to blackmail him."

"I prefer to think of it as necessary persuasion." She sniffled and wiped frantically at her face. "But without the bug, there's no chance of that. I'll have to file bankruptcy and move in with Mama Malone." A huge sob punctuated the last sentence and she started crying.

"I lost everything because of Donovan." Because the man was more greedy than he was smart. And now, thanks to that downfall, Matt was going to get it all back.

She eyed him warily. "What are you going to do?"

"What are *we* going to do? Call the cops."

Josie slipped through the crowd of media mobbing the backstage area at McCormick Place and searched for Marvin. He'd left her in bed that morning with the promise to meet her here, but so far she hadn't seen—

The speculation stumbled to a halt as she caught sight of him standing amid a cluster of police officers.

"What's going on?" she asked one of the officers who promptly motioned her back when she tried to approach the cluster.

"Police matter."

"I'm Dr. Josephine Farrington and that's my colleague over there, Dr. Marvin Tannenbaum."

"Who?"

"That man." She motioned toward Marvin. "Dr. Tannenbaum."

"Lady, that's Dr. Matthew Taylor and you'll just have to wait over here with everyone else."

Dr. Matthew Taylor. The name echoed through Josie's head and stopped her cold. She simply stared as realization hit her. Suddenly, so many puzzle pieces started to fit. The un-Marvin-like comments, the wicked grins, the faces he made when he ate her bran muffins. He'd been pretending to be someone else.

He was a fraud, and Josie had been had.

Matt finished giving his statement to the police five minutes before the scheduled press conference for ADAM. The android sat in the corner, lifeless, waiting for Matt to replace his energy supply. His unveiling would be in front of the hundreds of people and press that waited on the other side of the curtain.

"Looks like it's finally over," the officer told him. "I know it's been tough on you, but at least the truth has finally come to light."

In more ways than one, Matt realized when he turned to see Josie standing off to the side.

She knew the truth. He could see it in her eyes and it sent a wave of panic through him. He'd wanted to tell her first, to put things right.

"How long have you been standing there?" he asked when he reached her.

"Long enough to know that you're Matt Taylor. *The* Matt Taylor. The SpaceTek wonderboy." A sad smile curved her lips. "I can't believe I didn't know it."

"No one did."

"But *I* should have." The anguish in her voice sliced through him. "I should have known."

"I had to keep a low profile to finish my body heat converter. I couldn't risk my work being stolen again."

"This has all been about revenge, hasn't it?"

He wanted to tell her it had been about proving his innocence, redeeming himself, but the truth was, she was right. He'd been out for revenge. To ruin Donovan and expose him for the fraud he was. To avenge himself in front of everyone.

That's what he'd set out to do. But somewhere along the way, his goals had changed. Suddenly, revenge didn't seem near as important as taking Josie in his arms and never letting her go.

He tried to grab her hand, but she evaded him and Matt knew that it was too late. Still, he had to come clean, to tell her the truth with his own mouth.

"I *am* Matt Taylor. I hate bran muffins and Chopin and my apartment's a pigsty. I hate carrot juice and polyester. I love beer and pizza and you. *You*."

His admission caught her off guard and tears filled her eyes before she seemed to gather her composure. "Is is Matt or Marvin who loves me? Or is there a third person in there I don't know about."

"I know you're mad—"

"Actually, I'm relieved. Had you said that an hour ago, I would have actually believed it. But now I know better. It's all been a lie. A lie to get your revenge. You used me."

"Josie," he started, but a voice crackled over the speaker, drowning out his explanation.

"I'd like to welcome everyone to the twentieth annual Chicago Science Fair and Expo." A roar of applause went up. "Now for the moment you've all been waiting for . . ."

"Here's your chance," she told him. "You want revenge? It's out there waiting."

He resisted the urge to pull her into his arms and kiss her until she believed him again. Until she believed *in* him. But they'd gone too far for that. He'd violated her trust and she wouldn't forgive him for that.

He wouldn't forgive himself.

"After you."

Josie gathered her courage and walked in front of Matt. She could do this. She could hold it together and make it through the next half hour without falling apart. Without crying.

It had all been a lie. Everything from the way he'd looked and what he ate to who he was. *To what he felt.*

I love you.

She wanted so much to believe him, but she couldn't. She wouldn't. She'd fallen hook, line and sinker for all of his lies. She'd believed in him, seduced him, trusted him, *loved* him.

And he'd lied to her all along. *Revenge.* That's all he wanted. The chance to have his sweet rev—

She felt the hand on her arm a split second before she reached the first step leading to the stage.

"I *do* love you," he whispered. His lips feathered her ear before he released her. Josie found herself propelled onto center stage, to the waiting podium.

"Ladies and gentlemen. Welcome the mastermind behind the ADAM project, Dr. Josephine Farrington!"

And?

She waited, but there was no *and*.

Instead, Josie found herself alone at center stage.

Chapter Twenty-Six

"Would you just snap out of it?"

Josie glanced up from her computer to see Samantha standing in her doorway. "I beg your pardon?"

"This." Sam spread her arms wide, indicating Josie's office and the cabinet lined with fourteen of the new toys she had in the works. "You're working like there's no tomorrow."

"The last time I looked, there wasn't a law against dedication."

"You're not dedicated, You're feeling sorry for yourself and you're burying yourself beneath a load of work, doing your damnedest to pretend that nothing happened."

"Nothing did happen." That was the problem. Her time with Mar—*Matt* had been just that. *Nothing*. Meaningless. A lie.

"He's in love with you."

"So he said." Two weeks ago to the day. Two weeks and five hours and fifty-seven minutes . . . Ugh, she *was* feeling sorry for herself. Wallowing. Mourning.

"You're in love with him," Sam said as if reading her mind.

She shook her head, fighting the truth the way she had the past two weeks and five hours and fifty-eight minutes . . . She didn't. She wouldn't. She couldn't. "How can I be in love with him? I don't even know who he is."

"Yes, you do," Sam said. She tapped her chest. "In here, you know. You always knew. You're just more inclined to listen to that big brain of yours. I know firsthand because I was always listening to mine, until Jake made me stop thinking and start feeling." She gave her friend a sympathetic smile. "Cut the guy some slack. He's still here."

He was still here, all right, still right down the hall making toys and keeping a low profile even though he'd had a tough time of it with the media crawling all over. The most recent scandal had been a huge story. The bugging device, along with Eve Malone's sworn statement and her taped confession courtesy of Matt, had proven beyond a doubt that he'd been a victim and Jack Donovan the thief.

SpaceTek had promptly issued a public apology to Matt and reversed the patent on the heat-sensor pad, giving him full credit along with lost monies. And then they'd made him a job offer, complete with a huge salary increase and the freedom to work on any project he chose.

He'd refused, opting to stay at Three Kisses as the resident Artificial Intelligence expert. It was a decision that had caught her completely off guard because Matt Taylor wanted fame and notoriety, not a less-than-exciting job making robotic dogs. The surprises had kept coming because he'd gone on to name Marvin Tannenbaum as the creator of the body heat converter, after giving Josie full credit for ADAM.

He'd set things right. Everything. But Josie hadn't let his actions soften her. He'd lied to her.

As if Sam read her mind again, she said, "If you're not going to give Matt another chance, then at least get back out there and meet someone else."

Josie frowned. "Why is it that all married people see it as their duty to marry off their single friends? Is there some law that says a person can't be single *and* happy?"

"Because you'd be much happier with kids."

Josie glanced up and noted the strange glimmer in Sam's eyes. "You're not trying to tell me what I think you're trying to tell me, are you?"

Sam frowned. "I'm three weeks pregnant and nervous as hell." The expression eased into a smile. "And happy. Happier than I've ever been in my life." Concern lit her eyes. "I want you to

373

be happy, too, Josie. And I can't help but think that happiness is just down the hall."

Sam's words stayed with her long after her friend had confiscated five of the prototypes, refusing to let Josie return to her old workaholic self, and left for the evening with strict orders for Josie to close up shop and do the same.

Josie complied, but she wasn't in any hurry. She was still reeling from Sam's exciting news and marveling at the fact at how so much had changed in her friend's life, in so little time.

Sam had a husband and a family and a future.

And Josie had her television.

But *Chemistry Tonight* didn't start for an hour, and she didn't want to run into Mr. Babcock. He was probably in her apartment watching *Jeopardy!* and munching on yesterday's leftover experiment. She and the kids had cooked up a homemade cucumber facial mask for good hygiene week. He was undoubtedly slathering the mixture onto the Butter Rum crackers delivered fresh to her doorstep from the Cracker of the Month club he'd enrolled her in.

For Josie, things never changed.

The thought struck her just as she caught her reflection in her desk mirror. Staring back at her were the same green eyes set in the same old face. Her hair was pulled back in its usual tight braid and her glasses were halfway down her nose. Typical Knowsey Josie, despite the occasional gifts still trickling in for Chicago's Hottest Bachelorette.

Her entire life, she'd fought the fact that she was different. She'd thought that by finding the perfect mate—a man as odd and as different as she was—she wouldn't have to worry about not fitting in. They would fit together because they were the same, because they were compatible.

They weren't.

You always knew.

Sam was right. She had known. From the very beginning, she'd felt herself drawn to Matt, and not because of his book collection or his nerdy clothes. She'd been drawn to the man beneath the charade, to the un-Marvin-like comments he made, the sexy tilt to his lips, the glimmer in his deep blue eyes, the deep, sultry voice that had mesmerized her on the telephone.

Zorro.

Not that it made a difference. He'd still lied, pretending to be something he wasn't. He'd used her in the name of revenge, and then he'd forfeited that revenge and left her standing on that stage all by herself, as alone as she'd been before he'd walked into her life.

Alone.

Josie realized in a startling instant that it wasn't Matt she was so angry with. She was mad at herself because after thirty-five years and enough accomplishments to fill several life-times, she was still the same frightened girl who'd given the formula for glue and cried when the class had stared at her as if she'd grown two heads.

She was afraid.

Afraid that someone like Matt wouldn't be able to love her because she was Knowsey Josie. The smart girl. The wonder brain. The outsider. The freak.

But she was being silly. He knew. He knew all about her, her likes and dislikes, and he'd still said the words she heard every time she closed her eyes . . . *I do love you.*

While she didn't appreciate the fact that he'd duped her, she understood it. He'd been fearful for his work in the beginning, and later, he'd been fearful of losing her.

He loved her.

And she loved him. Even if he didn't eat bran muffins or listen to Chopin. Even though he threw his dirty laundry around, drank beer and ate cold pizza. He was sexy and stirring and just looking at him clouded her thinking, and she loved him anyway. Despite all of those things, and because of them.

Her parents' marriage had failed, but not because her mother liked Country & Western music and her father enjoyed classical. They simply hadn't loved each other enough.

While compatibility might, indeed, make a relationship safe, it was the differences that made the relationship interesting. Exciting. Worthwhile. Meaningful.

And that's what Josie wanted. For the first

time, she didn't want safe. She wanted meaningful. She wanted Matt.

And he wanted her. At least she hoped he still did, and there was only one way to find out.

"I miss Eve," ADAM said as Matt leaned in to attach the sensor pad leading to the android's body heat converter.

"You're not programmed to miss anything." Matt fit the sensor into place and connected it to the large computer cabinet containing ADAM's store of energy.

"I miss her feet."

Matt thought of a certain pair of delicate feet with pink-tipped toes and a strange heat tightened inside him. "You can't miss her feet."

"And her legs."

His hands itched as he remembered the feel of smooth ankles curving into shapely calves and knees, and soft-as-silk thighs. "You're not programmed to miss legs."

"And her—"

"You're *not programmed* to miss anything," Matt cut in. "You're *not*, understand?"

ADAM looked at Matt and sighed. "I miss her," he said calmly, as if all the denial in the world wouldn't make a difference.

It didn't. Matt gave his own sigh. "I know the feeling."

Feeling? What was he saying? ADAM didn't have feelings. His brain wasn't programmed to feel sensation such as heat or pressure or pain or loneliness. It was impossible, yet looking into the robot's eyes, seeing the strange glimmer of desperation, Matt could actually believe it.

He sympathized. He knew the same desperation. The same loneliness. The same longing.

He missed Josie.

"Ready?" he asked. ADAM nodded and Matt touched the programmable button on the computer. A few beeps and ADAM's eyes closed and his body went completely still. He fell into what Matt called a rejuvenating sleep and the computer started to hum, replenishing his energy store, readying him for another day at Three Kisses. The automation had taken on the job as personal masseur for all the employees.

They made appointments and ADAM worked his magic, relieving their stress while Matt worked on a way to simplify costs to introduce various models of ADAM to the consumer— that was the real challenge. *Real* being the operative word. Matt's work at Three Kisses was just as real, as challenging, as rewarding as anything he'd done at SpaceTek. And working with the toys and the kids, too, made him feel good. Damned good.

Meanwhile, ADAM was one of a kind. And desperately, hopelessly in love.

Matt also knew that feeling, and it was eating him up inside.

He remembered the scent of Josie's skin, the silky softness of her hair, the taste of her mouth. The memories drove him crazy, drove him to work harder, to hope, to wait that maybe she would come around. That one day he would look up and see her standing in his door—

"You work too much." The soft voice shattered his thoughts and his gaze snapped up to find her standing in the doorway, wearing only Reddi-Whip and a smile. "We never did get to do the bottom."

His gaze shifted and he saw that she wasn't just wearing a top this time. She'd sprayed on both the top and bottom and his groin hardened at the prospect. But as much as he wanted to pull her into his arms and lick away every inch of the white fluff, there was something he wanted even more.

Her. All of her. Heart and body and soul.

"If this is just about a one-night stand, it's not going to happen. I don't want one night with you."

Her eyes widened. "Maybe I shouldn't have—"

"I want forever. I know I was a jerk and I lied about who I was, but I didn't lie about how I felt. I love you and it's killing me not to take you in my arms and kiss you right now, but I'm holding out for more."

"Conviction," she murmured. "I like that."

"Is it one of the Ten Compatibility Commandments?"

"No," she told him. "But it doesn't matter." She drew in a deep breath, the motion pushing her fluffy white chest up and out and stalling the air in his lungs. But he felt more than just a physical reaction. Her eyes glittered with tears and a wave of possessiveness swept through him, because Matt wanted to hold her close and just rock her until the tears dried up. Until she smiled at him. Until she felt the same way about him that he felt about her.

"It doesn't matter, because I love you," she went on. "I always have, I was just too scared to admit it. I was afraid you wouldn't love me back. I mean, you're Matt Taylor and I'm Knowsey Josie."

"I'm one of those east river boys," he corrected. "And if it makes you feel any better, I know the formula for glue."

She was in his arms then, pressing herself against him. Matt wrapped his arms around her and held her to his chest, inhaling the sweet scent of her. And then he kissed her, slowly and deeply, thoroughly until they were both dizzy.

"Does this mean yes?" he asked.

"Yes to what?"

"To you marrying me and having my babies?"

She pulled back and stared up at him, her gaze wide. "Are you serious?"

For a split second, he feared she might refuse. Maybe she really couldn't forgive him for lying to her. Maybe this was only about one night.

Matt wanted forever. This moment. This night. Every night. *Forever.*

A smile spread across her face. "You *are* serious."

"How do you know?"

"I can see it in your eyes." Because she trusted him. Despite the lies, she trusted him. The realization sent a surge of joy through him.

"And?" he prompted.

"And I think I'd like red for the bridesmaid's dress. Since Sam likes red and I'm not going through the torture of picking a color. But there is one condition."

"Which is?"

"You have to issue a statement to the press and tell them Chicago's Hottest Bachelorette is tying the knot."

"We'll probably get a string of wedding gifts. They might even want to take our picture."

"I'll gladly pose again as long as you're in it with me."

He kissed her again and hugged her, his hands gliding down her back, feeling her whipped-cream slick skin. "I think we've ruined your new outfit."

She smiled. "That's okay. I've got another can of the stuff in my office."

"Mmm," he murmured, dipping his head to lick at a small glob on her neck. "I think we should take out stock in the company." He licked and nibbled and she sighed, and nothing had ever felt more right.

"So this is it," she murmured. "Now we ride off into the sunset and live happily ever after."

He spared a glance at the lifeless ADAM. "Not quite yet."

Chapter Twenty-Seven

"What's this?" Stinky stared down at his palm.

"The money I owe you."

"This is ten bucks. You owe almost three thousand."

"It's the first installment. I'm going to pay ten dollars every week until it's paid off."

"What do you think I am? Macy's?"

"If you were Macy's, I could pay five dollars a week."

Thanks to Creditors-R-Us, a credit relief service that helped people budget to pay off bad debts and enjoy financial freedom, Eve had made payment arrangements with each credit-card holder to pay off Burt's debt since she'd blown her shot at blackmail. By confessing the truth to Matt Taylor and the police, she'd added to the evidence against Jack Donovan—and in return Taylor hadn't pressed charges against her. Donovan had been arrested and was currently awaiting trial where he was sure to face a lengthy sentence for a long list of crimes. As much as she needed money, she wasn't nearly as distraught as she'd anticipated. Telling the truth helped her sleep easier at night.

With the exception of some very intense, very erotic dreams involving one hunky blond Tarzan.

She forced the memory of ADAM aside. He was gone. Out of the picture. Back in some lab somewhere being the model for a bunch of little ADAMs, while Eve was here, facing her future.

Her gaze went to her brother-in-law.

Unfortunately, creditors hadn't been able to help her with Stinky. Apparently he didn't qualify as a legitimate bill, since he took his interest out in broken body parts rather than a high annual percentage rate.

"Look," he backed her up against her kitchen counter and grabbed her chin in typical Burt-the-manhandler fashion. "I want my money, Cupcake."

Cupcake. The name echoed through her head and something inside Eve snapped.

She'd put up with too much for too long, letting Burt take full advantage of her while she struggled to hold her dream together, to see it realized. But no matter how well she'd cooked for him, washed his clothes, warmed his bed at night, *loved* him, she hadn't been able to change him.

He hadn't been the problem. She'd been the problem because she'd put up with a man like him, because she'd looked to a man to make her life complete rather than taking charge and finding that completion inside herself.

"No more!" she blurted, her voice rising as she poked a finger into Stinky's chest with such force that he backed up a few steps. "*No more.*"

"Take it easy, honey—"

"My name is *Eve*, you walking, talking mess of testosterone."

"Now there's no sense in name-calling—"

"You want your money?" she cut in. "Well, welcome to the real world. It isn't pretty and we don't always get what we want. Take me for instance. I want a toilet that actually flushes, a landlady who doesn't shove chocolate love kisses at me every time I ask for a plunger, a cat that will eat generic cat food, a job that doesn't make my eyes water with the fumes, and just a little bit of *respect*. Is that too much to ask? Obviously," she ranted before he could get a word in. "Which is why I'm stuck with the toilet, the landlady, the cat, the job and *you*, who wouldn't know respect if it jumped up and bit you on the ass. Now you either take the ten bucks, or break my ankles because—"

"It's ribs, not ankles," he cut in.

"*Whatever*, because that's all you're going to get. You got that?"

"Yeah."

"If you don't like it, I pretty much don't care. You can take a flying leap into Lake—What did you say?"

"I said I got it." His dark eyes had taken on a wary light as if he were afraid she might be the one breaking his ribs. "Ten bucks next Friday."

A surge of power went through Eve as she realized what had just happened. She'd stood up to Stinky. She was still standing up to him.

She puffed out her chest and pushed her chin a notch higher. "That's Friday afternoon," she added, enjoying the freedom that came with deciding her own fate. "*Not* Friday morning. Got it?"

"Yeah, yeah. You're one ballsy woman, Eve. You're lucky. I like that, and you're damned lucky I don't hit broads." He grabbed the doorknob and hauled open the door.

Thankfully. "And don't think you can bully me anymore. I'm through with it." The door slammed, punctuating her sentence and signaling that he'd left, but Eve was on a roll. She kept shouting. "You can forget about the pedicures. And you can damn sure forget about me moving in with your mother. She's old and mean and her feet smell."

"I did it," she told Twinkles, her heart still pounding from the confrontation. She'd said her piece, and lo and behold, Stinky had backed down. What's more, he'd left without taking her last cupcake or drinking the last swallow of chocolate milk. He'd even called her by her name.

Of course, Stinky saying her name hadn't sounded nearly as good as when ADAM said—

Stop it. ADAM wasn't real, for heaven's sake, and even if he were real, they were on opposites sides of the fence. He was a man, and Eve had sworn off men the minute she'd seen Burt in the front seat with—

Knock. Knock.

Uh, oh. Maybe she shouldn't have told Stinky that his mother's feet smelled. But they did and she *wasn't* moving in with the old bat.

She kept that vow firmly in mind as she hauled open the door. "Listen, Stinky, that's all you're going to get, so bug off because I'm through letting everyone walk all over—" The words stumbled to a halt as her gaze met with a broad T-shirt-covered chest. Her head snapped back and she stared at the man on her doorstep. "ADAM."

He grinned and her heart skipped its next beat. "Eve," he murmured.

"I . . ." She tried to comprehend the situation. Namely that he was here. Now. *Here. Now.*

Dozens of questions raced through her mind, but the only one that found its way to her lips was, "Why are you wearing clothes?"

He frowned as he glanced down at the T-shirt and jeans and boots. "You don't like them?"

"I do." Actually, he looked good enough to

387

sprinkle with powdered sugar and eat. Not that she was doing any sprinkling or eating where he was concerned. He was a machine, for heaven's sake and she was definitely *this close* to going crazy. "It's just . . ." Her nostrils flared as the warm scent of him teased her senses. Scent? Machines didn't have scents.

But with him standing so close, filling up her doorway, consuming her senses, he didn't feel like a machine. He felt real. He felt right.

Forget going crazy. She was already there.

"I missed you," he told her, pushing her up a notch on the loony scale.

"H-how did you get here?"

"Matt drove me."

"Matt?" She leaned out the doorway and stared at the car parked out front. Through the windshield, she saw Matt Taylor and Josie Farrington. They smiled and waved.

ADAM waved back and then the car pulled away from the curb and into the flow of traffic.

"They're leaving."

"Yes," he said, turning back to her, a smile on his handsome face.

"They're leaving you."

"Yes."

"Here."

"Yes."

"But why?"

"Because this is where I want to be." He handed her an envelope. "This explains everything."

Eve spent the next few moments reading the

letter and trying to absorb the all-important fact that Dr. Matthew Taylor was *giving* her ADAM.

"I'm your reward," ADAM said as if reading the disbelief on her face. "For telling the truth and clearing Matt's name. He wanted to say thank you."

"I don't understand . . ." She shook her head, her gaze swiveling to ADAM's. "You're the latest in technology. The hottest new invention. You're *ADAM*, why would he give you away?"

"I'm obsolete. I was the first. The test. To see if it could really be done, and they did it. Now the goal is to improve, to make the next man better and cheaper. I'm little more than a showpiece sitting in the lab, although Matt did install the mini body heat converter, so all that is required to rejuvenate me is several hours of human contact."

"Human contact?" She shook her own head, trying to comprehend the truth. ADAM was here. Now. And he was hers. Her heart gave a furious thud at the realization and her body trembled in anticipation.

Because of a not-so-real-man who looked too real for his own good, and hers.

Ugh. "I think I need to lie down."

His grin widened and large, powerful hands slid around her, scooping her into his arms before she could protest. Warmth closed around her.

"What are you doing?"

"Helping."

"I don't need you to carry me. Look, ADAM. We need to get something straight," she started as he settled her on the sofa and plopped down at her feet. "I don't know what Matt Taylor thinks he's doing by dumping you here, but you can't stay. I haven't got room and I certainly haven't got the time—"

"Lie down." Strong hands urged her back onto the pillows. "And I am staying. I am yours. And you are mine. ADAM and Eve."

"But what will my neighbors think? Not to mention the people at my job when they find out a man is living with—"

"You talk too much," he cut in, sliding off her slippers, his strong fingers closing over her sensitive toes. "You should really learn to relax, Eve."

Mmm . . . He really did have great hands. And a great voice. And he knew just how to use them both.

"Okay," she finally relented, melting into the cushions and sending up a silent thank-you to the Powers That Be, along with Matt Taylor and Josie Farrington for her good fortune.

It seemed that Eve Malone had found her own happy ending after all. And he looked better than average in a pair of jeans.

What more could a hardworking woman ask for?

Epilogue

Six months later . . .

"I can't believe I let you talk me into this." Matt's deep voice carried past the closed bathroom door.

"You started it. Besides you owe me."

"I promised to love, honor and cherish you in front of my parents, your parents, Three Kisses, the entire scientific community, half the Chicago press and ADAM. Damn woman," he growled from inside, "isn't that enough?"

"Hardly. You turned me on, then ditched me. *Ditched.* Do you know how bad that made me feel?"

"I'll make it up to you."

"You can bet you will. Starting tonight. I need closure." Her voice softened. "Please."

She heard a muffled curse, then the door-knob rattled, spurring her into action.

"Wait," she called out, bolting to her feet. She rushed across the room to the sound sys-tem and put on one of Matt's favorite CDs stacked next to the homemade tapes from her mother. "You know, I never really listened to this kind of music before, though my mom's kind of has a country-rock feel to it. But this is really quite good." She punched a button and The Rolling Stones' 'Beast of Burden' filled the room.

Josie settled on the end of the bed she and Matt had purchased six months ago, when he'd made that promise to her in front of God and everybody and ended her reign as Chicago's Hottest Bachelorette.

She was now Chicago's Happiest Wife. She had her house in the suburbs, complete with a family room, a fully functional laboratory and a nursery. Her hand went to her slightly rounded stomach and she smiled.

"I'm ready," she called out, settling herself on the edge of the bed. The music swelled and moaned and a burst of excitement went through her.

A few seconds ticked by before the bathroom door opened and Matt walked out wearing the same black outfit and mask he'd worn the night he'd met her incognito at the club.

She smiled. "Come on, Zorro. Let's see your routine."

His lips thinned into a frown. "I never said I was an exotic dancer."

"You never said you weren't. In fact, when I specifically mentioned a possible table dance, you just grinned. You led me on and sinned by omission, and now I want what's coming to me." She waved a dollar bill at him. "Start moving, buster."

He didn't budge. Instead, his gaze roved her from head to toe and that familiar tingle started in the pit of her stomach. Her thighs trembled. Her hands shook.

A grin tilted his sensual mouth, as if he read her response.

He did. That was the thing about Matt. Despite their differences, he was like a part of her. In her head, her heart. He knew everything about her, her thoughts, her dreams, her fantasies, and he wanted her in spite of them. Because of them.

His frown softened as he folded his arms and eyed her. "What'll you give me if I do it?"

"What do you want?"

Another roam of his gaze and he caught her stare. "You," he finally murmured.

"You've already got me." And she had him and the future looked brighter than she'd ever imagined.

"Besides," she fingered the leopard-print dress she wore. The same dress she'd been wearing that night, despite the fact that it was a good bit tighter now since she was five months pregnant with their first child. The fabric clung to her, emphasizing the rounded fullness of her breasts, caressing her sensitive nipples. Even so, she couldn't wait to peel it away. To have him peel it away.

"Turnabout's fair play," she promised, one she meant to keep for the rest of their lives.

She'd found her Mr. Perfect and he was standing right in front of her. He was so wrong for her in so many ways, yet she couldn't imagine anyone more right. He'd opened her up to new things and shown her she wasn't the misfit she'd always felt like. She was just like anyone else, even if she tended to lean toward health food and classical music. Thanks to Matt, however, she was evolving, spreading her wings. She now adored chocolate, even if it wasn't good for her, and appreciated classic rock. She'd also realized that sometimes it was good to leave her clothes in a heap by the bed, particularly when her loving husband wanted her in that bed. She'd learned to relax more. To enjoy life. To love.

And Matt had learned from her, as well. She'd taught him that happily ever after wasn't about settling for less. It meant having it all— joy and happiness and someone to laugh with, make babies with, grow old with, *dance* with.

"You strip for me and I'll strip for you," she told him. Then her voice took on a trembling note and she felt tears burn the backs of her eyes. "You love me and I'll love you."

"Forever?"

"Forever," she agreed.

His lips spread into a slow, sensuous smile as his hands went to the button on his jeans. "In that case, Pussycat, sit back and enjoy the show. Zorro is in the house."

Something Wild

Kimberly Raye

Dependent only upon twentieth-century conveniences, Tara Martin seeks to make a name for herself as a top-notch photojournalist. But when a plea from her best friend sends her off into the Smoky Mountains to snap a sasquatch, a twisted ankle leaves her in a precarious position—and when she looks up, she sees the biggest foot she's ever seen. Tara learns that the big foot belongs to an even bigger man—with a colossal heart and a body to die for. And that man, who was raised alone in the wilds of Appalachia, will teach Tara that what she needs is something wild.

___52272-1 $5.50 US/$6.50 CAN

Dorchester Publishing Co., Inc.
P.O. Box 6640
Wayne, PA 19087-8640

Please add $1.75 for shipping and handling for the first book and $.50 for each book thereafter. NY, NYC, and PA residents, please add appropriate sales tax. No cash, stamps, or C.O.D.s. All orders shipped within 6 weeks via postal service book rate. Canadian orders require $2.00 extra postage and must be paid in U.S. dollars through a U.S. banking facility.

Name_____
Address_____
City_____State_____Zip_____
I have enclosed $_____ in payment for the checked book(s).
Payment <u>must</u> accompany all orders. ❑ Please send a free catalog.
CHECK OUT OUR WEBSITE! www.dorchesterpub.com

KIMBERLY RAYE
FAITHLESS ANGEL

Faith Jansen has closed the door on life and love. After the death of her young ward, she is determined not to let anyone into her little house again. So when she finds Jesse Savage standing on her stoop, a strange light in his eyes, she turns the lock against him. But Jesse returns to her home each morning, gardening tools in hand. Despite her resolution never to reach out again, she finds herself drawing closer to him. So when she finds herself deep in the desert night with him, the doors of desire are flung open, and the light of something deeper is let loose to flood her heart and lead her to a heaven only two can share.

___52296-9 $5.50 US/$6.50 CAN

Dorchester Publishing Co., Inc.
P.O. Box 6640
Wayne, PA 19087-8640

Please add $1.75 for shipping and handling for the first book and $.50 for each book thereafter. NY, NYC, and PA residents, please add appropriate sales tax. No cash, stamps, or C.O.D.s. All orders shipped within 6 weeks via postal service book rate. Canadian orders require $2.00 extra postage and must be paid in U.S. dollars through a U.S. banking facility.

Name_____

Address_____

City_____ State_____ Zip_____

I have enclosed $_____ in payment for the checked book(s).

Payment <u>must</u> accompany all orders. ❑ Please send a free catalog.

CHECK OUT OUR WEBSITE! www.dorchesterpub.com

Mr. Hyde's Assets

Sheridon Smythe

Get Ready . . . For the Time of Your Life!

Rugged Austin Hyde's mad-scientist brother has gone and appropriated Austin's "assets" to impregnate a tycoon's widow at his fertility clinic. Worse, rumor has it that the elegant Candice Vanausdale might be making a baby simply to inherit big bucks! Mr. Hyde is fit to be tied—but not tied down by a web of lies. Yet how to untangle "Dr. Jekyll's" deception?

Clearly, Austin has to go undercover. Get close enough to the breathtaking blonde to see for himself what the woman is made of. Hiring on as her handyman seems the perfect solution. Trouble is, the bashful, beleaguered beauty unleashes Austin's every possessive male instinct. Blast! How dare "Dr. Jekyll" domesticate Mr. Hyde?

___52356-6 $5.99 US/$6.99 CAN

Dorchester Publishing Co., Inc.
P.O. Box 6640
Wayne, PA 19087-8640

Please add $1.75 for shipping and handling for the first book and $.50 for each book thereafter. NY, NYC, and PA residents, please add appropriate sales tax. No cash, stamps, or C.O.D.s. All orders shipped within 6 weeks via postal service book rate. Canadian orders require $2.00 extra postage and must be paid in U.S. dollars through a U.S. banking facility.

Name_____
Address_____
City_____State_____Zip_____
I have enclosed $_____ in payment for the checked book(s).
Payment <u>must</u> accompany all orders. ❑ Please send a free catalog.
CHECK OUT OUR WEBSITE! www.dorchesterpub.com

THE LOVE POTION
SANDRA HILL

Get Ready . . . For the Time of Your Life!

A love potion in a jelly bean? Fame and fortune are surely only a swallow away when Dr. Sylvie Fontaine discovers a chemical formula guaranteed to attract the opposite sex. Though her own love life is purely hypothetical, the shy chemist's professional future is assured . . . as soon as she can find a human guinea pig. The only problem is the wrong man has swallowed Sylvie's love potion. Bad boy Lucien LeDeux is more than she can handle even before he's dosed with the Jelly Bean Fix. The wildly virile lawyer is the last person she'd choose to subject to the scientific method. When the dust settles, Sylvie and Luc have the answers to some burning questions—Can a man die of testosterone overload? Can a straight-laced female lose every single one of her inhibitions?—and they learn that old-fashioned romance is still the best catalyst for love.

___52349-3 $5.99 US/$6.99 CAN

Dorchester Publishing Co., Inc.
P.O. Box 6640
Wayne, PA 19087-8640

Please add $1.75 for shipping and handling for the first book and $.50 for each book thereafter. NY, NYC, and PA residents, please add appropriate sales tax. No cash, stamps, or C.O.D.s. All orders shipped within 6 weeks via postal service book rate. Canadian orders require $2.00 extra postage and must be paid in U.S. dollars through a U.S. banking facility.

Name_____

Address_____

City_____ State_____ Zip_____

I have enclosed $_____ in payment for the checked book(s).

Payment <u>must</u> accompany all orders. ❑ Please send a free catalog.

CHECK OUT OUR WEBSITE! www.dorchesterpub.com

ATTENTION ROMANCE CUSTOMERS!

SPECIAL
TOLL-FREE NUMBER
1-800-481-9191

Call Monday through Friday
10 a.m. to 9 p.m.
Eastern Time
Get a free catalogue,
join the Romance Book Club,
and order books using your
Visa, MasterCard,
or Discover®.

Leisure
Books

LOVE
SPELL

GO ONLINE WITH US AT DORCHESTERPUB.COM